EVERYONE DIES FAMOUS

LEN JOY

BQB

Virginia

Published in the United States by BQB Publishing
(an imprint of Boutique of Quality Books Publishing, Inc.)
www.bqbpublishing.com

Printed in the United States of America

978-1-945448-72-0 (p)
978-1-945448-73-7 (e)

Library of Congress Control Number: 2020936303

Book design by Robin Krauss, www.bookformatters.com
Cover design by Rebecca Lown, www.rebeccalowndesign.com

First editor: Olivia Swenson
Second editor: Caleb Guard

PRAISE FOR LEN JOY AND
EVERYONE DIES FAMOUS

"A writer who speaks for the real lives of men. You can have your Italian and Scandinavian contemporary troubadours of modern life. Len Joy knows our American one. Especially, he knows men, and as a woman reader, I like getting inside men's heads. Strange as they are, they have troubles and desires and they make mistakes, oh boy, and when they figure that out, they have feelings, too. No fancy stuff. No mumble jumble interiority. This is Do Soimething, Find Out What Happens, Deal With It. In his own way, Len Joy is a fifties writer, no fluff; he isn't exotic. He's solid Americana."

— Sandra Scofield, National Book Award Finalist

"Len Joy's Everyone Dies Famous is a clear-eyed examination of how we live in an uncertain world. By creating imminently understandable characters and skillfully linking them to specific landscape, one that is so evocatively described, he shows us all the ways in which we're connected, how fragile those threads are. In clear prose, Joy does real work here. I'm grateful for it."

— Kevin Wilson, author of *Nothing to See Here*

"Mr. Joy sweeps us headlong into the swirling fury of lives buffeted not only by hail, rain, and wind, but even more so by disappointment, disillusion, and regret. He captures both physical and emotional dread with inexorable intensity."

— Joe Kilgore, author of *A Farmhouse in the Rain*

". . . The plot is entirely character-driven in this deftly paced story, and the characters are well drawn and endearingly flawed. Though their entangled personal connections sometimes strain credulity, the group portrait that emerges provides a striking depiction of small-town American at the dawn of the 21st century."

— Kirkus Reviews

"Len Joy's *Everyone Dies Famous* is a focused novel about regret and redemption. . . . True to life in a small town where everyone knows everyone, or has at least heard rumors about everyone, the story's complex characters, and their senses of shared history, give the book depth beyond its central disaster story. Nature forces them to focus on the future, especially on rebuilding relationships, and the book's conclusion is natural."

— Charlene Oldham, Foreward Reviews

"A tornado rains havoc and destruction upon the residents of a rural southern Missouri countryside, setting the backdrop for a gripping tale of remorse, hope, and new beginnings. *Everyone Dies Famous* draws you in slowly like a low pressure system, and creates a vortex that won't let you go until you turn to the final page. Len Joy has created captivating dialogue and authentic characters in the Stonemason and Landis families and their friends—folks I would recognize from my southern Indiana hometown."

— Phil Temples,
author of *The Winship Affair* and *The Allston Variant*

"Len Joy renders a small Missouri town full of heartbroken men, deferred dreams, and the kind of haunting regret that shapes lives. Love—complicated love—is frequently the motive behind flawed decisions, spawning consequences for generations. Joy inhabits multiple perspectives, giving us a diverse cast of characters fighting the natural elements outside and inside themselves. *Everyone Dies Famous* is a true lesson in empathy."

— Anne Elliott, author of *The ArtStars*

"In *Everyone Dies Famous* by Len Joy there's a storm brewing in Maple Springs, Missouri. The gripping opening charged the entire story with riveting tension. I was enthralled with the ominous undercurrents of what was to come. Joy's skillfully paced narrative never sagged. The vivid descriptions and sensory details brought this small town and its deeply flawed characters to life. Len Joy is a gifted writer and storyteller. I'm eager to read more of his work. Bravo, Mr. Joy."

— Gregory Lee Renz,
author of the award-winning novel *Beneath the Flames*

FOR SUZANNE

ACKNOWLEDGEMENT

I was fortunate that Rebecca Makkai (The Great Believers) recommended I enroll in the *StoryStudio Chicago's* Revise and Launch Workshop. The workshop led by Abby Geni (*The Wildlands*) with help from a great group of writers (Jennifer Collins Moore, Jaclyn Hamer, Kara Shroyer, April Nauman, Dorothy Lam, Dan Finnen, Dan Bacaredi, Anna Joranger, Lisa Tothstein, Marie Becker) provided me with the guidance and critical support to finish the book.

Special thanks to my tri coach Heather Collins and my training partner Cam Granstra for their unfiltered feedback and to my writer-friend Ania Vesenny and my lawyer-friend Jim Clark, who read everything I write (several times).

I am especially grateful to my publisher, Terri Leidich, and to the entire BQB Publishing team, for making this book a reality.

PROLOGUE

7:00 PM—July 18, 2003

Zeke Mesirow left his apartment in Crestview Manor as soon as Big John Thomas on KUKU-FM announced—using his serious radio voice instead of his fake hillbilly twang—that they were bringing the bodies to the high school gymnasium.

The tornado had arrived from the north, surprising the so-called experts. It cut an equal opportunity path of destruction through Maple Springs, flattening the black Baptist church on the west side where Zeke's very white ex-wife used to sing in the choir, and blowing away the sanctimonious Presbyterians on the east side. It pinballed down Main Street, chewing up the Tastee-Freeze, Hank Dabney's Esso Station, Dr. Manickavel's emergency care clinic, and the Main Street Diner, but sparing the useless bank, Crutchfield's boarded up general store, and the VFW Lodge.

As it roared out of town, it destroyed the Chevy dealership where Zeke's son had once worked and the fancy townhouse development project Ted Landis was building across the road from Crestview Manor.

Zeke wanted to call his son, but Wayne didn't own a cellphone. The road into town was impassable. Uprooted trees, overturned vehicles, chunks of concrete, twisted rebar, and pickup-stick configurations of aluminum sliding, roof tiles, and wallboard were strewn across the highway. It didn't matter—he couldn't drive anyway. His truck had disappeared.

A soft mist hung in the air like a wet fog, and it was eerily quiet as he started walking down the highway to the high school.

At the outskirts of town he saw a man, his dark business suit turned gray with grit, standing in his front lawn clutching an open briefcase and staring down the road like he was waiting for the bus. A few blocks farther on an old woman wrapped up in a ratty bathrobe swept brick fragments from her front stoop. The stoop was all that was left of her home. As Zeke turned on to Hill Street, a teenager on an ancient Huffy with a twisted front tire pedaled slowly by, weaving around the debris, his head swiveling like he was trying to figure out which pile of rubble was his home.

The high school at the end of Summit Avenue looked untouched. A highway patrol car and Sheriff Patrick Quinlan's cruiser flanked the driveway leading to the front of the school, and there were an ambulance and a fire truck in front of the entrance to the gymnasium. Two men were lifting someone off a stretcher into the ambulance.

Sheriff Quinlan leaned against the open door of his car like he needed it for support. Water dripped from the brim of his hat and his uniform was plastered to his skin. A mud-splattered Silverado rolled past Zeke and stopped at the driveway entrance. There were two body bags in the truck bed. Body bags just like they'd had in Nam. Quinlan waved the truck through.

As Zeke approached the sheriff, Quinlan held up his hand. "You have to go to City Hall, Zeke. The mayor's handling the missing persons reports."

Zeke Mesirow frowned. They had been friends once.

CHAPTER 1

14 hours earlier

DANCER

It isn't really darkest before the dawn, at least not in the hills of southern Missouri. And the morning air is not cool and refreshing, not in July. As the sun approached the ridge of the Caledonia River Gorge, the sky was storm-gray, but that was just an illusion. The storms had passed to the north, flooding Kansas City and St. Louis but offering the southern counties no respite from the month-long drought. Soon the sun would rise above the tree line and the hot-towel Missouri heat would wrap everyone in its sticky embrace.

Dancer Stonemason walked to the end of his son's driveway, sweat already trickling down his back as he stared at the LANDIS REALTY—SOLD sign planted in the front yard of Clayton's A-frame. He stuck his thumb and index finger in his mouth and whistled sharply for Russell, Clayton's Golden Retriever, and for probably the millionth time, he tried to ignore his three finger stumps. Last month, fifty years after losing those fingers, they had started to ache again, as they had in those first weeks after the accident. His doctor back then had called them phantom pains. "Your brain is confused. It will pass." And it had. So now maybe his brain was confused again?

Dancer bent over to retie his hiking shoes. He closed his eyes, took a deep breath, and then let it out slowly, like Dr. Manickavel had instructed him. "Controlled breathing will help you manage your grief," she said. Dr. Manickavel should have known better.

He had no more ability to manage his grief than he had of growing back his fingers. Clayton's death had ripped a hole in his gut that was never going to be filled. The ache of losing his son would be with him for the rest of his life, and no bullshit breathing exercises, meditation, or counseling were going to change that.

Russell, who had been sleeping on the deck, came shuffling around the corner of the house and stood in front of Dancer, tail wagging, slobbery tongue hanging out the side of his mouth. Russell had been a frisky pup when Dancer moved in with Clayton. Now he was an old dog—his joints creaky, his golden coat patchy and dull, and his muzzle flecked with gray.

"Why don't you go piss on that sign for me, Russell?" Dancer said.

Russell tilted his head. He padded a few yards toward the path that led down to the river, then stopped and looked back.

"I'm right behind you," Dancer said.

For the last ten years, Dancer had worked for Clayton and, to the surprise of everyone, lived peaceably in his home. Every morning before the workday began, Dancer hiked down to the river with Russell. When Clayton hadn't been too busy, he would join them. Dancer tried to keep up the tradition even with Clayton gone.

Dancer had been a baseball legend in Maple Springs but had left in disgrace. For thirty years he had bounced around the minor leagues—a journeyman pitching coach for teams like the Tucson Tigers and the Albuquerque Dukes, making barely enough money to get by. He and Clayton rarely spoke and Dancer thought he had lost his chance to have a relationship with his firstborn son. He'd been out of work for three months when he got a letter from Clayton asking for help with his new jukebox restoration business. With the letter was a photo of Clayton looking down at the river from the deck of his new home. Sandy haired, lean and tall, with an athlete's body, he reminded Dancer of himself at that age. Cocky, the world at his feet, with a wry half smile as though something amused him but he wasn't planning to share it. The truth was, Clayton was struggling with his new business and Dancer was desperate for work. They needed each other. Dancer returned to the town where he had achieved his greatest success and then thrown it all away.

At the first bend in the trail, Russell marked a bush and waited for Dancer to catch up. It used to take Dancer less than five minutes to make it to the river's edge. Now it was closer to fifteen. He was still fit—he could do twenty-five pushups without breaking a sweat and his legs were strong, his cardio off the charts according to Dr. Manickavel. But his eyesight was failing him. Even with his bifocals, it was difficult to make out the treacherous footing in the pre-dawn light. He moved cautiously, making his way down the path more by feel than by sight. This was his final trek to the river, and the last thing he needed was to slip and fall.

As he and Russell maneuvered the rocky path, Dancer could hear the roar of the water pounding the riverbank. Yesterday the river flowed languidly, the clear water burbling quietly along. But the weeklong rains up north had transformed this stretch of the lazy Caledonia into a swollen black snake, swallowing the trees and shrubs that lined its bank. Dancer stood at the edge of the water beside an uprooted tree and wiped his bifocals with the bottom of his T-shirt, which was already soaked with sweat. He slapped at the river gnats swarming around his knees and ankles.

Russell sniffed the water suspiciously and jumped back in surprise when a tangle of branches surfed past him, splashing his head. Down river, around the bend, a dog barked and Russell's ears perked. He abandoned his river exploration and scampered onto the high ground next to the partially submerged trail that bordered the river.

"Wrong way, Russell. We're heading upstream."

The barking dog was Ozzie, a pit bull mix who belonged to the two women who lived in the ramshackle cottage downstream beyond the bend in the river. The women wove willow baskets and sold them all over the country. Clayton said the basket ladies were famous. At least as famous as one could be in the world of willow basket-making.

The women, Phoebe and Lucy, had an early morning yoga ritual. Clayton had joined them occasionally. According to him, sometimes when it got hot like it was today, Lucy practiced topless.

Russell pranced farther down the trail, away from Dancer.

"Let the ladies be," Dancer yelled.

Russell ignored him. He would always be Clayton's dog. Dancer was like an indulgent grandparent who didn't require strict obedience. Most days, Russell and Ozzie would spend hours chasing each other up and down the riverbank.

As Dancer rounded the bend, he spotted Lucy in her black leotard on the grassy patch just above the riverbank. Russell's eyes were half closed as Lucy rubbed under his ears and throat. Lucy was in her late twenties, with cotton-candy-pink hair and freckled, fair skin that always appeared slightly sunburned. She had a healthy fleshiness—what Dancer's late wife, Dede, would have called chubby. Lucy patted Russell on the flank and he rejoined Ozzie, who had been waiting impatiently to continue their running game.

Lucy smiled as Dancer approached. "River's crazy today."

"It'll be worse tomorrow," he said. "Where's Phoebe?"

Lucy grinned. "She's angry at me." She grabbed her shirt

from the yoga mat where she'd been exercising and slipped it over her head. It was an Allman Brothers Band T-shirt with a silkscreen image of a flatbed truck carrying a giant peach on the front.

"Clayton liked the Allman Brothers," Dancer said.

Lucy glanced down. "Oh my God. I just grabbed it from my pile. It was Clayton's. He left it here, uh, last summer."

Last summer. His son's last summer. In their ten years working together, Dancer, to his great surprise, discovered he not only loved his son, but liked him, too. Against all odds they had become best friends. Dancer did everything he could to help Clayton make American Jukebox successful. They were a great team, and when Clayton started selling the refurbished jukeboxes on eBay the business took off. They were finally making money. And then Clayton was gone. Killed when he lost control of his truck on the interstate.

Dancer shook his head and tried to flush the memory of that August day. "T-shirt looks good on you, Lucy," he said, forcing a smile.

"Is Jim still trying to sell Clayton's house?" she asked.

In a family marked by failure and scandal, Dancer's second son, Jim Stonemason, was the exception. He had bought his first car lot before he turned thirty, and now he owned dealerships in Maple Springs, West Plains, and Mountain View. He was the largest GM dealer in southern Missouri.

Dancer stared down at his feet. "Jim sold it to Ted Landis." He scuffed the ground. The sick feeling in the pit of his stomach had returned. He glanced up when Lucy didn't respond to see her face had crumpled. It looked like she might cry.

After a minute, she took a deep breath. "Clayton would have never sold to that asshole. When do you have to move?"

Dancer pretended to be watching the dogs chase each other

down the river trail. He didn't want to meet Lucy's gaze. "Need to start moving the jukeboxes and spare parts today."

Lucy smacked him in the chest with the flat of her hand, making him look at her. "What the fuck, Dancer. Were you just planning to run off without saying good-bye?"

"Sorry. I should have told you. Guess I was hoping it wouldn't happen."

Lucy wrapped her arms around him and buried her head in his chest. "It's been such a shitty year." Hugging was Lucy's solution to most problems. "You got anyone to help you with the move?"

"Jim offered to send someone from the dealership, but I turned him down. Probably shouldn't have done that."

Lucy released him and hooked her arm in his, like he was an usher at a wedding. "You have to come to the house and tell Phoebe. I don't want to do it. She's already pissed at me."

Dancer grinned. "What did you do this time?"

"I brought a boy home from the bar. A soldier. He was too drunk to drive himself home."

"Good Samaritan, huh?"

"Exactly. And patriotic. Helping out a serviceman. I drove his truck and saved myself cab fare. A win-win." She paused to adjust her grip on Dancer's arm. "Phoebe doesn't like strangers sleeping over. He's still on our couch." She pointed toward the large screened-in porch hanging from the back of the cottage. "Hey. He could help you move. He needs work and he has a big pickup."

Dancer knew he didn't really have a choice once Lucy made up her mind, and he allowed Lucy to tow him toward the house.

"I need to get over to Jim's house before he goes to work," he said. "I'll stop in for a minute so you don't have to give Phoebe the news. Sounds like you've already got enough problems."

Lucy pulled open the porch screen door for Dancer. Five tables were staged inside, each topped with willow baskets in various stages of construction. In the far corner, a large overstuffed sofa held a lumpy form curled under a pink bedsheet.

"That's Wayne on the couch. He's just back from Iraq." She stopped at the first table and picked up the basket. It was a swirl of black- and copper-colored willow branches. "What do you think?"

"It looks like a cyclone. I like those colors."

Lucy smiled. "Me too. It has great contrast." She set it on the table and walked back to the sofa. "Hey G.I. Joe. Get up. I found work for you."

Dancer sighed. The last thing he needed was some drunk from Jake's Bar trying to help him. He'd been a drunk from Jake's. He knew that was a bad proposition.

The boy roused himself from the sofa, tugging up government-issued boxers. He had the lean, dirt-tanned look of a homeless guy and a military buzz cut gone fuzzy. He rubbed his hands over his face and head as though he were trying to wipe off his hangover. "You got any coffee?" he asked. Even from three feet away Dancer could smell the puke and stale sweat wafting off him. Dancer had smelled like that more times than he wanted to remember.

Lucy picked up a dingy white T-shirt from the floor. "Put your shirt on before Phoebe sees you," she said. "God. You stink." She stepped backward, almost knocking over Phoebe, who had come out from the kitchen.

"Watch out, Lucy!" Phoebe said.

Phoebe reminded Dancer of the woman from that American Gothic painting, only skinnier and less cheerful. Her brow furrowed as she stared at the figure on the couch. She nodded at Dancer and her frown slipped into neutral.

"Hello, Dancer," she said. "It's been a while."

Dancer hadn't seen Phoebe since Clayton's funeral. That was almost a year ago. He cleared his throat. "Wanted to let you know I'm moving today. Got an apartment over Jim's garage."

"Jim sold Clayton's house to that creep Landis," Lucy said.

Phoebe didn't act surprised at the news. "At least Jim's getting paid for Clayton's place," she said. "Landis wants to steal ours." She glared at Dancer like he was Landis. "He's trying to get the county commissioners to condemn our property. Hand it to him on a silver platter." She picked up a flyer from one of the tables. "And then he has the balls to invite us to that fucking riverboat extravaganza tonight." She stared malevolently at Lucy.

"It'll be a cool party," Lucy said. "A free concert on the riverbank for those who can't get onto the boat. A mystery group is playing. I heard it might be Kenny Chesney."

The soldier was paying close attention to the party conversation. "No way," he said. "Chesney don't do private parties anymore, unless you're an Arab sheik."

Lucy shrugged. "Well, it's somebody like him. And it's free!"

Phoebe slapped the flyer back on the table. "I can't believe you're thinking of going."

Lucy grinned mischievously. "Not thinking about it at all," she said. "Free concert, dollar drafts, loose slots, plenty of boys. Party time!"

"Party time?" Phoebe said, spitting the words. She turned toward Dancer. "What are we supposed to do if Landis takes our place? Move into one of his shitty apartments?"

Dancer stood silent. He agreed with her but hoped if he didn't say anything, he could avoid her ten-minute rant about the evils of capitalism.

"You said you got work for me?" the soldier said.

"Yeah." Lucy answered before Dancer could. "He has a bunch of jukeboxes and he needs help moving them into town."

The boy stared, confused. "Jukeboxes?"

Dancer was trying to figure out a way to extricate himself from this three-ring circus. He held out his hand. "Dancer Stonemason," he said. "I'm moving my jukebox restoration business. But I think I can handle it on my own."

"Are you *the* Dancer Stonemason?"

Dancer nodded. He knew what was coming.

The boy clasped Dancer's hand firmly. "Wayne Mesirow." He turned to Lucy. "This man's a legend."

While Dancer *had* been a local baseball legend, the boy was referring to the reputation Dancer had acquired after the cheering had stopped. The bad times.

"This man kicked ass in every roadhouse in the county!" Wayne said, still holding tight to Dancer's hand. Dancer tugged his hand free.

"Really?" Lucy asked. She stepped closer and studied Dancer's grooved face. "Such a handsome man. Not a mark on him."

Phoebe sighed audibly. She didn't have time for idle chitchat. "Dancer. When you see Jim will you ask him if he can help us with this condemnation suit? He made his deal, he doesn't have to help Landis take over the whole damn river for his fucking golf course."

Dancer saw his opportunity. "I need to drive over to his place this morning. I'll fetch Russell and go now." He could hear Russell and Ozzie barking at something at the river's edge, but he couldn't see them. He leaned out the porch door and whistled sharply, even though he knew Russell would ignore him. "I got to round up that damn dog."

"Wait," Lucy said. "What about Wayne helping you? He's got a cool truck. It's purple and it has huge tires."

"It's a '99 Dodge Ram Sport," Wayne said. He walked over to where Dancer was standing. "Five-point-nine liter engine, three hundred fifty horse."

"You in the army?"

The boy frowned. "National Guard. I was working at your son's Chevy dealership when I got called up. Lost my job."

"Must be more to that story," Dancer said, giving Wayne his bar brawling stare.

Wayne flushed and looked down at his shoes. "I got in a fight with one of the customer service reps. He started it."

Dancer shrugged. "Go see Jim. He's a fair man. He might give you a second chance."

Wayne nodded in a way that looked like he didn't really want to work there. "Need to make some money right now. I'm a good worker."

Dancer looked at the boy, remembering what it was like to be down and out. What the hell. He needed the help. "Okay. One day's work. A hundred bucks. My place is the A-frame above the gorge—43 Ridge Road. I've got some errands to run so I'll meet you back there at nine. Go take a shower."

Wayne scowled and it looked like he wanted to say something, but he just held out his hand. "You won't regret this, Mr. Stonemason."

CHAPTER 2

5:40 A.M.

WAYNE

The sun, ridiculously large, peeked over the horizon as Wayne turned into the driveway of the tired apartment building where his father lived. Crestview Manor, at the foot of the first hill east of Maple Springs, had been one of Ted Landis's earliest developments—hastily constructed to accommodate the influx of new workers hired by Caterpillar after they expanded the plant. It had been built in 1960 on what at that time was a sleepy county road but was now the main east-west artery between the interstates. All night long, fuel and dairy tankers and double trailers hauling walnut and maple logs throttled up and down that hill, their engines burping and coughing and their tires whining. The air in the apartments smelled of diesel and burning tires.

It was going to be another scorcher, and if he hadn't been so hungry, Wayne would have napped in his truck, which was comfortably chilled by the Dodge's powerful AC. The apartment would be stifling. Ezekiel "Zeke" Mesirow refused to use the air conditioning. He believed it weakened a man's resolve. His father had a code he lived by and it was pointless to argue with him. There were no gray areas for Zeke—things were good or bad, right or wrong. Ten years ago when Wayne got Anita Brown pregnant, Zeke told him he had to marry her because it was the right thing to do.

But when Wayne's mom left them, back when Wayne was

in grade school, the right thing would have been for Zeke to go after her when he learned she had joined up with some new age cult leader and all his women followers in Springfield. But Zeke wouldn't do that, so nine-year-old Wayne had stolen forty bucks from Zeke's sock drawer and bought a bus ticket. Against all odds, he had found his mother. He begged her to come back, and she told him she would, but that was a lie. She left him waiting in some seedy diner and the state troopers had to bring him home to Zeke.

Zeke had moved them to Crestview because he couldn't pay the mortgage on their home. Without his wife's income he could only afford to rent a one-bedroom unit, so Wayne slept on the living room couch all through grade school, junior high, and high school. Now, thanks to Anita, here he was back on the couch again.

He hadn't been a perfect husband. But he hadn't been the worst either. Not by a long shot. The first few years had worked out better than he expected. Daniel had been an easy baby— slept through the night after three weeks. Zeke got Anita a job at the Caterpillar plant where he worked, and Wayne found a job working for the county, which allowed him plenty of time to write music and practice his guitar.

He started playing lead guitar for the Ravens. They had regular gigs all around southern Missouri and even some in Arkansas. But when Kristi was born two years after Daniel, the wheels came off. Kristi was colicky and cried all the time. Anita got laid off and the Ravens broke up. Wayne joined the National Guard. He told himself it was for the extra cash, but the truth was he wanted to get out of the house. Those babies were driving him crazy.

Even after Anita got called back to work and the kids settled down, Wayne stuck with the Guard. It was like a weekend vacation every month. He bussed down to Fort Leonard Wood and then drove jeeps with his redneck buddies all around the Ozarks. Anita didn't seem to mind him being gone all that much, and things probably would have worked out okay, if it hadn't been for Iraq. The Guard got called up to support the invasion and he had spent six months in that hellhole. When he returned home a month ago, Anita told him she didn't want to be married anymore. So now he was living with Zeke again, not sure what was going to happen with his marriage or his kids.

Wayne unlocked the front door and stepped into the hallway. The familiar scent of Pine Sol made his nose twitch. Every Friday morning the old man mopped all the floors, like the apartment was a barracks. He could hear Zeke in the kitchen, rustling his newspaper, muttering to himself. Wayne tiptoed into the living room, trying to postpone the inevitable confrontation for a few more minutes.

His Gibson electric was propped against the cabinet where he kept all his classic rock albums. He picked it up and held it for a moment. He had planned to practice today. He hoped to get another tryout with the Confederate Pirates soon. He wanted to be ready, but he needed money, and guitar practice would have to wait. In Iraq, the Engineers had let him practice in the mess hall after dinner was over and everyone had left. Sanjay "Sonny" Patel would always tag along. He would sit in one of those uncomfortable metal chairs, nod his head, snap his fingers, and smile. Sonny had the greatest smile.

With his eyes closed, Wayne imagined he was back in the mess hall, Sonny grinning at him as he ran through his repertoire of guitar classics: "Stairway to Heaven," "Panama," "Dark Side of the Moon," "Sultan of Swing," "Hotel California," and always for his finale, "Juke Box Hero." Not really a classic, but it was Sonny's favorite because he knew the words. He'd sing along while Wayne played, and he'd point at Wayne and tell him that one day Wayne Mesirow would be a Juke Box Hero.

A sob nearly escaped Wayne's throat. His eyes were blurry. Fuck.

"Where you been, boy?" Zeke loomed in front of him. "Damn. You look rode hard and put away wet."

Wayne strummed a few more imaginary chords to recover his composure. He set the guitar down. "You got anything to eat besides goddamn corn flakes?"

"This ain't the Ritz. And you can't stay out all night hitting the bars and then spend the day playing with that damn guitar."

"I wasn't hitting the bars. Had a gig at Jake's." That wasn't a complete lie. He had talked to the bartender at Jake's about playing there for Happy Hour.

"Did you call on Jim Stonemason? You need to get your job back."

His father was obsessed with having a job. He had started working at the Caterpillar plant the day after he returned from Vietnam. He worked his ass off, never took a sick day, but still couldn't make enough money to keep the house when his wife deserted him.

"I don't want to work there," Wayne said, even though he knew it was the exact wrong thing to say.

"It's work. You're not supposed to like it. Man up." Zeke towered over him, standing too close, like the master sergeant who had tormented Wayne all through his reserve training. Zeke's feet were planted and his drab olive work shirt was pressed and tucked tightly into his work pants. His hair was grayer than when Wayne had left for Iraq, but combed perfectly—nothing out of place. Like his immaculately seedy apartment.

"I need to practice. I'm getting another tryout with the C-Pirates soon."

Zeke's jaw tightened, the vein in his forehead pulsing. "You can't support your family playing guitar for some hick band."

Wayne had been close to landing a spot with the Confederate Pirates—a country-rock band out of Rolla—when his reserve unit got sent to Iraq as part of Operation Iraqi Freedom. "They ain't a hick band. They're the real deal. They got a recording contract and they're touring with Brad Paisley in the fall."

His father's eyes narrowed. "Paisley? What the hell kind of name is that for a country singer?" He poked his finger in Wayne's chest. "You want to get your family back, you need a real job. Stonemason will give you another chance. You're a veteran."

Wayne snorted. "Pffft. Nobody thinks the reserves are real soldiers. All I did was help a bunch of asshole engineers build a fucking bridge no one needed."

"It was dangerous work. That Indian fella died helping with that bridge."

Wayne glared at his father. "His name was Sanjay."

"I'm just saying, people around here respect what you boys did. Jim Stonemason will take you back. You just gotta ask him."

Wayne stood up and tried to match his father's military bearing. "You don't know what you're talking about. Me and Anita are getting back together." Until he said it, he didn't know that was what he wanted. When Anita had told him she wanted out, she babbled about her self-esteem and made it sound like Wayne had held her back somehow. But that was Anita. She'd get a hair up her ass about something and say crazy things. He didn't believe her.

"Just like that?" Zeke asked, his eyes bugged. "After she kicked you to the curb? Do you even know why she did that? Have you talked to her?"

Anita had been hanging out with that older woman. Trudy

something. Wayne had heard they hit the bars every weekend while he was gone. He was willing to bet she was the problem. She'd confused Anita with a bunch of feminist bullshit. Wayne needed time to set things straight.

"I'm meeting her tonight," he said. He kicked himself for saying that. He was trying to stare down his father and it just came out.

Zeke scowled. He didn't believe him.

Anita and her bar-hopping friend would probably be at the boat party Lucy was all hot for. "We're hooking up at that riverboat party," Wayne said.

His father sniffed the air. "You smell like puke."

Wayne looked down at his T-shirt, crusty with dried vomit. He pulled off the shirt and tossed it on the couch. He dumped out his duffel bag, spewing clothes and gear on the floor. A handgun rattled out of the pile with a clank. His father picked it up and checked the magazine.

"It's not loaded," Wayne said. "I took it out of the truck last night because I don't trust that crowd at Jake's. Give it to me. I'll put it back."

"What are you doing with a Sig Sauer?"

"It was Sanjay's gun. I'm giving it to his father. Let him know what happened."

Zeke nodded. Soldiering was something he understood. "Be careful, Wayne. People think they want to know. But mostly they don't." He handed the gun back.

"Mr. Patel will," Wayne said.

"First things first, son. You need a job. Go see Stonemason."

Wayne laughed.

"What's so goddamn funny?" asked Zeke.

"I am going to see Stonemason. Dancer Stonemason. Helping him move some jukeboxes into town."

"Jukeboxes!" The word exploded from Zeke's lips. "That was Clayton Stonemason's big idea. Tell me how the hell you supposed to make a living selling old jukeboxes?"

"It's just a one-day thing. Where is this Clayton, anyway?" Wayne asked.

"Dead. Smashed his truck into a tree in broad daylight." Zeke squared himself up like the master sergeant used to do when he barked out the morning orders. "Listen up. Dancer Stonemason's a loser. Back in the early fifties she was the best pitcher in the minor leagues. Pitched a goddamn perfect game, for chrissake. He could have been a genuine major league ballplayer, but he pissed it all away. Had to go to work in the factory, like all the rest of us. You know how he lost those fingers?"

"Probably some badass bar fight."

Zeke grunted. "He cut them off. Tried to make it look like an accident. Get a big settlement. Company fired his ass." Zeke looked like he wanted to spit. "And then his wife left him for another woman and he still took her back."

Wayne wanted to say that losing your wife to another woman couldn't be any worse than losing out to some creepy guru with a dozen wives. At least Dancer got his wife back. But he stayed silent. Nothing to be gained by poking the old man.

"Dancer and Clayton Stonemason," Zeke said. "Those guys were nothing but trouble. But Jim Stonemason? He's different. A pillar of the community. You get your job back with him and then you can work on getting your kids back. And your woman. If you really want her."

CHAPTER 3

7:30 A.M.

ANITA

Anita Mesirow added a leaf of kale to her protein shake and switched on the blender. The high-pitched whine added to the symphonic chaos in her kitchen. Her son, ten-year-old Daniel, was sitting at the kitchen counter holding a doll over his head chanting, "Barbie sucks toads," while his sister Kristi shrieked for him to give it back. With all the noise Anita didn't connect that the ringing sound in her head was from her doorbell until she heard the door knocker bang several times.

"Shit!" She flipped the blender speed to low and moved toward the front door. "I'm coming, Trudy! You kids shut up! Daniel, put the doll down. Kristi, finish your cereal." She flung open the door as Trudy Bennett, dressed in her official U.S. Postal Service Bermuda shorts and top, was about to give the door knocker another try. Trudy was twenty years older than Anita, but with her trim bod, pixie haircut, and little-girl face, she didn't look it.

"Oh my God, Trudy. Is it too early to start drinking? Thanks for helping me out."

From the kitchen Kristi screamed, "I hate you, Daniel!"

Trudy laughed as she followed Anita into the apartment. "Sounds like you have everything under control. Except the blender. What's that glop?"

The protein shake had whipped into a froth that was bubbling out of the top of the blender. Anita ran to the machine and turned it off.

"My goodness, Daniel," Trudy said, walking over the to the table. "I think you've grown another inch since last week."

Daniel, clutching Kristi's doll like it was a weapon, stood ramrod straight—a soldier lined up for inspection. "I'm almost as tall as you," he said.

"Forget about me. In another year you'll be taller than your mama."

Anita was nearly six feet, a good four inches taller than her husband, Wayne.

"A big boy like you has to look out for his little sister," Trudy said. "Why don't you give me the doll?"

Daniel beamed and immediately handed over the doll. He ran to the TV set and picked up his dad's old acoustic guitar. He pretended to strum it, though it had no strings, and he lowered his voice as he sang, "I can't get no satisfaction. I can't get no—"

"Daniel!" Anita yelled. "You put that guitar down this minute. I don't want to ever hear you singing that song."

Daniel huffed dramatically and plopped down on the couch to play with his Gameboy.

Trudy sat down at the kitchen counter next to Kristi. "I'll watch Barbie while you finish your cereal."

"That's Felicia. She's Barbie's second-best friend," Kristi said.

"Who's her best friend?" Trudy asked.

Kristi pulled a cocoa-colored doll from her pink backpack. "Tiffany! She's Barbie's bestest friend in the whole world."

"Ooh. She's bare naked!" Daniel said.

Kristi pouted at her brother. "I'm dressing her when we get to Grandma's."

Anita walked over to the table. Trudy made a face as Anita sat down next to her with her green shake. "That looks awful."

Anita sighed. "I know. I'd kill for a sausage biscuit. But look." She tugged on the waist of her jeans. "These used to be my tight jeans. Now I can wear them for work. I've lost ten pounds since the boob job."

"If you get any skinnier, people will mistake *you* for Barbie."

Anita sucked in her stomach and thrust out her chest. Sounding like a ring announcer for a title fight, she said, "In this corner, Platinum 'Nita—Barbie's third best friend!"

Trudy laughed.

Two weeks after Wayne left for Iraq, Anita had received a registered letter from an attorney in Indiana informing her that her father, who she had not seen in twenty years, had died a year ago. The lawyer had determined that Anita was his only heir. The net proceeds of his estate, after the lawyer's fees and the taxes, amounted to $4,785.43. A certified check was attached.

Her mother was surprised. Not that her ex had died, but that he had managed to have any estate at all. "Must have won the lotto and croaked before he could piss it all away," she told Anita.

The next day, while Anita was over at her mom's dropping off the kids, she glanced at a copy of the *West Plains Bugle*. On the back page between the ads for liposuction and how to lose ten pounds in ten days was an ad for "Dr. Gupta's Breast Enhancement Special" for $3,999.99. It seemed like an omen. When she told her mother her plans, she just grinned ruefully. "Your father would be proud."

Anita was a B cup so she enhanced herself up to a D, got a stylish shag haircut, and changed her hair color from mousy to platinum.

A month later she met Trudy.

Anita was in the parking lot of Graham's Country Station

outside of West Plains, screaming at Kit Rollins as he peeled out of the parking lot. He had brought Anita to the bar but dumped her when he ran into his old high school girlfriend. It had started to rain—a freezing, stick-to-your-skin Missouri rain—when Trudy pulled up in her little Camry and told Anita to get in the car. They had been hanging out ever since. The friendship had been good for both of them. Wild Anita gave Trudy a social life again, and cautious Trudy kept Anita from getting completely out of control.

Now Kristi looked up from her cereal and grinned. "You can be Barbie's best friend, Mom. Tiffany won't mind."

"That's great. Now go brush your teeth. You too, Daniel. I can't be late for work again."

The kids' sneakers made thwanging sounds on the threadbare hall carpet as they raced down the hall. "Thanks a bunch for helping me out, Trudy. The locksmith should be here by 8:30."

"Have you sent in your school application yet?"

Trudy was pushing Anita to apply to Southwest Missouri State. They had a night school program where she could get an associate's degree.

"I'm still thinking on it," Anita said.

"Anita. I thought you said you were going to take control of your life." Trudy was staring at her with her lips pressed tight. Sometimes she was worse than her mother.

"I am taking control," Anita said.

"You need to do more than get a boob job."

"I think breaking up with Wayne is a pretty big move." Anita went over to the sink to rinse the blender carafe. She filled and dumped the contents, mesmerized as the water turned from kale green to clear.

Her marriage had been a mistake. Wayne, the geeky munchkin musician whose mother abandoned him for a cult, and

Anita, the gawky ugly duckling, taller than most of the boys. They dated each other because they had no other options. Then Anita got pregnant and Wayne's father made him marry her.

Wayne loved his kids, but he wasn't ready to be a father—he wanted to be a rock star. Then the reserves got called up and he was sent to Iraq just when Anita was ready to tell him she wanted out.

"Hey, we're in a drought here," Trudy said. "I think your blender thing is clean enough." She wrapped her arm around Anita's waist. "I don't mean to be a bitch about school. I know it hasn't been easy. But you need to look to your future as a single mom. I'm glad you're changing the locks. Wayne's not stable."

Anita turned off the faucet and set the carafe back in the blender base. "He's just confused."

Trudy retrieved the carafe and dried it with the dish towel. "He's so confused he can't remember to pick up his kids?"

Working out the visitation had been a problem. There wasn't any room at Zeke's house for the kids to sleep over. There was hardly room for Wayne. He had taken Daniel and Kristi out for the day several times since he'd been back, but in the last two weeks he had cancelled three times at the last minute. That was hard on them, especially Daniel.

Anita had been hopeful they could have a soft landing, but the other night after she had told Wayne he couldn't schedule another visit until next week, he had left a message on her cell, drunk and angry and making threats. Trudy convinced her she should get the locks changed.

"What do you want me to do with the new key?" Trudy asked.

"Just put it under the mat in the back," Anita said. "The locksmith shouldn't be more than an hour."

"That's cool. I don't have to start mail sorting until ten. I'm glad your AC is working. It's brutal out there." She looked over her shoulder to see if the kids were returning. "You don't think Wayne will show up here, do you?"

Anita shook her head. "Victor called me last night. He was bartending at Jake's. Said Wayne had been there all evening. He was talking trash on me again and got so shitfaced Victor had one of those basket-making gals drive his truck to their place. Probably won't be conscious until noon."

"Which one?" Trudy asked.

"Which one what?" Anita asked.

"Which of the basket chicks? Bubblegum head or the librarian?"

Anita shrugged. "I don't know. Those gals are weird. Hippies. Or maybe witches." She grabbed a yogurt and an apple from the fridge and packed them in her lunch bag. "The skinny one started a petition. Tried to stop Ted from docking his steamboat in the gorge." She giggled. "She obviously didn't know who she was dealing with."

Trudy poured herself a cup of coffee and moved over to Anita's couch. "Are you gambling on the riverboat tonight, or just trawling for more boyfriends?" she asked.

"Ted says if we gamble, we should play craps. It has the best odds. Stay away from the roulette wheel."

"Does your mom know you're boffing her biggest customer?" Trudy asked.

Anita's mom, Johnine "Johnnie" Brown, had built a thriving business scavenging for old furniture, dishes, and farm implements. She knew what city folks wanted to make their fancy second homes look appropriately country. Ted Landis bought her stuff for his model homes, and when he started turning his riverboat into a floating casino, Johnnie became his primary vendor for all those vintage and kitschy items he needed to give the steamboat an authentic look. In the last six months he had been stopping by every week and that's how Anita became friends with him. Her mother didn't know about the relationship.

"You think he's too old, don't you?" Anita asked.

"I don't know." Trudy shrugged. "I guess so. But what do I know?"

Anita sighed. "I know he's old and I'm worried he's getting too serious. But he's a lot of fun. Like tonight. He's giving us priority passes for the riverboat. Free food and drink."

"Us? I get the red-carpet treatment too?"

"Of course. You're my wingman." Anita grinned coyly. "Maybe you'll meet someone on the boat you can bring to the Stonemason wedding tomorrow."

Kayla Stonemason, daughter of Jim Stonemason who owned the Chevy dealership beyond Landis Mall, was marrying an out-of-town boy on Saturday. It would have been the social event of the month if it hadn't been eclipsed by Ted's riverboat party. Years ago, right after high school, Trudy had dated Clayton Stonemason. Anita's mom told her it had been the talk of the town when Clayton dumped Candy Landis—Ted's beauty queen daughter—for trailer trash Trudy Bennett. They were together for five years but broke up soon after Clayton returned from Vietnam.

"I don't know why I got invited," Trudy said. She scooped up two Barbie dresses and a handful of Barbie high heels. "God, I hate those little shoes. They're everywhere." She dropped the doll accessories on the coffee table. "Clayton had a dozen girls after me. Two dozen."

Her face had darkened. She didn't like to talk about herself.

"Because you were the love of his life," Anita said. "Everyone says so."

"Everyone?" Trudy scoffed. "You mean your mother."

"Hey. When it comes to town gossip, no one knows more than Johnnie Brown. She told me Clayton once took on a whole biker gang defending your honor."

Trudy shook her head slowly and looked up at the ceiling. "It was two skinny bikers and they were so drunk I could have whipped their ass. If your mom has such a good pipeline, you better figure she knows about you and Ted."

"We're very discrete," Anita said. She grabbed a Tupperware container that was half filled with doll clothes. "Anyway, I like Mom's version better."

"Clayton got a week in jail and it cost him his job. He went to Nam just to get away from his father. When he came home, most people couldn't see it, but he had changed."

"Angry?" Anita asked.

Trudy bit down on her lip. "That was the thing. He didn't seem angry—he even got along with his father, which he had never done before—but he could lose it in a flash. There was no predicting what would set him off. Broke my heart to let him go."

"Why did you?" Anita asked.

Trudy exhaled slowly. Her face was tight. "I was afraid he might kill us both."

"Wow," Anita said softly. No wonder Trudy was so worried about what Wayne might do.

Kristi started shrieking in the kids' bedroom. "I hate you, Daniel!"

Anita put the doll clothes container back on the counter. "So much for our quiet coffee break. Kristi! Stop leaving your doll stuff all over the house!"

Trudy frowned. "I'm not going to that wedding. Too many memories."

"Come on," Anita said. "It'll be fun. More free food and

drinks. If you don't find someone tonight you can bring me as your plus one." Anita batted her eyelashes in her best Southern belle imitation.

"You think any place where there's booze and men is a good time."

Anita laughed. "And your point is . . . ?"

Trudy walked over to the sink and rinsed out her coffee cup. "I'll think about it." That was her stock answer whenever she didn't want to say no.

The phone on the kitchen counter rang as the kids rambled back into the living room.

"Let's go, Mom," Daniel said. "Hey, Kristi, I'll bet Grandma makes us pancakes again." He ran out the front door.

Trudy walked over to the counter. "Do you want me to answer this?" she asked.

Anita frowned at the phone. "No. I'm cutting off the service at the end of the month. The only calls we get on that phone are people selling stuff I don't want or from guys wanting Wayne to play in their band. Anyone I want to talk to has my cell."

"Wayne doesn't have a cellphone?" Trudy asked. "I told you he was crazy."

Anita lowered her voice to a whisper. "Not crazy. Confused. He'll come around. He'll see that breaking up is the best thing for all of us. He doesn't really want to be married."

Trudy sighed. "Whatever you say. For sure, he'll be confused when he tries to get in this apartment and his key doesn't work."

CHAPTER 4

7:40 A.M.

DANCER

Dancer drove without enthusiasm to the house of his younger son Jim to pick up the new sports jacket Jim's wife Paula had bought for him. She didn't think Dancer's twenty-year-old blue blazer was good enough for her daughter's wedding. Jim and Paula lived twenty minutes away in a renovated farmhouse, northeast of Maple Springs.

Even as a boy, Jim had been the dependable Stonemason. Not self-destructive like his father or reckless like his brother. Clayton had been the star athlete, popular with the girls. Jim was clumsy, struggled with his weight, and never had a girlfriend until he met Paula.

They were perfect for each other. Paula Castignetti was from a large Italian family in Springfield. Her family was opinionated, volatile, and numerous. She was a wild party girl with a broken heart who was trying to turn her life around. Jim, from a family that never shared their feelings, was the conscientious good citizen who was trying to overcome his social awkwardness. They were married six months after their first date, and it was a storybook marriage, except for the inconvenient fact that the man who had broken Paula's heart was Clayton. That became one of those Stonemason family secrets that everyone knew but no one shared.

Jim's dealership empire was growing. He was a natural businessman. Paula had been a good partner for him—supportive of his dreams but practical, able to temper those dreams with a heavy dose of reality.

Three years ago, when Jim had wanted to buy one of the overpriced McMansion style homes in Camelot Square—Ted Landis's new upscale development—Paula convinced him to buy the McClellan farmhouse after McClellan had sold off all his farmland to Ted Landis for some future development. Paula had taken charge of the renovation and transformed an old-fashioned box house into an extraordinary living space.

As Dancer pulled into the long driveway, now lined with majestic willows and birch trees, he thought that the house looked like something out of *Gone With the Wind*. Paula had added an attractive columned portico to the front. She had knocked out walls, created large bedroom suites, and opened up the main floor so that the small kitchen, dining room, and den were now a large open family room with a cooking island, a fireplace, and a large flat-screen television.

Dancer drove up to the front of the detached garage where he would soon be living. There was a basketball hoop over the garage door where Kayla, who was getting married tomorrow, used to practice her jump shot.

Through the family room door, Dancer could see Paula, back from her morning run, hunched over the coffee table. She was still wearing her running shorts and a black sports bra, and her dark hair was gathered in a scrunchy.

She looked up, not frowning, but not smiling either, as Dancer stepped into the room. "Your jacket's hanging in the hall closet. In the Dillard's wrapper."

"Thanks," Dancer said, leaning over the board. "That looks like a battle plan." Paula was arranging colored name tags on a large poster board that had a series of rectangles, squares, and circles drawn on it.

"Sort of," she said. "It's a seating arrangement for Stone-masons and Castignettis. I want to avoid a repeat of the graduation debacle."

Four years ago, at Kayla's high school graduation party, Tony Castignetti, one of Paula's nephews, had asserted that Rocky Marciano was the greatest heavyweight champ of all time. Clayton, just to stir things up, insisted Muhammed Ali was superior. When the argument was over Tony had a broken nose and a chipped tooth and Jim had a thousand-dollar assessment from the Maple Springs Country Club for damages.

"Hillbillies and mobsters don't mix well," Dancer said.

Paula gave him a look. The locals had gossiped for years that her late father had been in the mafia.

"Just kidding," Dancer said, grinning.

Paula sighed. "Of course without Clayton, there shouldn't be any . . ." She stopped and closed her eyes like she was in pain. "Sorry, Dancer. I'm not thinking clear today."

"It's okay. You're right. Without Clayton around, I don't see anyone who's likely to light the match."

Paula dabbed at her eyes and looked around to make sure Jim had not come down the stairs. "Look what I found when I cleaned out the garage for your apartment." She picked up a framed photograph from the counter. "That's Clayton on your shoulders, right?"

It was the photograph that had been on their family hutch until the day the family imploded. Clayton riding on Dancer's shoulders as he and Dede paraded around Crutchfield Stadium after Dancer had pitched his perfect game as the crowd shouted, *Dancer! Dancer! Dancer!* When he closed his eyes, he could still feel Clayton's cotton-candy sticky fingers clinging to his neck.

That game should have been Dancer's ticket to the major leagues, but the baseball gods are fickle. Dancer never made it to the Show. Instead he made mistakes. Big mistakes. The kind you can't make right. And for a boy who thought his father was perfect, that was unforgivable.

"I thought Dede destroyed this," Dancer said. He handed the frame back to Paula.

"Jimmy must have saved it." She studied the photo. "Clayton looks so happy." She sniffed and put the photo back on the counter. "God, I miss him. I wish I hadn't been such a shit to him all these years."

Dancer swallowed hard. Dr. Manickavel said he should talk about Clayton. "Share your memories with your friends." That was better than her deep breathing idea, but he didn't really have any friends so it wasn't much help. Paula was family and for most things she was easy to talk to, but not about Clayton.

"I miss him too," he said finally. "He was always a hard case. It was easy to be shitty to him. I think that's what he wanted."

He hadn't thought that before, but now it seemed right. Clayton could never take the easy path. Never keep his mouth shut. He and Paula would have never survived as a couple. Neither would give an inch.

He looked over Paula's shoulder at her seating chart. "I didn't think Kayla wanted any help with her wedding."

"I reminded her about her graduation party and she decided she could use my expertise on the Italian side of the family. She'll have her hands full this evening just getting the showroom ready for the reception."

"Can't some of Jim's crew help her?" Dancer asked.

"She didn't want to ask them because she knows they all want to go to that Landis riverboat party. She has that obsession with not accepting any favors because she's the boss's daughter."

Dancer nodded. That was Kayla. She had started working for Jim the day after her high school graduation. From the beginning, she refused any help that might appear to be favoritism. She started as a gofer, doing menial chores like fetching coffee, keeping the break room clean, and organizing the dealer manuals. She worked her way up one step at a time. Like her father, she was a natural salesman. Six months after she moved into used car sales, she was his number one sales rep.

"Those guys she works with adore her," he said. "They'd help her in a heartbeat if she asked. How'd she ever get so stubborn?"

Paula gave him her look again. "Yeah. I wonder." She pinned the last name tag to the board. "I think this will work." She walked over to the kitchen nook and turned on the gas burner. "How many eggs you want? Two or three?"

"Didn't know my place came with a meal plan," Dancer said. His new over-the-garage apartment had a mini-kitchen so he could cook his own meals. Clayton had done most of the cooking, and Dancer had not yet adjusted to life after Clayton.

"Dr. Manickavel says you've lost ten pounds in the last six months. You're not eating regular, are you?"

"Whatever happened to doctor-patient confidentiality?" Dancer asked. Paula was a nurse three days a week in Doctor Manickavel's emergency care clinic, which wasn't just for emergencies. It was for anyone who needed medical help and didn't want to drive all the way to West Plains. Dancer had seen her last week for the physical exam Clayton used to insist he have every year.

Dr. Kuzhali Manickavel. Stout, with dark, lacquered hair. Smiling didn't come naturally to her, which Dancer appreciated. Most doctors, in his experience, smiled way too much. After a battery of measurements and lab tests, Dr. Manickavel had studied the clipboard of results the nurse handed her and then looked at Dancer and frowned. He had reckoned that even Kuzhali, with her limited people skills, would toss a few softball questions at him before she got down to business. But she came in hot with a ninety-mile-an-hour fastball aimed at his chin.

"Do you think about suicide?" she asked.

"Every time I walk out on that goddamn deck of Clayton's," Dancer said.

"What stops you?" Dr. Manickavel's expression never changed. She would have made a great poker player.

Dancer hitched his shoulders. "It seems sort of chickenshit. I've never been able to come out of a game early, even when I should."

"Don't you feel you have much to live for?"

"I did. Helping Clayton to make his business a success. That was cool. I would have done that for as long as he'd have me." He sighed. "But now . . ."

"But you have Jim and Paula and Kayla. They care deeply for you."

"I know. But they don't need me. I'm just taking up space. It would be a lot easier for them if I were gone. But don't worry, Doc. I'm not jumping."

"Good."

"Fall probably wouldn't kill me anyway," Dancer said. Dr. Manickavel almost smiled when he said that. Almost.

"Two or three, Dancer?" Paula held up an egg like she was ready to throw it at him.

"Two eggs would be great," Dancer said. Food had lost its flavor, but he knew better than to argue with Paula. She was way more stubborn than he was.

"Would you turn on the TV?" she asked. "I want to hear the weather forecast. Hoping there's a break from this heat wave. That church will be a steam bath."

An up-tempo music promo blared from the speakers as the

Channel 3 news crew from Springfield flashed their glaringly white teeth for the viewers.

"Don't the Methodists believe in AC?" Dancer asked.

Paula, who had been absentmindedly stirring the eggs in a bowl, started whipping more vigorously. "They probably won't turn it on. We're not members. Half the folks in this town still think of Jim as the son of the notorious Dancer Stonemason and me as the Godfather's daughter." She laughed to herself. "Actually, my dad would have been thrilled. He loved Marlon Brando."

"I think most folks have forgotten me," Dancer said.

"This is a small town, Dancer. Everyone dies famous here."

On the television the anchor was happy-talking with the weather gal. They always wasted half the news hour with their banter.

"I've outlived my fame," Dancer said. He reached for the remote to turn up the sound.

Paula scrunched her eyes, perplexed. "Well yeah, they've forgotten about your big game, but they still remember all the bad things you did. People love to talk shit."

No one would ever accuse Paula of being a Pollyanna.

The smiling weather gal used a laser pointer to identify the string of tornados that had touched down in Kansas and Arkansas. Nothing was expected in southern Missouri. The region would continue to bake, with no break from the record heat wave. She smiled while she delivered that news, like only someone who lived all day in air-conditioned comfort could do.

"It's supposed to stay hot, according to Miss Accu-Weather," Dancer said to Paula, who was sliding his portion of scrambled eggs on to a plate.

Jim came thudding down the stairs. He lumbered into the kitchen with his briefcase in one hand and his sports coat in the other. Despite Paula's exhortations (or nagging, according to Jim), he now weighed close to three hundred pounds. He poured the coffee into his Starbucks mug and glanced sideways at Paula. "I'll grab some breakfast at Gillespie's office."

Paula wrinkled her face. "Yeah. Your lawyer will have a great selection of Dunkin Donuts. Just what you don't need."

Jim had built up Paula immunity. He absorbed her comments without response.

Paula wasn't done. "Don't forget. You have to give me a ride home after my shift. Kuzhali's working late."

By the pained expression on Jim's face it was clear he had forgotten. "What time?" he asked.

"Three o'clock. So you'll have plenty of time to rest up for your daughter's wedding."

Jim turned to Dancer. "Hey, Dad. Those two jukes you got in last week? The ones from that country bar in Licking?"

"What about them?" Dancer asked. He knew he wasn't going to like the answer. Jim had never understood Clayton's business. Never wanted to. But after Clayton's death, Jim had cancelled all the out-of-state trips Clayton had planned. Dancer continued to run the operation, working down the inventory and buying boxes locally. But they couldn't keep doing that. He wanted to talk to Jim about Clayton's plans for the business. After years of struggle, they had finally turned the corner. American Jukebox would be Clayton's legacy. Dancer could keep it growing, if Jim would let him.

"I sold those boxes to Landis for two grand. You need to deliver them this morning."

Dancer felt that tightness returning to his stomach. The

mouthful of egg he was chewing had turned to sawdust. He swallowed it with difficulty.

"For both of them?" Dancer said, his voice rising. "That's no good. Those are Seeburgs. We can get twice that once I pretty them up. Landis is stealing them."

Jim frowned. He didn't know the difference between a top-end box like a Seeburg and a cheap Wurlitzer. "Dad, I don't have time to debate it with you. This saves you having to lug those jukes back here. It's a done deal. Landis needs them for that riverboat party tonight." He looked at his watch and his frown deepened. "One more thing. Landis bought a couple crates of antiques from Johnnie Brown. I told him you could stop by her place and pick them up when you deliver the jukes. It's practically on your way."

Dancer looked down at his plate. He had lost what little interest he had had in the eggs. Jim was selling stuff at cost. He wasn't expecting Dancer to continue operating American Jukebox. He was liquidating Clayton's company.

"You know those women who live down by the river?" Dancer asked as Jim snatched his briefcase and headed for the door. "The basket gals?"

"What about them?" Jim asked, glancing at the clock on the wall.

"They were hoping you might help them. Landis is trying to get their property condemned."

Jim grimaced as if Dancer had handed him a sack of warm shit. "They should have taken his offer. Nothing I can do."

He was about to make his escape when Kayla entered and the whole atmosphere of the room changed. "Grandpa!" she yelled. She ran over to the table to give Dancer a hug.

Kayla was an effervescent, freckled blonde with tomboy short hair and a killer grin. Dancer couldn't help but smile when she was around.

"Not taking the day off before your big day?" Dancer asked with a wink.

Paula laughed. "What kind of crazy talk is that? Take a day off from selling cars. Has Hell frozen over?"

Kayla punched her mother lightly in the shoulder. "We all have our addictions, Mom. How many miles did you run today?"

Jim, still holding on to the doorknob, ready to leave, said, "Hey, Kayla. I'll be late. Make sure all the guys know to push the Silverados. We have to—"

"I know, Dad. The 2004s are coming. Message received: Silverados out the door."

Jim smiled, bemused. Now that Clayton was gone, Kayla was the only person who could still get away with giving him shit.

"You need to be careful of Landis," Dancer said, unable to let the matter rest, but Jim was already out the door. If he heard him he didn't acknowledge it.

Dancer tried not to play the what-if game. But it was hard not to speculate on how different the Stonemason family might have turned out if Landis had set up shop somewhere else. Dancer's wife, Dede, had been a free spirit. If she'd been born a decade later, she would have fit in perfectly with the free-loving hippies and flower children of the sixties. But in the uptight, Bible-thumping self-righteous world of Maple Springs in the 1950s, she was out of place. Lonely. So was Ted Landis's wife.

The two neglected wives found each other. They became friends and then somewhere along the line they became more than friends. When Dancer discovered them in bed, Dede told him it was just "girls having fun." If he had only accepted that, everything might have been different. There wouldn't have been any accident at the plant. He wouldn't have become a drunk and a brawler. Dede wouldn't have kicked him out, and he wouldn't have lost Clayton.

Now, fifty years later, Ted Landis was still fucking with his family.

Paula stood at the kitchen sink and watched as Jim walked across the driveway to his Cadillac parked next to Dancer's truck. "He needs to get serious about his weight," she whispered.

Kayla grabbed a yogurt from the fridge. She draped her arm over Paula's shoulder. "Maybe after the wedding, when things settle down?" she said.

"It'll be even harder for him after the wedding. You know that," Paula said. She studied her daughter's face. "You feeling okay? You need to eat more than just that yogurt."

Kayla wrinkled up her face and shrugged. "A little queasy, you know?"

Paula sighed. "When are you going to tell your father?" She spoke softly, as if she didn't want Dancer to hear. He tried to oblige her by sitting down in front of the television and turning the channel to ESPN.

The top sports story of the day was that an NBA superstar had been indicted for felony rape in Colorado. It seemed like those announcers spent more time talking about how much money the players made or what crimes they committed than talking about sports.

"Think that will ruin his career, Grandpa?" Kayla said. She clearly saw the TV as a convenient escape route from the whisper-argument she was having with her mom.

"Won't help," Dancer said.

Paula frowned at the screen. "Pfft. He'll be fine. Rape a woman? That's a misdemeanor in professional sports. Now if they'd caught him in bed with a man or if he beat his dog, then he'd have a problem."

Kayla grinned at Dancer and rolled her eyes. She set her half-finished yogurt on the table and grabbed her car keys from the pegboard by the door. "I'll be home late, Mom. Barry and I have to fix up the showroom."

"Talk to your father," Paula said as Kayla opened the kitchen door.

"Yeah, yeah. See you, Grandpa," she said and was out the door.

Dancer didn't say anything. He knew Paula would tell him what it was he wasn't supposed to hear. She wasn't good at keeping secrets.

"Kayla's pregnant," Paula said.

"Oh," Dancer said. He was more surprised by Paula's matter-of-fact tone than by the news.

Paula shrugged as she watched Kayla peel out of the driveway in her red Chevy Camaro. She drove home a different dealer car each week. "That's the way kids do it these days," Paula said. "Sometimes they wait until after the baby is born."

"Jim doesn't know?" Dancer asked.

"No. Not yet. He doesn't need to know until she starts showing."

Dancer felt like he had missed a page somewhere. What had Paula been encouraging her to talk to Jim about if not the pregnancy? "So—?"

"Kayla and Barry are moving to New York in September. Barry got a big promotion. Kayla hasn't told Jim yet, and she says she doesn't want to until after the wedding. But by the time they get back from their honeymoon, she'll only have a month until she moves. She doesn't appreciate how little time she has left here. Jim needs to know they're moving now."

Barry was a CPA with some kind of computer expertise. He worked out of the regional office of Coopers Accounting in West Plains, twenty miles from Maple Springs. Two years ago, Jim

Stonemason hired Coopers to help him with his computer system and controls. Barry headed up the project, and Jim gave Kayla the job of answering all of Barry's questions about dealership procedures. Barry must have liked her answers.

As far as Dancer knew, the couple was planning to buy a house between West Plains and Maple Springs. Jim was expecting Kayla to keep working for him at the dealership. Those plans obviously would need to change.

"Sounds like a great opportunity," Dancer said. He carried his plate to the kitchen sink and dumped the remainder of his scrambled eggs in the garbage.

Paula was still staring out the window at the driveway as though she expected someone to pull up. "Absolutely," she said. "If I were them, I'd leave this town and never look back. But it will be a real blow for Jim."

"Jim's resilient," Dancer said. "He had to be, growing up with me and Clayton and Dede. He'll get over it."

"I'm not so sure," Paula said. She faced Dancer and her expression was serious. "That's another reason I think your moving here will be good for him. And for you." She drilled him with her dark eyes.

"Why's that?"

"He never talks about Clayton. It must be a Stonemason thing. You men pretend like nothing happened. It's okay to cry, you know."

Dancer shrugged. "You sound like Dr. Manickavel. Crying won't bring him back."

"That's right. He's gone. I'm angry as hell at Clayton for what he did, and it's hard for me to get over that anger when the man I'm living with acts like his big brother has just gone off on a long vacation. Clayton's fucking dead!" Paula's eyes welled with tears.

"It was an accident, Paula." Dancer had heard the rumors. Busybody bullshit gossip. Just like when he lost his fingers. There always had to be a reason. Someone to blame. Couldn't just be an accident.

Paula sighed like she didn't have the energy or the will to argue anymore. "Okay, Dancer. I really am glad you are here. With Kayla leaving, Jim needs someone he trusts to talk to about the business."

"What about American Jukebox?"

Paula's face clouded with disappointment. "Dancer, Jim kept that place afloat for ten years. It was never going to be viable. It's time to move on."

Kept it afloat? Clayton had told Dancer they were making money. He'd paid Dancer a decent salary for the last three years. Was that all Jim's charity?

"I didn't know Jim was funding the company. Clayton never told me that."

When Dede was having her affair, he'd been totally clueless. Clearly nothing had changed. He had reveled these last few years in Clayton's success and the new relationship they had forged. Had it all been a lie?

"Clayton didn't want to disappoint you," Paula said. "He was trying so hard to make it work." She paused, obviously uncertain whether to continue. "You could be a great help to Jim. He'd never say so, but I know he feels you've always favored Clayton."

Dancer stared at Paula, not believing what he had heard. Favored Clayton? What had he done or not done to make Jim believe that? When Dancer and Dede broke up, Clayton had hated his father. Deservedly so. But Jim had never taken sides. He'd been a rock, always. Everyone in the family depended on Jim. Especially Dancer.

He stared down at the floor. It felt like all the blood had left his face. "I came back to Maple Springs and spent all my time trying to repair the damage I'd done with Clayton. Helping him to build his company." He slowly shook his head. "I guess I did take Jim for granted. I didn't mean to," he said, his voice barely a whisper.

Paula squeezed his hand. "It's okay. You're right. Jim is resilient. But he'll need your help after Kayla leaves."

Dancer hitched his shoulders and straightened up. He had work to do. The clock on the wall said 8:10. "I need to get back out to the house. I've got a kid coming out there to help me move."

CHAPTER 5

8:15 AM

ANITA

Ted Landis was about to pull out of Johnnie Brown's driveway onto Sundance Drive when Anita drove up with her kids. He rolled the window down on his metallic blue Porsche 911 as Anita stopped opposite him.

"Good morning!" he said. His smile made his eyes disappear.

Anita had never met anyone so obviously happy to see her. She knew that no one in town really liked Ted, not even her mother, but he always made her feel special. He didn't do it with money—he wasn't a big spender. For sure he wasn't movie-star handsome, but they looked good together. Ted was big, not fat like Trudy claimed. He was the first man Anita had been with who was taller than her. Ted's size made her feel more feminine. She liked that he shaved his head instead of hanging on to some pathetic comb over. He had a nice shaped head—he looked sexy bald.

The sex wasn't bad either. Wayne had more endurance, but he treated sex like it was an item on his to-do list. Ted tried harder—he took double doses of Viagra and he would go down on her, something Wayne refused to do. Trudy was probably right that he was too old for her. But still.

"Hi, Ted. Is the boat ready?" she asked.

"Thanks to Johnnie. Your mom's a miracle worker. Tried to convince her to come out tonight, but she says she gets seasick. Didn't seem to care that the boat isn't going anywhere."

Anita didn't really want her mom on the party boat and Ted probably knew that. "She's Missouri stubborn," Anita said. "Be careful pulling out of here. Don't want any dings in your car."

Sundance Drive was gravel and potholes for the two mile stretch back to the highway. Not a road built for a sports car.

Ted did another eye-closing smile. "I'll see you tonight. I have a special surprise planned," he said as he eased on to the road.

Anita took a deep breath. She wasn't sure she wanted a surprise right now. If Ted had not been so obviously intent on moving their relationship to the next level, Anita would have been happy to just go along as his secret lover, at least for now. But it was becoming increasingly clear from all the hints and plans he was making that Ted wanted to close the deal.

She continued up the driveway. The Ford LTD dashboard clock indicated it was 8:15, but she knew Trudy had advanced the clock five minutes to help Anita get to work on time, so she had at least twenty minutes before her shift started.

She pulled up in front of her mom's house. Johnnie was on a step ladder rehanging the living room window shutter. She was tall like Anita, but where Anita had the fleshiness of her father and a pampered complexion, Johnnie had hard ropy muscles and skin weathered like a cowboy's. She wore baggy work jeans and an old denim work shirt with the sleeves hacked off. Her unruly, gray-streaked hair was partly covered by a red bandana.

Daniel jumped out before Anita had put the car in park. "Can I help, Grandma?" he yelled as he ran across the lawn.

Anita opened the rear car door. Kristi unbuckled her booster seat and handed her pink Barbie backpack to her mom. Anita kissed the top of her daughter's head. Her light brown hair was soft and had that sweet smell of little girl sweat. "You be a good girl now. Mind your grandma."

Kristi slipped out of her mother's grasp and ran toward Johnnie. "Grandma!" She hugged her around the waist.

"Are you hungry for pancakes?" Johnnie said.

"Pancakes!" Daniel said to Kristi as he clapped his hands together. He tugged on the strap of his sister's backpack. "Race ya!" Before Anita could yell for him to grab his stuff, he ran up the porch steps with Kristi following like a puppy.

She snatched his backpack from the car and walked toward her mother, who was staring at the house, her head tilted as she studied her handiwork. Johnnie had been working on that house for twenty years. Anita would never forget the night her mother, with her lip split and both eyes black from her latest beating, had plucked Anita from her bed and packed her and one tiny suitcase in a car she had borrowed from her brother. She drove for two days, only stopping for gas, food, and bathroom breaks. They escaped a backwater one-horse town in southeast Ohio and ended up in Maple Springs, Missouri—another map dot. A place folks moved from, not to. Johnnie promised they'd be safe here and she'd been right.

When they moved in, the house was hardly more than a shack with running water. It had belonged to one of Johnnie's recluse cousins who had died years ago.

Anita never saw her father again. She sometimes thought she should miss him, but she had no good memories. Nothing that made her wish he was a part of her life. Her mother took a job as a cashier at the Foodliner. She had to leave Anita home alone at night while she worked—but they survived. And after Johnnie started her antique scavenging, she had enough income to transform that shack into the loveliest house on Sundance Drive.

"I like that blue," Anita said, squinting at the freshly painted shutters.

Her mother wiped her brow with her bandana. "I need to finish this job before the storm hits."

Anita peered up at the clear sky. "Storm?"

Her mother was always predicting a change in the weather. Eventually the weather invariably cooperated, so Johnnie believed she had a gift for weather prophecy, even though her timing was abysmal.

"You'll see. This heat wave is about to break." She folded up the step ladder. "You don't think it's too bright?" she asked as she set the ladder down next to the porch.

"It looks pretty, Mom."

"I was tired of that dark green. I thought this would brighten things up a little."

"Can you keep the kids overnight? I'm going with Trudy to Ted's riverboat party."

Johnnie clicked her tongue. "That man is something to behold."

Anita remembered what Trudy had said about her mom's pipeline. She was sure that her mother didn't know about her and Ted, but she didn't want to get into a conversation with her about him. "I can pick them up before noon."

Johnnie wasn't done talking about Ted. "He's like an expert fly fisherman. Makes himself a pretty little lure and all the folks who by rights ought to hate his guts are falling all over themselves to get on his boat."

"Fly fisherman?"

"Yeah. A good fisherman gets a big trout on the line, he don't try to reel it in right away. He lets it run. Damn fish doesn't realize until it's too late that it's been hooked. That's what Ted does. Folks are naturally suspicious of him. For good reason. But he always seems to convince them he's not the way people think he is. They fall for it and then bam, they're hooked." Johnnie bent over and plucked a weed from her flower bed. "Didn't think

it could happen to me, but that man's a master. I never wanted
to be dependent on one customer, but now Ted Landis is fifty
percent of my business. I got hooked before I knew what hit me."
She looked curiously at Anita, expecting her to comment, but
Anita wasn't going to be hooked by her mom.

"So you're okay with the kids?" Anita asked.

Her mother dismissed that notion with a wave of her hand.
"I'll keep them all weekend. We'll go to the farmer's market
tomorrow. Sunday I'll drive them out to the holler. I have a lead
on some stuff. Gotta replenish inventory."

"They would love to stay here for the weekend. Your place is
way more fun," Anita said.

Johnnie pursed her lips and Anita knew what was coming.

"What have you done about the Wayne situation?" Her
mother almost choked on the name.

Anita shrugged. "Nothing yet. He's staying at his daddy's
place."

Her mother had never liked Wayne. Johnnie had been a
cashier at the Foodliner when Wayne got caught shoplifting a
package of Ho Hos. She brought up that incident after Anita had
started dating Wayne. "Don't make this a regular thing," she
said. "That boy's not worth it."

"He was only eleven, Mom."

Her mother had looked at her like she was the clueless one.
"People have walked out of the Foodliner with full-dressed
turkeys and that boy can't steal a lousy two-pack of cupcakes.
Throw him back."

When Anita got pregnant, Johnnie didn't want her to get
married. Told her she could live at home with her baby and
get her diploma. Together they would make it work. But Anita
didn't want to be a single mom living with her mother, so she
rolled the dice with Wayne.

Her mother gave Anita her stop-wasting-time look. "I talked to Mr. Gillespie. He said for you to call him. I'll pay his fee."

"Maybe we won't need a lawyer. If he got his own place so he could have the kids a couple days a week, I think we could just agree to split up. No harm. No foul."

Johnnie sighed. "He's an itinerant musician, playing one-night stands for chump change. He can't afford a place of his own. And he sure can't support anyone. The boy's a dreamer, not a worker. You need to think about Daniel and Kristi."

"Wayne loves his kids. He's not violent. I'm not running off in the middle of the night. This is different."

"It's always different until it ain't. That boy was never any damn good. I see him driving around town in that ridiculous truck." Her face twisted into a disgusted frown. "Crazy."

Once her mother got started on Wayne it was hard to get her to stop. "Okay, Mom. I'll talk to Mr. Gillespie," Anita said. "I'm thinking about enrolling in night school at Southwest. Get my associate's degree. Could you loan me the tuition? It's six hundred dollars for the semester."

Her mother's jaw dropped and she was, for a very brief moment, speechless. "You get yourself unhitched from Wayne and I'll give you the goddamn tuition as a gift. And I won't even say anything about how you shouldn't have wasted your daddy's inheritance on a boob job."

"Thanks for not saying anything, Mom." Anita looked at her watch. "Shit. I gotta go. You sure you're cool with having the kids for the weekend?"

Johnnie shrugged. "Maybe one of these days I'll join you on one of these girls' night out. I'm only a couple years older than Trudy." Her mom batted her eyes. "I'm kidding, darling. Go have your fun. Don't shake your new tits in every man's face."

CHAPTER 6

9:10 A.M.

DANCER

The soldier was a no-show. That was no surprise to Dancer. He hadn't wanted to hire the kid, but he could really use some help to load those two Seeburg jukeboxes. They were heavy-duty, and all he had was a finicky hoist to lift them up into the pickup. He thought about asking Lucy, but to drive over to their place would take fifteen minutes and then he'd probably be cornered by Phoebe again, wanting to know if Jim would help them with Ted Landis. That would suck up another hour.

Clayton had converted the three-car garage at the edge of his property into his jukebox workshop and warehouse. The five jukeboxes that had just arrived and the Seeburgs that Landis had bought were stored there. There wasn't enough clearance in the garage so they always had to wheel the boxes out of the garage to load them on the truck.

It wasn't an easy job, even with two men. Dancer stood in the center of the garage contemplating the two Seeburgs. They were quality pieces in good operating condition. With just a little work, Dancer could have made them sparkle. They would have sold for at least two grand, probably more on eBay, where there were plenty of rich city folks looking for something retro. Now Dancer would have to bust a gut just so he could deliver them to that asshole Ted Landis. Fuck.

Fortunately the boxes had not been unpacked. He could

use the heavy-duty strapping as a handle for the hoist. Dancer positioned the lift cart. Clayton had always tipped the jukebox forward while Dancer slipped the lift cart under it. Now Dancer had to do it all himself. He leaned over the cart and pushed on the top of the jukebox crate. It weighed over three hundred pounds. He couldn't get enough leverage with the cart between him and the box to tilt it. It was barely nine a.m. and the garage was already sweltering. Dancer leaned on the crate and tried to catch his breath.

There was a discarded sofa in the back of the garage. He dragged it over to the Seeburg and pushed the lift cart out of the way. With knees bent like a linebacker, he leaned into the crate with all his strength. His biceps and triceps twitched, and the jukebox finally tipped forward. He was able to prop it against the back of the couch. He quickly positioned the lift truck underneath the box and pulled the crate back onto the lift cart.

"Not perfect, but good enough," Dancer whispered. He and Clayton had adopted that as their catchphrase. They didn't have to make the jukes perfect. Just good enough to satisfy their customers. It had become their performance standard for work and for life.

Paula was wrong. Clayton wasn't gone. He was in Dancer's head and he would be there forever. All Dancer had to do was close his eyes and he could feel Clayton clinging to his neck as they paraded around Crutchfield Stadium the day Dancer pitched his perfect game. On that day, they both had been perfect.

Dancer repeated the procedure for the second box and was feeling unreasonably smug as he wheeled it out to the truck, until he remembered all the times Clayton would swear a blue streak grappling with the temperamental hoist.

Dancer slipped the hoist hooks into the strapping. He

had just started cranking when a purple half-ton pickup with cartoonish, over-sized tires rumbled up the driveway. Wayne Mesirow, dressed in camo Army fatigues, jumped out.

"Why you using that freaky old hoist?" he asked. "Don't you have a liftgate?"

Dancer stopped cranking. He was exhausted and the jukebox had barely moved. "If I had a fucking liftgate I wouldn't be using the goddamn hoist, would I?" He wiped his brow and glared at Wayne, angry at the situation more than at the boy. "What's with the fatigues?"

Wayne grinned sheepishly. "Don't have any clean clothes."

Dancer had been there before too. "Jump up here and do the cranking. I'll steady the box. Jim sold these to Landis, so I need to deliver them, pronto."

"Hell, I can deliver them for you. I got a liftgate. No need for you to bust your ass."

The kid made sense, but no way would Dancer let him drive off with two jukeboxes. "Okay. We'll use your truck, but I have to go along. Ted Landis is a hard ass."

It was no sweat, literally, to load the boxes with the liftgate. The tailgate descended like an elevator until it was flush with the pavement. With the push of a button, the jukes were lifted up to the truck bed. Dancer changed his sweaty T-shirt while Wayne worked on the second box.

When Dancer walked back out to the driveway, the boy had both jukeboxes loaded and tied down. He was sitting in the truck with the engine rumbling like a bull ready to bolt out of the chute. With the giant tires, the truck was so high a kid could probably walk under it without ducking. Dancer stared dubiously at the bully step, which was at least three feet off the ground.

Wayne rolled down the window. "If you need a boost, I got a stool here I use for the ladies."

Dancer ignored the gibe as he grabbed the handhold and hoisted himself up into the cab. "You expecting a flood?"

Wayne smirked. "Those are thirty-seven-inch nitro trail grapplers with heavy-duty struts. I can drive through anything, and I like the view from up here. So where we going?"

Dancer settled into the comfortable bucket seat—a nice upgrade from Clayton's tired old Ford with its duct-taped upholstery. "A few miles southeast of Pomona," he said as he buckled his seat belt. "Landis has his riverboat moored at a place he calls Landis Landing. It used to be the Jesse James Water Park."

Wayne turned left out of the driveway onto Ridge Road. "That's the party boat Lucy was talking about? What's Landis want with that shitty water park? Place is a dump."

"Water park's gone. He's turning that whole section of the river from Maple Springs to West Plains into a giant development project: golf course, condos, restaurants, a whole bunch of factory stores. The riverboat is just the beginning."

For the last year, Landis had been buying up property on both sides of the river. Clayton had refused to even talk to him and so had the basket ladies, but most of the other landowners had sold out.

"A riverboat on the Caledonia?" Wayne said. "Sucker's hardly three feet deep most places." He shifted into overdrive as they turned onto US 63. The engine whined and Dancer had to admit the elevated view was cool.

"Jim says Landis got the law changed. Damn boat doesn't have to go anywhere. Just has to float."

On the southern horizon, a long row of eerie yellow clouds emerged, looking like a distant mountain range. "I heard there was a tornado spotted outside Fort Smith yesterday," Wayne said.

"Bad weather all around us. All we get is this damn heat and humidity. Glad the AC is working," Dancer said.

"Hell, this ain't nothing compared to Iraq. No wonder those fuckers are always fighting. Place was unlivable."

"You got sent to Iraq with the Guard?" Dancer asked.

"Yeah," Wayne said. He had a tight smile on his face—a look of regret—and for the first time he seemed at a loss for words. "Big mistake."

"The war?" Dancer asked.

Wayne shrugged. "Don't know shit about the war. Hell, I still couldn't find that place on a map. Should have never joined the Guard. Just did it to escape. A weekend out of town every month. Didn't think they'd call us up. Stupid, huh?"

Dancer stared at Wayne, bemused. "Trust me. On the stupid ladder, that's barely the first rung."

"My old man said you were a ballplayer."

"Long time ago. Your father must be old."

"Not as old as you. He said you pitched a perfect game and you should have made it to the majors but you screwed up."

Paula was right—folks were never going to forget the bad shit.

Dancer adjusted his seat so he could stretch out his legs. "I got the call to report to the Cardinals just before I pitched that game. They wanted me for the Labor Day doubleheader in three days. Manager didn't want me to pitch, but my son was in the crowd and it was the first time he'd seen me play, so I convinced the manager to let me go three innings."

"So you wouldn't be worn out?"

"That was the plan. But I was young and strong. No reason to take me out. I was cruising. Everything was working. Three innings went by and they hadn't even hit the ball out of the infield. My manager didn't like it, but I convinced him to let me pitch until they got a hit."

"And they didn't get one, right?"

"That's right. Only problem was I developed a blister on my throwing hand. Cardinals figured I wouldn't be ready to pitch again in three days, so they brought someone else up."

Wayne squinted at the rearview, then tapped the brakes to make space for a Budweiser truck pulling onto the highway. "So, if you'd come out of the game like they planned, you'd have made it to the majors?"

"Maybe. But I couldn't quit with a perfect game on the line. I was disappointed, but I figured I'd get another shot. It didn't happen."

"That sucks. Do you wish you'd come out of that game?"

Dancer smiled. Every drunk in the county had asked him that question one time or another. "I made more than a lifetime of mistakes, but that wasn't one of them," he said. "Not everything happens for a reason. Life isn't that simple."

"My wife wants to dump me," Wayne said. He gunned the engine and passed a tractor trailer loaded with hickory logs. "If I hadn't gone to Iraq that wouldn't have happened."

"Really? What would you have done different that would have changed her mind?"

"If I'd been here, she wouldn't have been hanging out with that Trudy woman. Bitch is a bad influence. Got Anita out to the bars every weekend."

"Trudy Bennett?" Dancer asked.

"That's the name. You know her?"

"She's my mailman." He could have said more, but he stopped himself.

Of all the women Clayton had been involved with, Trudy had been Dancer's favorite. If they had stayed together, the boy might have escaped. Started over with her someplace where he wasn't haunted by the Stonemason legacy. But that wasn't on

Trudy. Clayton returned from the war a different man. Angry and out of control. A hard man to love.

Wayne's face was pinched. "My wife said she found someone new. But I don't believe her. She might have hooked up with someone, but it couldn't have been serious. I'd have heard about it. Can't fool around in this town without someone talking."

What had Paula said? People in town loved to talk trash. If Wayne hadn't heard anything maybe his wife wasn't cheating on him. Or maybe he wasn't paying attention. That had been Dancer's problem.

"But she says she wants out?" Dancer asked.

Wayne hung his head. "I screwed up with Anita. Took her for granted. I just want another chance."

Dancer studied the kid. He didn't seem half bad. Not as much of a fuckup as he had suspected. "There's no shortage of people who will tell you how to fix the problems you've taken a lifetime to create. I don't intend to be one of those folks, but you might as well talk to your woman. What do you have to lose?"

"My old man says first I need to talk to your son about getting my job back. But I hated that job. No offense. Mr. Stonemason treated me fair."

"What kind of work you looking for?"

Wayne peeked over his shoulder and then passed another log hauler. "I had a chance to play lead guitar with the Confederate Pirates, but I got called up and they hired someone else. My old man doesn't understand. I can make a living playing guitar, I just need a break."

Dancer nodded. He understood. "Doesn't do any good to give up your dream if it messes you up so you're no good for your family. I learned that lesson the hard way. Take the exit for Fort Hill Road."

"I thought we were going to Pomona?"

Dancer's face stiffened. Just the thought of having to do a special favor for Ted Landis made him angry. "We have to pick up some junk for Landis from one of those antique dealers. She's over on Sundance."

"Johnnie Brown?" Wayne asked.

"Yeah. You know her?"

Wayne laughed bitterly. "Johnnie's my mother-in-law. She hates my guts."

CHAPTER 7

9:15 A.M.

JIM

Jim Stonemason drove west on US 60, headed for the meeting with his attorney, Matt Gillespie. For the first time since Clayton had died, he was feeling hopeful. The tightness in his chest that had dogged him these last six months was almost forgotten.

He felt even more pride than normal as he cruised past the tall retro neon sign for STONEMASON CHEVROLET. When he spotted the entrance to Landis Mall a mile down the road, he chose to see Landis and his mall not as an evil force, but as a necessary development in the renewal of his hometown. A renewal that would be led by Jim Stonemason. Today was the first big step.

Jim turned off the highway onto Harris Street and then onto Main. He rolled past the storefront that used to be Ivy Drugstore, where as kids he and Clayton had bought their freeze pops and candy bars. It was now a Tae Kwon Do center. Next door, after Campbell Jewelry left their home of fifty years, a succession of businesses had tried and failed to make a go of it in the building, from a takeout Mexican restaurant to a discount cigarette outlet. Bernie Campbell, the son of the founders, had given Jim a special deal on Paula's engagement ring, but six months after two national jewelry chains opened in the new mall, Bernie was out of business. The current occupant was Ruby's Nail Emporium.

Jim remembered those hot summer days when he had

perched on the handlebars of Clayton's bike as they rolled down Main Street. Clayton had been fearless. He looked out for his little brother and protected his mom, even when she didn't need protecting. Clayton was smart too, even though he refused to admit it. He could have had it all, but his anger at their father poisoned his life for decades. All those years when Dancer was out West trying to hang on as a pitching coach, Clayton never reached out. Jim and Paula had taken Kayla out to Albuquerque during Easter vacation one year when Kayla was nine and they spent a long weekend visiting. Jim had asked Clayton to come along, but he said he was too busy.

Then Dancer returned, and against all odds, he and Clayton rebuilt their relationship.

Without Jim.

Jim had hoped that once he got the Saturn dealership up and running, he could bring Clayton into his business. Dancer too. With Kayla running Saturn, it would be a real family operation. The Stonemason team would be unbeatable.

But now that could never happen. Clayton was gone, and Dancer resented Jim for not wanting to waste more money on Clayton's damn jukebox business. Winning the Saturn dealership and launching his plan to save downtown should have been the moment when Jim got to bask in the spotlight like Dancer and Clayton had so many times. But there would be no cheers from Clayton or Dancer. Not even Paula seemed to care about his plans anymore. She had been a different woman since Clayton died.

Kayla was now the only bright spot in Jim's life. The one person who could truly appreciate his work.

The Gillespie law offices were on the second floor of the Scribner Stationary Building. Every September Dede had dragged Clayton and Jimmy to Scribner's to stock up on school supplies. Now the space was occupied by a second-hand clothing store.

Jim parked in the empty Crutchfield lot across the street from the law office. Weeds had forced their way through the crumbling asphalt. When Jim's mentor, Seymour Crutchfield, had dropped dead at his desk back in '89, his daughters had sold the Crutchfield General Store chain to a real estate developer who leveraged everything and was broke in ten years. Now graffiti-scrawled plywood covered the front windows. For years the town council had been trying to find someone to take over the space.

Five years ago, Ted Landis offered to buy the property and convert it into a park, honoring his late ex-wife. Joyce Landis had left her husband after her affair with Dede Stonemason had come to light. She wanted Dede to run away with her, but his mother had refused so Joyce escaped to Scottsdale, Arizona, where there was more tolerance for gay relationships than in Maple Springs, Missouri. Unfortunately, the town council had not been prepared to have a park named after someone who one council member had described as a "notorious lesbian." In a rare defeat for Ted Landis, they rejected his proposal.

That fateful decision had prompted Landis to build Joyce Landis Memorial Mall on the outskirts of town. He anchored it with Wal-Mart and added national chain jewelry, dining, and auto parts outlets. It didn't take long for the downtown merchants to regret their decision.

Now Jim had the plan that would lead to the town's rebirth.

The thrift store took up most of the sidewalk with this week's summer sidewalk sale. The sun was already strong, and Jim was sweating in his too-snug sports coat as he sidestepped a rack of men's suits and started up the stairway to the law offices. He paused to catch his breath and wipe his brow in front of the door with "Gillespie & Gillespie" stenciled on the nubby glass panel.

The office was refreshingly cool and smelled faintly of disinfectant. For Jim it was like stepping back in time. He had spent many days after school in the Gillespie conference room.

Matt Gillespie had given Dede a job after she and Dancer had split up, and his mother worked there from the time Jim was a baby until she died in 1973. During those early years when his father had been struggling to find his way, Matt had been like a second father to the boys. Matt was also separated from his wife at that time. His wife had been involved in the 1960 presidential campaign. "Crazy for Kennedy" was how Matt had described it. Crazy enough that when Kennedy won, she left Matt and got a job in Washington.

Clayton told Jim that their mother and Matt would've married if President Kennedy's assassination hadn't caused the return of Matt's wife. Jim wasn't convinced that Dede was going to marry Matt. Clayton always acted like he knew more than he really did. If it were true, Jim was glad it never happened. Dancer moved back home when Dede got sick. If she hadn't died, they'd still be together.

Matt Junior walked out of his office. "Let's go to the conference room, Jim. Dad will be right with you. Do you want coffee?"

"No thanks. Had mine already."

The Gillespie son was a few years younger than Jim. He had joined his father's firm after law school, as his father had done thirty years earlier. He walked across the bullpen area and reached over the empty receptionist desk to shake Jim's hand. "So tomorrow's the big day. Getting nervous?"

Jim smiled. "Kayla doesn't allow anyone to get nervous. She and Barry are running the show. Didn't want any help and no fuss. It's easy for me, but I think it's killing Paula. She would love to plan the fancy wedding she never had."

Matt Senior bounded out of his office carrying a sheaf of papers in one hand and a cup of coffee in the other. With his country club tan and a full head of hair as dazzling white as his teeth, he looked like a cruise ship hustler.

"Hey, Jimmy!" he said. "You ready to sign some papers?"

Jim was buying the headquarters property of Crutchfield General Store. He planned to tear down the Crutchfield building and replace it with a brand-new Saturn dealership. But it wouldn't look like a typical dealership. In the architectural drawings he had commissioned, it resembled an upscale boutique hotel.

GM had launched Saturn as a separate company—a revolutionary new car design and a revolutionary way to sell cars without all the hassling and dickering that most consumers hated. Every Saturn dealership in the country would be selling the models at the same fixed price, just like buying a steak or a hammer or a new suit. Saturn dealerships were in high demand, and Jim Stonemason, as a hugely successful GM dealer, was granted one of the franchises.

Matt pushed a document across the tabletop. It was earmarked with several red "Sign here" tags. "This is your escrow agreement. Do you have the check?"

Jim pulled the envelope with the fifty-thousand-dollar cashier's check from his jacket breast pocket and handed it to his lawyer.

Gillespie inspected it. "I have an escrow account set up with First National . . ." He grinned ruefully. "I mean Barclay's. Getting old, Jimmy. Can't keep up with all these changes. Please tell me you've at least talked this over with Paula."

Jim signed his name on the front page. "As soon as the

wedding is over. Before the kids take off for Hawaii." He flipped to the next signature page. He didn't want to look at Matt. He didn't need another of his well-intentioned fatherly lectures.

Gillespie got up from the table and stared out the front window at the remains of the Crutchfield's headquarters. "I won't miss looking out at that eyesore. Do you need any help from me on the Saturn dealership?" he asked.

"Not yet. I have their proposal. I'm meeting with Ted Landis today to show him my plans. I'm counting on his support."

Gillespie looked at him like he couldn't believe he had heard him correctly. "Seriously? Ted Landis? He's done everything he can to destroy Main Street."

Jim wasn't surprised by the reaction. That was typical lawyer thinking. "Landis doesn't have a vendetta," he said. "He's a hard-nosed businessman. A robust downtown won't hurt his river project. It will make it stronger. Two plus two will equal five."

Gillespie didn't argue with him, but Jim could tell he wasn't convinced. "Four dealerships. That's a lot of work for you," he said.

Jim hadn't planned to tell anyone until he had it all buttoned down, but he couldn't resist. "Kayla will head up the whole Saturn project."

Gillespie's jaw dropped. "Wow. That's a huge job for a young woman. How old is she?"

"Twenty-two. But she knows the business and she's really smart. She's going to do great." It made Jim feel good every time he thought how Kayla would react when he gave her the news. It had to be the best wedding present she could ever imagine.

CHAPTER 8

9:25 A.M.

WAYNE

Wayne hadn't been to his mother-in-law's house in over a year. From the road, Johnnie's little Cape Cod always looked perfect. Like one of those country homes they feature in magazines for rich folks. Siding and shutters freshly painted, windows sparkled, flower gardens edged and weeded, lawn groomed like a golf course. Even her gravel driveway looked like it had been raked. But the backyard was a different story. That was pure hillbilly. Scattered across two acres, there were weather vanes, birdbaths, shiny colored globes, dozens of lawn boy sentries, and a small army of gnome statuary. A lawn ornament cemetery. It made for a great playground. As Wayne pulled into the long driveway, he could hear a child screaming shrilly in the backyard.

"Sounds like someone's being tortured," Dancer said. He opened the truck door and climbed down from the elevated cabin.

"That's gotta be my daughter," Wayne said. "Johnnie takes care of the kids while Anita works." He was torn. He wanted to see his kids, but not with Anita's mom around.

As though on cue, Johnnie emerged from the far side of the house on a Caterpillar lawn tractor. She frowned deeply as she spotted Wayne's purple truck. She turned off the mower and walked briskly toward them. Wayne's stomach churned.

"She doesn't look too happy," Dancer said softly, speaking out of the side of his mouth.

There was a hitch in her step when she noticed Dancer standing next to Wayne. She blinked rapidly as she tried to make sense of their joint appearance. As she resumed her march, Daniel and Kristi scampered around the other corner of the house.

"Daddy!" Kristi screamed. She ran up to him and jumped in his arms.

"Hey sweetie!" Wayne lifted her high above his head, twirling her around. She squealed with delight. As he set her back down Daniel grabbed him around the waist. "Hey, Dad! Are you taking us some place?"

Wayne tousled his son's mop of hair. "Can't today. But we'll get together next week for sure. Today I'm working with Mr. Stonemason."

Wayne introduced his kids to Dancer. Kristi wasn't really interested, but Daniel stared at Dancer's maimed left hand. "What happened to your fingers?" he asked.

"I was careless. Didn't watch what I was doing," Dancer said.

Johnnie had made it across the lawn. "Hello, Wayne," she said. Her voice civil but cold. She turned to Dancer. "Mr. Stonemason." She nodded formally. "I was very sorry to hear about Clayton. I used to run into him at the swap meets and auctions all the time. He was a good man."

"Thank you," Dancer said. "Jim said you had some stuff for me to deliver out to Landis's place?"

Johnnie waved her hand dismissively. "That man. Don't know what he's thinking. Drives out here in his fancy sports car with a trunk that hardly has room for a shoebox. It's just some brass lamps and sconces." She pointed to two packing cartons on the front steps.

"I'll load them," Wayne said. He wanted to get away from

Johnnie. He never felt comfortable around her. She didn't believe he was good enough for her daughter. "Hey guys. Help me carry these boxes."

Johnnie turned to Dancer. "I have some paperwork for Ted. Why don't you come in the house while I gather it up? Get out of this heat."

Wayne knew she just wanted to get Dancer alone so she could learn why he was employing her good-for-nothing son-in-law, but he didn't care. Once she was out of his sight he immediately felt better. He picked up the first carton—it didn't weigh more than twenty pounds. He groaned dramatically and staggered down the steps. "Help me, I'm going to drop it."

Kristi and Daniel giggled and ran over, jostling each other. "I got it, Kristi," Daniel said. "Get out of the way."

Wayne grinned at his daughter. "No yelling," he said quickly, before she could blast her brother with one of her train-whistle screams. "Daniel, you hold one corner. Kristi, you hold the other. Teamwork. It's important."

They positioned both cartons in the back of the truck and Wayne strapped them down.

"What's in those?" Daniel asked, pointing.

"Jukeboxes," Wayne said.

"What's a jute box?"

"Juke, not jute. It plays old fashioned vinyl music records. You know. Like they have on *Happy Days*."

"When you pick us up, can we go to McDonald's?" Kristi asked. "I want a Barbie Happy Meal."

"Those are stupid," Daniel said.

"Are not!" Kristi said.

She was getting close to scream-level again and that would bring Johnnie back out to rescue the kids from their evil father.

"Hey, guys," Wayne said. "Next week, you want to go to a concert down in Pomona? A real rock band. There'll be lots of cool stuff like cotton candy and sno-cones."

"Neat!" Daniel said. "That's better than a stupid Happy Meal."

"Can Mommy go too?" Kristi asked.

Daniel looked at Wayne expectantly. The kids wanted them back together. Wayne swallowed hard.

Johnnie and Dancer walked out onto the porch. Dancer had the paperwork in his hand. It was time to go. Wayne picked up Kristi and twirled her again. "Maybe. I'll ask her. Now y'all be good. Mind your grandma."

Wayne hugged Daniel and nodded grimly at Johnnie. He pulled himself up into the truck and started the engine.

Dancer settled back into his seat. "You're right. She does hate your guts."

Wayne shrugged. "Didn't use to be like that. When she was the checkout lady at the Foodliner, she was downright friendly to me. Always talked to me about my music—my band would play dances at the high school. But once Anita got pregnant and we got married, I couldn't do anything right. She thought I was wasting my time, trying to be a musician. Thought I should work at the plant like Anita and Zeke and everyone else."

The engine hummed as Wayne pulled onto the highway. "She's wrong about my music. So's my old man. I just need a break." He shifted into third and brought the truck up to cruising speed. "Holy shit!" He pointed at a huge billboard. "The Madman's opening a store in West Plains!" Pictured on the billboard was a frizzy-haired guy with his hands raised over his head. Above him a banner read: *Grand Opening—Southern Hills Shopping Center. The Electronics King of Joplin is coming to West Plains!*

"What are you talking about?" Dancer asked, frowning.

"Madman Patel, the Electronics King of Joplin! You've seen his commercials. He's on all the late-night shows."

Dancer shrugged. "Don't watch much TV."

"Can we stop? It's on the way."

Dancer stared at Wayne like he was crazy. "Are you kidding? We got work to do."

"Madman Patel is Sonny's old man. Sonny and I were the only guys from our unit assigned to the Engineer Corps."

Dancer's expression softened. "Clayton was in the Engineers in Vietnam."

"No shit. What kind of work?"

"They were supposed to be helping the Army build roads, but Clayton told me he spent most of his time selling cigarettes on the black market. He wasn't gung ho for the war, he just wanted to escape."

"Escape from what?"

Dancer had that half smile on his face, like whatever he planned to say wasn't really funny. "He was trying to get away from me. My bad reputation. I was glad he left. This town was no good for him. He shouldn't have come back." He looked at Wayne. "What did you do over there?"

Wayne settled back in his seat and exhaled slowly, remembering those precious days with Sonny. "We did recon for the Seabees and Army Engineers. Spent our whole tour patrolling the Tigris River in a powerboat while they built a fucking bridge nobody ever used."

"What happened?" Dancer asked.

"Sonny drowned." His voice caught. It was the first time he had actually said those words. "I just want to pay my respects to his father," he said softly. "I won't take too long."

Dancer looked at his watch and shrugged. "I guess Ted Landis can wait.

CHAPTER 9

9:30 A.M.

KAYLA

Kayla was waiting to greet any customers who ventured out of their air-conditioned offices to go car shopping. She positioned herself in the shade of the Stonemason Chevrolet sign, but there was no escape from the heat. The morning sun had already baked the asphalt enough so that the soles of her running shoes made slurpy sounds as she walked across the tacky surface. She craned her neck to look up at the sign. It was older than she was. Her father had planned to replace it a decade ago but had changed his mind. Now the midnight blue oval and the bright red neon with its 1960s script created a cool retro look.

She had grown up under that sign and now she was leaving. She wondered what she would do in New York City. The only job she had ever had was selling cars. What kind of work could a small-town hick get in the big city? She studied the sign as though it might have some answer for her. Uncle Clayton used to say that his brother could have saved a lot of money on neon if he just named his dealership "Jim's."

Her uncle had been cool. When he wasn't in one of his dark moods, he made all the family gatherings more fun. He loved to tease her father about how hard he worked, but anyone could see he was proud of his brother's success. Kayla missed Clayton, but not like her parents did. Her mom cried for a week when he died. Ten months later she still wasn't the same person. She was too nice now. Kayla missed the opinionated, sarcastic mother she grew up with.

Kayla had hoped that her wedding, with all of her and Barry's "screwball notions," would bring back the old acid-tongued Paula, but it hadn't. She had agreed without protest to all of their ideas, even having the reception in the showroom.

Her father's reaction to his brother's death was more upsetting. He was so controlled—took care of all the arrangements for the visitation, funeral, and the military burial. His eulogy for his brother had brought everyone to tears. Everyone except him. Whatever he was feeling, he hadn't shared it with anyone.

Stu Collins, acting as assistant GM today, strolled out to where she was standing. With his trim brush cut and a beer gut that was starting to become serious, he looked like a jock gone to seed, which he was. He tugged up his Dockers and pretended to wipe his brow. "Come inside, Kayla. Too hot for folks to buy a car today. Save your energy for your wedding night," he said. He leered at her but in his usual good-natured way.

"It's Barry that needs to rest, not me," she said. She could hold her own with any of those salesmen. "And it's not too hot if you need a car."

She *would* sell a car today. That would be her sign everything was going to be okay: New York, Barry, the baby, her father. Especially her father. She got a sick feeling in the pit of her stomach as she thought about telling her dad she was leaving. "And look at that. My next sale just arrived."

Oscar Hancock rattled into the lot in his ten-year-old S-10. Oscar was a short-order cook at the Main Street Diner. He was a magician on the grill—his burgers, omelets, and hash browns were to die for, but he was not so magical on mechanical matters. His truck engine was overheated. It continued to clank and sputter after he turned off the ignition. Normally that would be a good buying signal, but Oscar had been coming in for the last six weeks with that sputtering wreck. No one had walked him into the box yet. Oscar was the kind of guy Paula would call a gentleman. Tipped his hat, always said yes ma'am and yes sir. Played Santa Claus at the Toys for Tots gala every December. With his round face and pillow-sized gut, he was perfect for the part.

"Hey Oscar, how are things?" Kayla held out her hand, offering him her most enthusiastic smile.

Oscar took off his Cardinals cap and patted down a few wispy long hairs he had wrapped around his bald head. He clutched his hat, staring down at his feet like Bashful, the dwarf from *Snow White*. He didn't seem to know whether he should take her hand or not. Finally he gave a quick up-and-down handshake.

"Hello, Miss Kayla. Can't complain. Wouldn't do no good anyhow."

Kayla searched her memory for something she could hook Oscar with. She had a recollection of him pushing a tandem stroller down Main Street when she was still in high school. Twins. He had twins. "How are those twins, Oscar?" She couldn't remember if they were boys or girls. "I'll bet they're a handful. What are they now, six?"

Oscar's worried looked morphed into a broad smile. "Nine years old last month. They're in the Rotary Soccer League over in Landis Park. Belinda's top scorer. And Melinda, she's a defensive star. Coach separated them, so he could tell them apart."

Kayla offered him her wide-eyed, totally amazed look. "Nine years old. They grow up fast, don't they?" She put her hand on his shoulder and pointed toward the lot, where her father had all the 2003 Silverados on display—the ones Jim wanted gone before the 2004s arrived. "I want to show you something,

Oscar. Your S-10 is a great *little* truck," she said, making sure he caught her emphasis. "But it's too small for your family, and it's not safe enough. Take a ride with me in this new Silverado. It's got your extended bed with your club cab so you can haul your gals to every game with total peace of mind."

Normally she would have started slower, but this would be her last chance to sell Oscar. She started to stroll toward the Silverados, but Oscar didn't move. She looked back and he was staring at her like he'd forgotten why he came.

"Did anyone ever tell you that you look like Hayley Mills?" Oscar asked.

Oscar was a master at going off on tangents. Kayla smiled, pretending she hadn't heard him. "Come on, Oscar, check out this truck."

"She's the daughter of John Mills, the great English actor."

Kayla tried not to sigh. "Never heard of her."

Oscar wrinkled his forehead as though he were trying to decide whether her ignorance of Hayley Mills made her an unworthy salesperson. "We rented the *Parent Trap* the other day. Helen and I wanted the twins to see the original version, not the one with that new girl, Lindsay Lonigan. You have the same blond hair and freckles."

"You mean Lindsey Lohan? Hayley Mills looks like Lindsey Lohan? Isn't she like ten years old in that movie?" Feigning great offense at that implication, Kayla put her hand on her hip and gave her head a Valley girl tilt. Oscar's cheeks reddened liked they'd been slapped.

That was her opening. Kayla marched toward the Sport Red Silverado with a sticker price of twenty-eight nine ninety-nine, and Oscar, hat in hand, head down, followed her like she was Snow White. "Check out this suspension, Oscar. Safety. That's what this truck is all about . . ."

Thirty minutes later she had him in the box.

Selling cars was a game. The box was a bare cubicle—no phones, no windows, two folding chairs, and a beat-up card table—in the back of the showroom. They sat down and Kayla pulled out the 4-Square, their negotiation worksheet. There was one square for the list price, one for down payment, one for monthly payment, and one for trade-in. By the end of the negotiation, the 4-Square would be littered with so many numbers most customers had no clue as to what they had actually agreed to.

Oscar watched as Kayla wrote $28,999 in the list price box. She wrote it big and bold, with perfect penmanship, the way her father had taught her. Oscar scooted to the edge of his chair. "I can't pay twenty-nine for that truck. No way." He folded his arms across his chest.

"Don't fret, Oscar. I'm filling in the form the way the boss tells me to. Now how much did you want to put down?"

Kayla kept Oscar answering the easy questions as she filled in the blanks. Address. Insurance carrier. Date of birth. Down payment. Monthly payment capability. She took her time because the longer he sat in that chair the better her chances were of closing the deal.

"I can't pay more than twenty-six and I need a grand for the S-10," Oscar said as she finished filling in the boxes. He leaned forward, elbows propped on the table. His ball cap was clutched tightly in his hands.

That was perfect. They would get a minimum of two grand for the truck at auction and dealer invoice on the Silverado was twenty-three five, so she was already in the money and the negotiations hadn't started. She glanced up at the mezzanine and nodded at Stu Collins. A minute later he strolled over to the table.

"Hey Oscar, my gal Kayla treating you okay?"

They shook hands. Oscar exhibited none of his earlier handshake uncertainty. He settled back into the rickety folding chair. "Miss Kayla's doing fine. We were just beginning our discussion." He wanted Stu to go away, which was good.

Stu picked up her 4-Square where she had written Oscar's counteroffer. He threw it back on the desk like it had burned his hand. "Twenty-six?" he said, his voice breaking like a teenage boy. "Call the cops, Kayla. Oscar's trying to steal this truck," He took a step back from the table. "Oscar, do you think Jim Stonemason is going to give this vehicle away just because his little girl's getting married?"

Oscar looked at Kayla—his mouth and eyes were perfect circles in his round red face. "You're getting married? When?"

"Hell, Oscar, where you been? She's getting hitched tomorrow to some bean counter. There's a rumor she might wear a dress."

Kayla's stomach started to feel queasy. Being pregnant made her hungry all the time, and she was getting more and more stressed as she realized she could no longer put off telling her father about the move to New York.

"Congratulations!" Oscar reached over and clasped her hand between both of his. He smiled as if he were the one getting married.

When Oscar finally let go, Stu came up behind Kayla and squeezed her shoulders. "Yes sir. Kayla's getting married on Saturday, probably be back on the job on Monday."

"You're going to keep working?" Oscar asked.

"Yes," she said with a smile she hoped appeared demure and unflappable. She twisted her shoulders out of Stu's grip and gave him her I'll-kill-you-if-you-don't-shut-up look as she said sweetly, "Stu, Oscar and I can work this out." She leaned in.

"Okay, now Oscar, do you want the flashy Sport Red or the more subtle Sierra Mist?"

Fifteen minutes later they had a deal. Kayla began filling out the paperwork for financing and ownership transfer on Oscar's S-10. "Can you give me your driver's license? I need to copy the ID number."

Oscar's wallet was two inches thick and crammed with business cards and snapshots of the twins. A creased business card tumbled out. Kayla picked it up off the floor. It was faded and fuzzed along the edges like it had been through the wash more than once. Without really meaning to, she glanced at it as she handed it back to him:

KENDALL COLLEGE OF CULINARY ARTS
Evanston, IL
Stephen Matthews—Dean of Admissions

"Are you applying to cooking school, Oscar?" The question escaped her mouth before she could stop herself. It was a rookie selling mistake: Never ask a personal question you don't know the answer to.

Oscar blushed, but not like before. This time his look was more resigned than abashed. "I don't know why I'm still holding on to that card."

Kayla started transcribing his driver's license number on to her form. She felt like she should say something more but didn't know what.

Oscar sighed. "I had a full scholarship to Kendall, but when Helen got pregnant we decided it would be a mistake to move to Illinois right then. Better to stay in Maple Springs where we had family to help us with the twins. Two babies are a lot of work."

Kayla stared at him. It would probably sound lame for her to tell him how much she loved his eggs Benedict.

Oscar hung his head. "I wanted to become a real chef, not just a lousy grill man. Always figured I'd go to Kendall after things settled down." He looked at the card again and shrugged. "Maybe I will someday."

CHAPTER 10

10:15 A.M.

WAYNE

Madman Patel—the Electronics King of Joplin—knew how to get attention. For the opening of his new store, he had set up a mini carnival in the parking lot. There were free rides for the kids on a tiny roller coaster and an old-fashioned carousel, and there were cheap eats for everyone. Fifty-cent hot dogs, nickel sno-cones, and nachos for two bits. Red, white, and blue pennants and balloons ringed the parking lot.

"You want out here?" Wayne asked Dancer. "I'm parking over in that corner, away from the crowd. Don't like people messing with my truck."

"Sounds good. I already got my hike for the day. I'll look around the store and meet you in front in fifteen minutes." He pushed open the door and eased himself down to the pavement. For an old guy, Dancer moved pretty well.

Wayne parked as far away from the commotion as he could. He grabbed Sonny's Sig from the glove box, tugged it from its holster, and pressed the grip against his face. It smelled of gun oil and was cool on his cheek. He slipped the re-holstered Sig into the deep hip pocket of his fatigues.

He wove his way through the carnival crowd. As he walked past the food stand, the sweet smell of cotton candy blended with the cheesy aroma of nachos. He should have been hungry—he hadn't eaten all morning—but his stomach was churning with nervous apprehension. He had been certain that giving Sonny's gun to Mr. Patel was the right thing to do. Now he wasn't so confident.

Wayne shivered even though the sun-blistered asphalt was steaming. He straightened up and squared his shoulders, like Sonny was always reminding him to do. Mr. Patel would understand. He would appreciate the risk that Wayne had taken to deliver Sonny's gun to him. Wayne, a trusted friend, delivering the sword of a fallen warrior.

At the entrance to the store, Wayne was welcomed by four pompom-toting girls with long shiny black hair. They cheered everyone who entered, but still it made Wayne feel special. The cheerleaders were probably Sonny's younger sisters. Sonny had five, but he told Wayne that the oldest one had run away when he was ten and he never saw her again.

For weeks he had been rehearsing in his head what he would say to Sonny's father when he gave him the gun. Then, as he marched into the store, there was the Madman. Wayne's heart raced. But it was just a life-size cardboard cutout of the man, his arms extended over his head like the crazy man he pretended to be.

Wayne stepped around the cardboard Electronics King and headed up the middle aisle. Crazy or not, he was selling Magnavox VCRs for $99. People were grabbing boxes off the shelf like he was giving them away. Next to the VCRs was a huge inventory of VHS tapes. *The Gladiator* with Russell Crowe was marked down to $6.99. If Zeke had owned a VCR, Wayne would have bought that tape. The Gladiator was cool. Fearless. Honorable.

At the end of the aisle there was a bank of televisions all tuned to CNN. On the screen, some white-haired pretty boy with chilly blue eyes was standing in front of a burned-out storefront in Baghdad reporting on the latest terrorist incident. Iraq was turning into a huge clusterfuck. Around the corner from the televisions was a bank of electric guitars. They were all cheap beginner sets. Nothing that compared with Wayne's Gibson.

Wayne startled as he felt a hand squeeze his shoulder. "See anything you like, my soldier friend? We have much larger inventory in the warehouse."

The hand belonged to Sonny's father. He was taller than his cutout and his hair was neatly combed, not frizzed up. He had the same smell as Sonny had when he got himself cleaned up. It must have been some kind of special Indian cologne. A spicy, bakery-like smell.

The man extended his hand. "Welcome to my store. Vikas Patel, proprietor." His skin was the color of mahogany, just like Sonny's. His hands were surprisingly soft, like they'd been pampered, but his grip was firm, confident. He made good eye contact and then glanced down at Wayne's chest pocket where his name and unit ID were sewn.

He let go of Wayne's hand and his face clouded. "You are with the National Guard?"

Wayne tried to remember what he had rehearsed. "I'm pleased to meet you, Mr. Patel. Wayne Mesirow. I was a friend of Sonny's. I mean Sanjay." Fuck. He was already screwing up. Sonny had told him his old man hated it when someone called him Sonny.

"A friend?" Mr. Patel's mouth twisted like it pained him to say the words. "What kind of friend?"

"We worked for the Army Corps building a bridge over the Tigris. Sonny, uh, Sanjay, was a great guy. He taught me to swim. Well, not really swim, not like him, but at least I could—"

"What are you babbling about?"

The Madman in the TV commercials was so happy-go-lucky. Funny. He acted like someone who would be easy to talk to. This neatly combed and dressed man wasn't like that at all. He acted crazy in a scary kind of way. He looked at Wayne like he was a turd someone had tracked into his pretty new store.

"I . . . I tried to save him, Mr. Patel." This wasn't how he had planned to deliver the news. He wanted to present Sonny's gun to him and tell him what a great friend Sonny had been.

Mr. Patel's lips curled into a sneer. "Save him from what? Himself? You fags make me sick."

Fag? Wayne took a step back. It felt like all the air had been sucked out of his lungs.

"I'm not a fag."

The Madman looked at him with disgust. "That's the only kind of friends he had." He looked like he wanted to spit on Wayne's boots. He shook his head, muttering to himself as he walked away.

Wayne shouted at his departing back. "Sonny wasn't gay. He had a girlfriend. Whitney wrote him every week."

Mr. Patel stopped walking and wheeled around. "You silly poofer. Whitney was his boyfriend. Broke his queer little heart and he couldn't take it so he killed himself. He was a fag and a coward. Now get out of my store before I call security."

"Sonny didn't kill himself, Mr. Patel." Wayne grabbed the Madman's sleeve as he started to walk away. "It was an acci—"

With surprising speed and strength, the old man grabbed Wayne around the throat. "You don't know what you're talking about, you little homo." His eyes were wild, his grip powerful. It didn't feel like he had any intention of letting go. Wayne instinctively raked his arms up hard to break the stranglehold. Mr. Patel stumbled back into a stack of GE toaster ovens, still in their cartons. The display model on top of the stack crashed to the floor.

Wayne hovered over the man. "I'm sorry, Mr. Patel. I just want to explain—"

Two men grabbed him roughly and pushed him down, twisting his arms behind his back. His eyes, nose, and lips were smooshed into the shiny storeroom floor, and his shoulders felt like they were going to pop out of their sockets.

"Get him out of here," the Madman yelled as he extricated himself from the pile of cartons. He carefully repositioned his hair, which had started to look more Madman-like from his tumble into the toaster ovens.

The two security guards yanked Wayne to his feet and frog-marched him toward the store entrance. He didn't resist, but he was having trouble getting his feet under him as they raced out the door past the pompom girls. Wayne expected them to release him once they were out of the store, but they dragged him across the parking lot.

"Let me go," Wayne yelled.

The larger of the two guards tightened his grip. He said to his partner, "Call Barrow and find out what he wants us to do with this son-of-a-bitch." He twisted harder on Wayne's arm, sending shooting pains from his shoulder to his elbow.

The smaller guard loosened his grip as he reached for his walkie-talkie. Wayne whipped his arm free. He whirled around and punched the larger guard in the side of his head, knocking his ball cap off. He staggered backwards, letting go of Wayne's arm.

"Fuck!" The guard rubbed his ear and stared at Wayne in disbelief.

Wayne started to run, but the guard with the walkie-talkie tripped him from behind, and he hit the pavement hard. As he was scrambling to get to his feet, the other guard kicked him hard in the ribs.

"How's that, asshole?"

Wayne could feel his ribs crunch the instant before he felt the excruciating pain. The blow knocked him on his side. He tried to roll away as the guard brought his leg back for another kick.

"Want some mo—"

There was a soft splat followed by a sound like a bag of air deflating, and the big guard was face down on the pavement next to Wayne, his jaw already starting to swell from the punch Dancer had landed.

The other guard, a panicked look on his face, backed away from Dancer. The searing pain in Wayne's gut made him nauseous as he struggled to stand up. The guard was desperately tugging on his revolver, but he had failed to unsnap the holster cover. Wayne pulled the Sig from his pocket and walked toward him. "You got something more to say to me, asshole?" he said, pointing the unloaded gun in the guard's face.

The guard held up his hands. "Don't shoot!"

Someone in the crowd shouted, "He has a gun!" People started running in all directions.

"Give me the gun, Wayne," Dancer said, his voice calm, like he was asking Wayne to hand him a pair of pliers.

Wayne meekly handed it to Dancer. They started jogging for the truck, which Wayne wished he had parked a hundred yards closer. Every jarring step felt like a knife stabbing him in his gut.

When they reached the truck, he handed the keys to Dancer. "You drive." He shuffled around to the passenger side and screamed in pain as he hoisted himself into the cab.

Police sirens whined in the distance as Dancer pulled out of the parking lot.

CHAPTER 11

10:20 A.M.

KAYLA

Ominous storm clouds had formed on the southern horizon and the inert, sauna-like air that had suffocated the town for weeks began to stir. But to Kayla, standing in the shade of the neon sign and watching Oscar drive off in his new Silverado, the whisper of a breeze offered no relief. She'd almost lost the sale when she proposed the financing. Kayla had shown Oscar that with a sixty-month loan, his monthly payment would be $449.43, which he could afford even if his wife remained at home with the twins. But his face clouded with disappointment.

"I was hoping to have it paid off sooner. Maybe forty-eight months?" he asked. There was no way that would work, but Kayla dutifully plugged the numbers into her loan calculator. "That will make your monthly payment $554.32," she said. They both knew he couldn't afford another hundred dollars a month.

"You need this truck, Oscar. I mean that sincerely," she had said, and she was being sincere. She liked Oscar, but not enough to give him more than a grand in trade-in for his decrepit old truck. "Why put it off? That S-10 is going to die on you any day. You could be stranded out in the middle of nowhere with your family. The Silverado will last you ten years, easy. Sixty months financing is right for you."

He sighed, accepting her verdict with a look of resignation. "By the time the truck's paid off, the twins will be getting ready to go to college."

Kayla knew he didn't really have a choice. He had to replace his truck. He couldn't abandon his family obligations. He had been Kayla's age when his twins were born. If not for them, he might have become a chef. Moved to Chicago or New York or even Paris. Who could say? His life had possibilities then. Now, ten years later, there was no off ramp from the road he had taken. He would live out his life in Maple Springs, Missouri—the best short order cook in the county. A good husband and father. A good man. He seemed happy enough, but that wistful look as he slipped the card from Kendall College back into his wallet haunted Kayla.

Now she looked up as her father rolled into the lot in his mint green Cadillac. He parked in his designated spot next to the showroom and waved for Kayla as he climbed out of the car. Jim was smiling—a real smile, not the salesman smile he could produce for anyone who might be in the market for an automobile.

"Was that Oscar Hancock driving off in a new Silverado?" Jim asked, his booming voice easy to hear even from across the lot. Kayla knew it was a rhetorical question. Her father had a great eye for any detail that affected his business. For other stuff, like her mother's profound unhappiness, his vision wasn't so great.

Kayla gave him a thumbs up.

"Come inside," he said. "There's something I want to talk to you about." He pushed open the double doors and walked back toward his office, not stopping to survey the action in the showroom as he usually did.

Kayla's stomach clutched. Could he have heard about Barry's new assignment from someone else? He wouldn't be smiling like that if he had. Whatever he wanted to talk about, it couldn't be that. As soon as he told her his news, she would tell him about the move to New York. She couldn't put it off any longer.

Jim had settled in behind his huge desk when Kayla walked into the office. His face was flushed and his blue oxford button-down had sweat stains around the neck and under his arms. He motioned for her to close the office door.

"Can't believe you were standing point outside in this heat," he said, his expression deadpan serious. If there wasn't a thunderstorm raging, Jim insisted that there be a salesperson outside to greet any potential customer.

"You've pitted out that shirt," Kayla said.

"I know. I'm changing to the white." He nodded toward the long-sleeve white shirt hanging on the doorknob to his closet. "But first, I've got some news." He pulled out a fat manila folder from his briefcase. His face could barely contain his smile. Kayla hadn't seen him that happy since she told him she wanted to come work for him. "GM has granted us a Saturn dealership," he said.

"Holy shit." Kayla understood better than anyone what this meant. GM had been pursuing their Saturn project with missionary zeal. It was their Toyota-killer. Built in America, but not in Detroit. A new approach to manufacturing with a hassle-free approach to sales. Many of the old-line dealers hated the concept. But her father knew that the old guard were afraid to change. He wasn't.

"That's fantastic, Dad," she said. "I thought they wanted to keep it away from the established dealers?"

Jim smiled like he had been expecting that question. "Yes, that's their general approach. I convinced them there was another way."

Kayla remained silent, waiting for the big reveal.

"You're going to be in charge, Kayla." He stood up, towering over her. "You're young and smart. You understand the generation that wants to buy that car."

Kayla lost her voice. She needed to say something, but she stared dumbly at her father.

"There's more," he said, sounding like one of those late-night TV hucksters. He plucked another file folder from his briefcase. "I just agreed to take over the old Crutchfield property. That's where we're putting the dealership." He pulled out a heavy sheet of architect-style drafting paper and unfolded it on his desk. It was a mockup of Main Street. "Saturn will be the first phase in a total renewal and renovation of downtown Maple Springs!" He swept his hand across the drawing. "And you'll be my point person for the whole project."

Kayla would have never thought it could be possible to feel excitement and dread at the same time. She needed to tell her father about Barry's new job and their move, but this was huge. She wanted to talk to Barry first. Her stomach churned.

"Wow," she said, but her voice was weak, not wow-like at all. "So this is the secret project you've been working on."

"Had to keep it under wraps. Those GM guys are nervous as kittens."

Kayla made a show of looking at her watch. "I'm meeting Barry for lunch. I can tell him about your plan, right?"

"Of course. He's going to love it."

Kayla, still in a daze, hustled out of Jim's office. Stu Collins cut her off before she could get to the employee lot. "Hey. Nice job with old Oscar. How about lunch at the pub? My treat."

"Thanks, Stu. Can't do it, I'm meeting Barry at Valencia's."

Stu scoffed. "You're not driving all the way to West Plains to eat in that dump."

Kayla gave him the evil eye.

He held up his hands. "Okay, none of my business. But hey. You need to be back here by four. Your dad's taking off early. I want to go over the logistics of the showroom transformation."

Stu always took himself way too seriously whenever Jim left him in charge. But she had too much on her mind to argue with him.

"We'll be back by four," she said.

"You know you could have just rented the American Legion. They put on a nice spread."

That was the last place Kayla would have held her reception. Dank and dark, with the air reeking of cigar smoke. The food in the high school cafeteria was better. "I'm a car girl, Stu. It has to be here."

CHAPTER 12

10:45 A.M.

WAYNE

Dancer drove onto the frontage road for US 63. Two West Plains cop cars approached, sirens blaring. He pulled the truck to the side of the road.

"What the fuck you doing?" Wayne screamed. "We have to get out of here."

Dancer gave him a look. "Obeying the rules of the road. With this goddamn purple truck we don't need to be drawing any more attention to ourselves."

The cops raced past and turned into the shopping center parking lot. Dancer drove on down the road at an excruciatingly slow thirty miles per hour. He took the ramp for US 63 headed south toward West Plains.

Wayne's ribs throbbed with every bump in the highway. He unbuttoned his fatigues and pulled up his T-shirt. There was a purple, crescent-shaped bruise on the left side of his lower back. He twisted in his seat trying to find a comfortable position. He could feel the bone shift when he leaned back in his seat. "I think that asshole broke my rib," he said.

"Most likely," Dancer said. "Why the hell did you pull that gun?" He had the same disgusted, incredulous look Zeke used to have when Wayne fucked something up.

"It wasn't loaded."

Dancer stared at him like he couldn't believe what Wayne had said. The man had a bunch of looks, all of them some variation of grouchy, disgusted, or annoyed. "Pointing an unloaded gun at somebody, especially someone in law enforcement, is a really good way to get yourself killed. Along with anyone stupid enough to be with you at the time."

He was right. Wayne could have gotten them both killed. "I wasn't thinking straight. Thanks for decking that guard. You lived up to your legend, old man."

"Fuck you," Dancer said. But he had the trace of a smile. "What'd you do to get him so pissed off?"

"Sonny's old man said Sonny was gay. Said he killed himself because his boyfriend broke up with him."

"Is that true?" Dancer asked as he took the exit ramp for Siloam Springs.

The road to Siloam Springs was rough—it should have been resurfaced years ago. Wayne tried to brace himself. "Aarrww. Fuck! That hurts!" He puffed out a breath like Anita had done when she was delivering Daniel. It didn't help. "How long we got to be on this road?" he asked through gritted teeth.

Dancer looked over at him and frowned, as though he were actually concerned. "At least another twenty minutes. I'm dropping you off at Zelda's. She can take care of you while I deliver the jukes."

"Who's Zelda?"

"Fortune teller. Calls herself Madame Zelda. She's also a tattoo artist."

Wayne felt hot and cold at the same time. Sweat beaded his forehead and upper lip. "I think I'm going to be sick."

Dancer slowed down to twenty miles per hour. "Breathe, son. Nice and easy." He turned up the fan on the AC.

Wayne took a deep breath and let it out slowly. The wave of nausea passed. "I didn't know," he said.

"Know what?" Dancer asked.

"That Sonny was gay. He got a letter every week from Whitney. I thought she was a girl. Fuck, I'm an idiot."

"Tell me what happened to Sonny. It'll take your mind off the pain."

For the last two months Wayne had felt crushed by the heavy burden of Sonny's death. He had failed his friend and he wanted to confess to someone, but no one would listen. The Army didn't want to know what happened to Sonny. The investigating officer had prepared a report labeling the death an accident. He had insisted Wayne sign it. "It's war, Mesirow. Men die. End of story."

When Wayne returned home his old man wasn't interested in that "Indian fella." And now this. Not even Sonny's father wanted to hear how he died. How Wayne tried to save him. And failed.

"My reserve unit got called to active duty for Operation Iraqi Freedom in January. They bussed us down to Fort Hood for our assignments. Everyone but me and Sonny were assigned to support the Marines leading the battle for Baghdad. We got sent to help the Engineers and the Seabees build a damn bridge over the Tigris River at Zubayidiyah."

"Where?" Dancer asked.

"Zoo-bay-ih-die-ya. It's not hard to pronounce after you to have say it a couple hundred times."

"Sounds like good duty," Dancer said.

Wayne buttoned up his fatigues. The pain had dulled. "We took a lot of shit from the other guys in the unit because they were supporting the Marines. They'd be part of the real war. I was bummed, but Sonny knew it was a sweet gig. He told me we'd get our own powerboat."

"Really? What kind?" Dancer asked.

"Twenty-eight foot inboard/outboard. Two hundred horsepower Merc. That fucker could haul ass. All day long we patrolled up and down the Tigris, two miles in both directions from the bridge, keeping an eye out for hostiles. It was obvious after the first week that no one was going to attack. Hell, the locals *wanted* us to build that fucking bridge."

Dancer pulled over to the side of the road to let another pickup pass. "From the news reports, it sounded like the Iraqi army just went home when they started dropping the bombs."

Wayne nodded in agreement. "It got boring as hell. I'd spend the day plotting guitar arrangements in the logbook and Sonny would read his weekly letter from Whitney. He said Whitney lived in an apartment in Provincetown—a really cool town on Cape Cod, according to Sonny. He talked about how he'd be free there to do whatever he wanted. He hated Joplin. Didn't want to go into his father's business."

"He didn't want to work for a madman?" Dancer asked, a trace of a smile creased his face.

Wayne shifted his position. "Sonny said his father was the least crazy man he'd ever known. Said he was hardcore."

Dancer raised his eyebrows and glanced at Wayne's damaged ribs. "Hardcore, huh? I guess so."

Wayne leaned forward and directed the louvered air vents so more of the chilled air blew on him. They were driving east and the sun was intense on the windshield. "When we started our tour in January it was hot, but bearable. But by April the temperature never fell below 110 during the day. We baked in that fucking boat, so every afternoon we patrolled downstream and weighed anchor out of sight from the bridge. Sonny would dive in and swim from one side of the river to the other and I would crawl under the deck to escape the sun and try to sleep, but there was no way with that heat."

"Not a swimmer?" Dancer asked. The road had smoothed out some and he was careful to avoid most of the major potholes.

"Couldn't swim a lick. But Sonny was made for the water. The guy was movie star handsome and he already had a great tan, you know, being Indian and all. If there had been any women around, they'd been all over him. If it weren't for Sonny, I'd have never got out of that damn boat."

Dancer stopped at the outskirts of Siloam Springs. "I think Zelda's place is this way. It's been awhile." He turned left on to another beat-to-shit road. "Sonny taught you how to swim?"

"The basics: how to kick and breathe. I couldn't swim like Sonny, but I could splash around the boat and cool off while he did his thing."

Dancer's face was screwed into a puzzled frown. "None of this looks familiar." The road to Siloam Springs cut through a dense forest. Other than a few hillbilly trailers and shacks the road was deserted.

"There," Wayne said, pointing to a faded, hand-painted sign that had been nailed to a large spruce tree: MADAME ZELDA'S TATTOO PARLOR—1 MILE.

Dancer nodded vigorously. "I remember now. Her place is just past the main drag."

Wayne looked at the near deserted roadside. "I don't think this place has a main drag." He raised the seat's back so he could have a better view of the road.

"We aren't lost. Keep talking," Dancer said.

Wayne sighed and settled back in his seat. "One day Sonny swims all the way to the shore and walks into the trees along the bank. Next thing I know he comes screaming out of the brush and starts swimming like he's on fire. I'm expecting a bunch of crazy Iraqis to bust out of the trees, but there's nothing. Sonny scrambles back into the boat, grabs his .44, points it at the shore, and yanks the trigger. Luckily the gun jams. He starts screaming about snakes and cursing his gun."

"He wanted to shoot at the snakes with his .44?"

"He was scared shitless of them fuckers. The next day he went into Z-town and bought the Sig Sauer P220 and two hundred rounds of ammo."

"That's a lot of bullets."

"Cost him fifteen hundred dollars, but that included the Bengal tiger tattoo he got on his arm. Gun dealer told him it would bring him luck." Wayne laughed bitterly. "Great fucking luck."

Dancer was peering over the tops of his glasses, staring intently down the road. His face creased with a frown. "Can't read those road signs with these fucking glasses."

"There ain't any signs to see. You sure you know where we're going?" Wayne asked.

"Keep talking, boy. I'll do the driving."

"Okay. You're paying me for the day even if we never make it to that damn water park."

"Talk."

Wayne sat back in the seat and closed his eyes. He had never told anyone this part of the story. "The first week in May Sonny gets his Whitney letter. It's only a single page. I know by his face that's it bad news. He don't say nothing, just folds it up, sticks it in his pocket. Tells me he's going to drive the boat. We cruised up and down the river—fucker drove slower than you—and he kept eyeballing the riverbanks like he expected them to be crawling with bad guys. Or snakes."

"He didn't say anything about the letter?" Dancer asked.

"Nope. And I didn't ask. For two weeks he was a different man. Didn't swim or tell any stories or joke around. Just sat in the goddamn boat staring at the riverbank, clutching his Sig."

Wayne paused, remembering.

"Then, boom," he said. "The old Sonny returns. It was like

he'd had a fever and now everything was back to normal. Tells me to drive again. Late in the afternoon he has me stop at our swimming place and he strips down to his cargo shorts and hands me the Sig. 'Take care of my gun,' he says, and he has this weird smile on his face."

Wayne reached up and pulled down the visor, but it didn't help much. The sun was blinding, just like it had been on that late afternoon.

"Sonny starts swimming into the sun, heading downstream, not toward shore. I yell, 'Where you going, Sonny?' and he stops swimming and looks back at me with that killer smile and tells me that he's trying to get back in shape. Says I should take a nap because he'll be gone at least an hour."

Just saying the words out loud made Wayne realize how naive he had been.

"It's late afternoon, hottest part of the day, so I do what he says. I crawl under the deck and go to sleep. I wake up when I hear Sonny yelling for help. I look down the river and I'm blinded by the sun reflecting on the water. Sonny's out there somewhere, but I can't see him. Then I hear him. He's calling my name, asking for help. He sounds desperate. I crouch low in the boat and shade my eyes and I see a splash and a dark shadow in this sea of gold. Sonny's in the middle of the river at least a hundred yards downstream. I yank up the anchor and punch the starter. Nothing. The battery's dead."

Wayne paused as Dancer slowed down to avoid a hopscotch of potholes. How did the battery go dead? Did Sonny disable it, so Wayne couldn't save him? He took a deep breath and continued.

"Sonny calls out to me again. His voice is weaker and I know I have to do something fast. I yell that I'm coming and I stand up in the boat and wave my arms hoping he sees me. He calls again. His voice is weaker. More desperate."

Wayne swallowed hard. The Madman was wrong. Sonny wanted to live. He didn't want to die in that river.

"I jump in and start swimming towards him. The current's a lot stronger than I'm used to and in no time, I'm fucking exhausted."

The memory of that cold sick feeling flooded Wayne's mind. He had wanted so desperately to be brave. To save his friend. But he was terrified of drowning.

"I'm not getting any closer and the boat's drifting free about twenty yards behind me. I swallow a mouthful of water and start choking. I know I'll never be able to reach Sonny so I turn around and flail my way back to the boat. I grab the Sig. Fire it into the sky until it's empty. Then I start screaming for help."

Screaming. That was all he could do for his friend.

"In less than five minutes a crew of Seabees rounds the bend in the river on a motorized raft. But it's too late. Some raghead farmer finds Sonny's body three days later, caught among the reeds and stumps, a mile downstream from the bridge. Two weeks later we're shipped home. Mission fucking accomplished."

Dancer stopped scanning the highway for Zelda's parlor and looked at Wayne with actual concern. "Did you tell Sonny's father what happened?"

"He didn't want to hear it. It was like he hated his son for being gay. Hated anyone who had anything to do with him," Wayne said, shaking his head slowly. "Hey. There's Zelda's. Next to that taco stand."

Dancer pulled off the road and parked in front of a white cottage with blue shutters. "This is the place. I told you I knew where it was."

"Yeah, I never doubted you."

Dancer jumped down from the truck and bounded up the steps. There was a note pinned on the front door. "Says she'll be back in ten minutes," he said. He looked around. There was a Baptist Church across the street next to a Texaco Station and a taco stand. "I'll see if she's over at El Charro."

Wayne eased himself out of the truck and walked slowly up the steps to the shaded porch of Madame Zelda's Tattoo Parlor. He settled carefully into the wood rocking chair on the porch. "I'll just wait here. Could you get me three beef tacos while you're over there?" he said. "And a beer?"

"This is a dry town."

"Fuck me. This ain't a town. It's barely a crossroads. Lots of hot sauce on the tacos, too."

"Anything else?" Dancer asked, giving him that look again.

"Dr. Pepper. No ice."

Dancer walked away, shaking his head. A few minutes later he was back with three tacos and a can of Dr. Pepper. "She wasn't there. They haven't seen her." He looked up and down the highway, but it was deserted. "You stay here. Enjoy your tacos and I'll be back in an hour or so. If Zelda shows up, just tell her you know me. Don't let her con you."

Wayne raised himself up in the chair, indignant. "What the fuck. I ain't stupid. I'm not getting fleeced by some two-bit hillbilly fortune teller."

Dancer squirreled up his face again. "Right. I forgot. You're a man of the world." He pulled himself up into Wayne's truck like he'd driven it all his life.

CHAPTER 13

11:15 A.M.

DANCER

Ten miles down the road from Zelda's Tattoo Parlor was the cutoff for the Jesse James Water Park. Ted Landis, in his race to get his riverboat casino launched, had not had time to replace the billboard of a menacing fifty-foot-tall Jesse James pointing his Colt 45 in the direction of the water park. The Budweiser truck that Dancer had been following for the last ten minutes made the turn ahead of him.

The road down to the river was a mile-long downhill with a dozen switchbacks. In the two years the water park had been closed, the road, which had been oiled dirt, had gone untended and now, after the month-long drought, it was dusty and rutted. It was a good thing he had left Wayne behind, because with all the dust the beer truck kicked up, it was impossible for Dancer to steer around the rough patches.

Ever since the phantom pains in his missing fingers had returned last month, he had tried to use his left hand as little as possible. But with all the switchbacks he had to twist the steering wheel continuously. By the fourth switchback the hand was throbbing. He glanced in the rearview mirror to check on the jukeboxes. Wayne had done a first-rate job of securing them. A flatbed truck hauling port-a-johns was right on his tail, the driver probably not too pleased with Dancer's cautious driving as he navigated the curves.

Finally the switchbacks ended. Straight ahead was the

entrance to the park. Another fifty-foot cowboy, maybe it was Frank James, pointed to the right for the parking lot. The huge parking lot—a testimony to the unrealistic expectations of the water park developers—was a bevy of activity. Security personnel in neon lime vests were busy placing orange cones to funnel cars to the southeast corner of the lot. In the northeast corner, the port-a-john folks were unloading the outhouses, and along the west side of the lot a swarm of food and drink vendors set up their booths. Outside the parking lot, in the shadow of what had been the largest water slide in the state, a soundstage had been assembled where the mystery band would play. Roadies were crawling all over the stage arranging electronic gear and checking power connections.

Next to the bandstand, a crew was raising a big-top tent. It had a blue-and-white roof just like the one the Baptists used every summer for their big revival in Pomona. A sudden gust billowed the tent and one of the men holding a guideline lost his grip. The vinyl dome flapped wildly. The straw boss dropped his bullhorn and managed to grab the line at the same time he chewed out the boy who had let go.

At the entrance to the parking lot, a husky man with a trim beard and mirrored sunglasses was talking on his cellphone. He waved the Bud truck through, but raised his hand, directing Dancer to stop. He frowned at Wayne's huge tires. "What do you want?" he asked.

"Got two jukeboxes for Landis," Dancer said.

"We've been waiting for you. Hold on." He lifted his cellphone to his ear. "Hey, Mr. Landis. Jukeboxes are here." He holstered the phone and said to Dancer, "Drive through to the loading dock. You'll see Landis on the boat deck. We'll unload the boxes."

Dancer drove forward to the very front of the parking lot. He paused for a moment to rub the feeling back into his damaged hand. The thunder clouds that had formed in Arkansas had rolled into the valley and temporarily blocked the sun. A fat drop of rain splattered on the windshield, making a dusty streak. Dancer turned on the wipers, but there were no more raindrops. The sun re-emerged. The wipers screeched on the dusty windshield and Dancer pulled the window washer lever to clean off the grime.

There was an exit from the parking lot with an access road that led down to the riverboat. From the elevated truck seat he could see Ted Landis standing on the deck of his riverboat waving for him.

Landis was a few years younger than Dancer. They'd never been friends but were linked forever by their wives' notorious affair. Their paths hadn't crossed in the ten years that Dancer had been back in town. They'd only had one significant conversation. It had taken place two weeks after the calamity that changed the story of Dancer's life from that of the hometown hero who almost made it to the majors to the man who tried to scam his employer and ended up cutting off three of his fingers. Both stories sucked, but at least the first one was true.

It had been one of those insufferably hot summer days, just like today. He had left work at lunchtime to surprise Dede at her new job helping Joyce Landis show prospective home buyers through the model unit at Landis's new housing project. It was more of a surprise than he counted on when he walked into the bedroom to find Dede and Joyce making love. Dede tried to explain it away, but Dancer had raced away from the scene. Without a clue as to what he should do, he returned to work.

An hour later he was shearing plate steel on the Pexto, angry and distracted. His hand slipped. It hadn't been intentional. Today they would have some fancy name for it, some post-traumatic stress bullshit. But he never defended himself. He never told anyone what really happened that day. Most folks in town believed he had done it on purpose.

The only folks who knew the truth were Dede, Joyce, and Ted. Joyce told Ted just before she packed her bags and left him for good—two weeks after Dancer had discovered her in bed with Dede. That had been the reason Ted had come by their house. He wanted to talk to Dede, but she wasn't home. Instead, he found Dancer sitting on his chaise on the back deck, drinking whiskey. That had become his daily routine as he tried to recover emotionally and physically from the accident. With an athlete's dedication he maintained the drinking part of that routine for the next ten years.

Ted had bounded up the three stairs of the deck and stood glowering at Dancer. His face was puffy, his eyes red, like he'd been crying. He pointed a shaky finger at Dancer and said, "Tell your trailer-trash cunt of a wife to stay away from Joyce."

Dancer had set his drink down and got to his feet. He'd had more than a few drinks and was a little wobbly as he walked over to Ted. His hand was still heavily bandaged, and maybe with the wobbling and the bandage he looked like a cripple to Landis. Someone he could intimidate or boss around, like one of his lackey employees.

Landis was Dancer's height but outweighed him considerably. The two men stared at each other and then Dancer put his bandaged hand on Ted's forearm. As Ted looked quizzically at the bandage, Dancer drove his right fist into the big man's gut, dropping him to his knees. He made inhuman wheezing sounds as he sucked to refill his lungs with air. Dancer grabbed him by the collar of his shirt and said, "Tell her yourself, asshole," and then he went back to his chaise and poured himself another drink.

That was forty years ago, but it had been a short conversation. Dancer was confident Ted Landis had not forgotten.

CHAPTER 14

11:30 A.M.

WAYNE

Wayne had finished the first taco before Dancer was out of sight. He polished off the other two and chugged the Dr. Pepper. He stood up gingerly, shuffled over to the edge of the porch, and dumped his can and taco papers in the trash basket. As he stood there, a gum-chewing girl on a rusty Schwinn pedaled up to the porch. She was skinny and flat-chested and at first Wayne figured her to be a teenager. But the once-over glance she gave Wayne as she parked her bike made him figure her to be in her mid-twenties. She was wearing tattered jeans and a Grateful Dead T-shirt. Both arms were covered from wrist to shoulder with matching serpent tattoos.

"You look like you could use a nice cold glass of masala chai," she said. She had a serious hillbilly twang that made it sound like she was talking through her nose.

"No thanks. I'll stick with beer," Wayne said, unconsciously slipping into the same twang she had used.

"Not in this town, mister. Step inside. Get your fortune told and I might have something better than beer." She took a key out of her hip pocket and opened the door to the store.

Wayne looked at her and then at the sign above the door. "Are you Zelda?"

"What? You expected some fat chick in a veil?" Zelda snortled and that made Wayne laugh too. She held the door open, expecting him to follow her.

"I just figured a friend of Dancer's would be, you know, older."

She smiled, revealing a slight gap between her front teeth. It made her look interesting. "You know Dancer Stonemason?"

"I'm just working for him today. He told me I could wait here while he made a delivery. How do you know that old fart?"

"My granddaddy played baseball with him."

Wayne took a couple of steps toward the door. His back was throbbing again.

"You're hurt," Zelda said.

"Got kicked in the ribs."

Zelda nodded, as if she already knew. She stepped into his personal space, just like Zeke and that asshole drill sergeant during basic training. Her intent wasn't intimidation, but it still made Wayne uncomfortable. He broke eye contact to glance at her skinny, tatted arms. "Does it hurt getting your arms inked like that?"

"The pain lasts a minute, but the art endures a lifetime. Don't you have any tats, soldier boy?"

Wayne shook his head, embarrassed that he didn't. "My name's Wayne."

"Come on in, Wayne. I won't bite. Get out of that hot sun. I'll give you a reading, on the house. It's the least I can do for a friend of Dancer's." She pulled open the door and gestured for him to walk in.

Wayne didn't move. "I don't believe in that stuff."

"You don't have to believe, darlin'. I ain't Tinker Bell."

Wayne rolled his head from one side to the other. He remembered Dancer's caution, but that was the warning of a tired old man, not the fearless bar brawling legend. "What the hell. Can't hurt." He walked through the door Zelda held open. There was a huge tabby cat parked on the counter where she checked in her customers. Behind the counter, a red-curtained doorway.

"This is Jerry Garcia," she said, scratching the cat behind his ears. "He's my bodyguard." Zelda plucked the note that said she'd be back in ten minutes off the front door and flipped the sign that hung on the door from *Open* to *Closed*. She pushed aside the curtain that led to the back room. Wayne was relieved that the cat didn't move from the counter.

The back room was cool and dark like a cave. In the middle of the room was a black recliner that looked like a dentist chair. Tattoo art lined all the walls.

"Who did your tats?" Wayne asked.

"My ex, Rory. He was good. Taught me everything I know. But I got a better eye. I won't ink someone if it ain't right for them."

"What do you mean?"

"Sit down on the table. I'll show you."

Wayne sat sideways on the edge of the recliner, his legs dangling off the side. Zelda stood in front of him and took hold of his hands. She stared into his eyes. "Now Wayne, if you were to tell me you wanted a skull and crossbones, I wouldn't do it. That's for macho freaks who have to flash how tough they are. I can see that you are loyal but mysterious. You're strong, but you don't go looking for trouble."

Wayne could feel his face getting warm. She was conning him, but she was good at it. "What kind of tat should I get?" he asked.

She let go of his hands and tugged off her T-shirt. "Maybe this," she said as she turned around to show him the ink on her back.

Wayne gasped. Reclining regally, just above Zelda's pink bra strap, was the same Bengal tiger tattoo that Sonny had gotten from the gun dealer in Zubayidiyah. "That's wh . . . wh-what I want," he stammered.

Zelda took up his hands again and looked deep into his eyes. "I think it might be right for you. But let me give you a reading first, so I can be sure."

Wayne winced as she gently pushed him back on to the recliner.

"I can't fix your rib, but I can give you something that will take away your pain." From a porcelain teapot she filled a shot glass–sized cup with a dark liquid. "Drink this. It will help you relax." It was cool and had a minty, bitter taste. She lit an incense candle and switched on her CD player. The sweet, burnt odor of the incense seemed to fuse with the music, which sounded like the bubbling of a cool mountain stream.

Zelda pulled up a chair next to the recliner. She traced the surface of his palms with her index finger. Her touch was soothing. Wayne's eyelids felt heavy, his body pleasantly numb, as though he were lying in a feathery cocoon. Zelda had taken off his shoes and slipped off his fatigues. He was lying on the recliner in just his T-shirt and boxers. She pulled up the T-shirt and tugged it over his head. Wayne tried to help, but his arms were so heavy he couldn't lift them.

He could hear Zelda murmuring, but she sounded far away.

Wayne opened his eyes. In the dim light of the barracks he could see a man standing at the foot of his bed, wearing a broad-brimmed Panama hat that shadowed his face. He was smiling—his teeth blindingly white—and strumming his fingers like he was playing a guitar.

"Are you a jukebox hero, Wayne?"

It was Sonny. Wayne's heart felt like it would burst. "Sonny! You're alive." He reached out his arms toward his friend. Sonny's hips undulated sensually as he danced his way toward Wayne. He stopped just out of reach.

"Are you a jukebox hero, Wayne?" he asked again.

Wayne tried to speak, but he couldn't make a sound. Sonny continued to smile at him, but now he was sliding away. Wayne tried to get up from his bed, but his legs wouldn't move. As Sonny disappeared, Wayne shouted, "Yes. Sonny. Yes. I am a jukebox hero."

Wayne was on his back and Sonny was on top of him, teasing Wayne with his beautiful smile. Wayne cupped Sonny's face in his hands and they kissed. A long, devouring kiss, their tongues probing. Sonny tasted like Juicy Fruit.

Sonny broke the kiss but he had become Anita.

"Surprise!" she said. She smiled, but not like she was glad to see him.

Wayne gasped for air as she slowly drew a knife across his neck. "I'm a bad girl, Wayne." She laughed with malevolence.

Wayne opened his eyes. Zelda was leaning over him, chewing her gum vigorously and scratching something on his chest.

"It's okay, Wayne. I'm just sketchin' an outline so you can see what the tiger would look like."

"I guess I fell asleep."

She held up a hand mirror. "What do you think?" she asked. He could see the outline of the tiger over his left breast. Anita would definitely take notice.

"I like it. How much?"

Zelda picked up a binder and flipped to the tiger tattoo artwork. "This is custom work. I usually charge five hundred," she said. "Because you're a friend of Dancer's, I'll do it for three fifty."

Wayne sighed. He really wanted that tat but that was too much. "I don't have three fifty."

Zelda stared at him, as she had earlier. It was as if she were trying to read him. She smacked her gum and smiled like she had just had a revelation.

"You can pay me a hundred now and leave that ring as collateral. Bring me the balance next month and I'll give you the ring back."

He and Anita had bought their wedding bands at Campbell's Jewelry. Platinum bands and two diamonds to "signify their union," Anita said. The retail price was five grand for the pair, but Bernie Campbell had given them his "young lovers" discount and charged them $2999.99. Now Campbell's was gone—a victim of the new mall on the outskirts of town. The young lovers' union was not looking so good either.

Wayne felt woozy. His back was numb, but the pain was almost gone.

"Your wallet's on the table there," Zelda said. She pointed to the lamp table next to the recliner. "It fell out of your pocket when we took off those overalls."

Wayne picked up the wallet and peeled off five of the six 20s he had "borrowed" from Zeke's underwear drawer this morning. He twisted off his wedding ring and handed it to her. "I'll be back for this," he said.

Zelda smiled at him and eased him back on the table. "I'm sure you will, darlin'. Drink this." She handed him another shot glass of the minty drink. "Now tell me about Anita."

CHAPTER 15

11:45 A.M.

KAYLA

Kayla balanced the Taco Bell takeout bag on top of the cardboard tray of Cokes and pushed the buzzer for Barry's apartment at Seminole Gardens. Seminole was a tacky apartment building on the south side of West Plains. Barry, in typical Barry fashion, had spent all of two hours looking for an apartment when he moved here from Chicago. It had probably seen better days, but in Kayla's estimation, even on its best days, Barry's studio apartment would have sucked. The appliances were cheap and barely functional, the wallpaper was some version of puke green, the carpeting was threadbare and reeked of cigarette smoke or something worse. Living there, even now, for the few weeks before they moved to New York, filled her with dread.

They had planned to buy a house between West Plains and Maple Springs and were about to start their search when Barry learned he was being promoted in September. Kayla had been depressed at the prospect of five more weeks in this dump, anxious about having a baby, and agitated at her mother's insistence that she tell her father immediately about the move to New York. Of course none of those things could compare to the emotional bombshell her father had just dropped on her.

On the twenty-mile drive to West Plains she had fantasized about staying in Maple Springs and running the Saturn dealership. The more she thought about it, the more convinced she was that they needed to reconsider their move to New York.

If those cars were half as good as GM claimed, she was confident she could build a great dealership. She'd be the youngest dealer in all of GM by at least ten years. Okay, Barry had been given a huge promotion, and the idea of moving to New York was exciting, but wasn't her opportunity much bigger than his?

The plan had been for Barry to drive up in the late afternoon so they could start getting the showroom ready for the reception. But when Kayla had texted Barry to see if he would like to meet for lunch, she had been surprised to learn he had stayed home. HOW ABOUT TAKEOUT TACOS? he had replied to her text.

This had become their code for "noontime quickie?" Kayla smiled as she imagined Barry reclining on his bed, in his boxers, his soft caramel-colored curls splayed on the pillow, texting with one hand while holding some boring corporate document with the other. He had been on the gymnastics team in high school and had strong, sloping shoulders and a well-defined, smooth chest, which was probably why she always imagined him half-dressed (or less). She liked that he was not pathologically tall, like the Stonemason men. She could kiss him without a step stool and look directly into his dreamy brown eyes.

But first they needed to talk.

As she'd waited in the Taco Bell drive-through line, she formulated a strategy for persuading Barry that this could be a "huge" opportunity for both of them. She would start by casually mentioning that her father had been awarded the Saturn dealership and had a plan to revitalize Maple Springs. Barry was clever and compassionate; he would connect the dots and see how those projects could develop into an exciting, lucrative situation. It was always easier to sell the customer if he thought it was his idea to buy the car.

Barry buzzed her in, and she walked to the end of the dingy hall. His door was open and he was sitting at the kitchen counter talking on his cellphone. Unlike fantasy Barry, real Barry was wearing cutoff jeans and a sweat-stained purple Northwestern T-shirt. Much of the floor of the tiny studio was covered with packing cartons. Something was wrong. They had nearly two months until their move, and Barry was a last-minute guy. He wouldn't pack even a day in advance.

Barry winked at Kayla as he said into his cellphone, "It's Kayla, Ma. Looks like she's brought us a gourmet lunch."

His parents weren't coming to the wedding. Barry's dad had dementia and his mother wouldn't leave him, even for a weekend.

"Ma says hi, Kayla. Okay, Ma. Say hello to Dad. Next week I'll give you the wedding blow by blow. Love ya."

Kayla slipped past him and walked over to the bed, which was covered with new car brochures. "You're replacing your junky old Beemer?" she asked.

"No way. Those are for you," he said, grinning. He grabbed the bag from her and kissed her hard. "You're a lifesaver. I'm starving."

"Why are you packing now?"

He extracted the tray of crunchy tacos from the bag. "Where's the . . . Never mind, I see it." He grabbed a handful of sauce packets from the bottom of the sack.

Kayla picked up one of the brochures. The tagline read, *Welcome to Life Quality BMW—Proudly serving Bay Ridge and Dyker Heights*. "You're buying me a Beemer?"

Barry continued his I'm-so-cool grin as he squeezed the packet of sauce on a taco. "My new boss sent those to me. That place is in Brooklyn. He knows the owner. He can get you a job."

Damn. So much for her grand strategy of laying out her opportunity so Barry could connect the dots. He had beaten her to the punch with his own dots.

Kayla unwrapped a bean burrito. "Fifty-nine cents. We could live on these. Think of all the money we'd save."

"He'll set up an interview for you," Barry said. He grabbed the brochure and flipped through it. "If you were working there, maybe I would trade in the old car. Let you sell me this new turbo model."

"What's the rush? We're not moving for a couple months."

The grin vanished and Barry's face went into bad news accountant mode. "Remember that douche bag, Blake?" he asked. "He was at the Christmas party."

Kayla dug through the bag, trying to find a packet of hot sauce. "Why do they always give me the mild stuff? Is it because I'm blond?" She found a packet of Fire Hot sauce and ripped it open. "All your auditor buddies look alike to me."

"He was the only one wearing a suit."

"Oh him. The guy from the New York office. He was an asshole, not a douche bag."

"Yeah, that's Blake. What's the difference between a douche bag and an asshole?"

"Douche bag is a natural state. Assholes have to work at it."

"Blake thought he should get the job. He's not happy I'm going to be his boss."

She dipped the burrito in the hot sauce and took a huge bite. The burrito burst and the bean stuffing and sauce splattered her white polo shirt. "Shit!" She yanked off the shirt and rushed to the bathroom to run cold water on the stain. "Damn, why'd I have to wear the white one." She scrubbed it with a washcloth but a faint pink splotch remained. She hung it over the shower rod.

"My new boss says it would be a good idea if I could get out there by Monday," Barry called.

"Monday! We'd have to leave right after the wedding." Kayla

hustled out of the bathroom, flicking water off her hands. She took a large gulp of Coke and started to reach for her busted burrito, then began unsnapping her jeans. "Fuck it. I'm not spilling anything on these jeans. They're the only ones I can still wear." She sat down on the edge of the bed.

"We can't go on Monday," she said as she peeled off the jeans. "I haven't told anyone about New York. I thought it was, uh, you know, still up in the air." That was a lie, and not a very good one. She picked up her burrito and took another bite.

"Up in the air? Are you kidding me? Coopers is committed." His face was a mask of confusion as he searched his memory for how she could have misunderstood their plans. "We're committed!"

"But what about Kauai? Our honeymoon?"

A look of relief erased his confusion. "I found someone in the New York office to take our spot. We won't lose a dime on the reservations. We can go in January or February and it will be even better!"

The honeymoon in Kauai had been Barry's idea. She hadn't even given it much thought, but now she was pissed. "You changed our honeymoon reservations just like that? Did you think about asking me first? We're having a baby in January, in case you've forgotten, so I don't think it will be even better then."

Barry winced. He had a habit of forgetting about the baby. Of course, he didn't have morning sickness every day to remind him. "I'm sorry, Kayla. I wasn't thinking."

She crammed the rest of the burrito in her mouth, wadded up the paper, and threw it at the waste basket under the television, but missed by a foot. "GM awarded Dad a Saturn dealership."

That got his attention. "Wow. That's good, isn't it? I heard they had a long waiting list."

She sat down cross-legged on the bed and faced him. "He wants me to run it."

Barry's face scrunched up as he tried to process this. "I don't understand."

"He's buying the Crutchfield property and putting the dealership in there. He has a wonderful plan for revitalizing Maple Springs."

"But we're moving to New York." Barry shook his head and then kept shaking it, trying to reconcile plans that were irreconcilable.

"It's an incredible opportunity, Barry. I'd be the youngest dealer in GM's whole network."

He stared at her, a confused frown creasing his face. "But what about my job?"

"Couldn't you keep running the office in West Plains? You said there was a chance you could become the regional manager."

Barry sighed. "If you turn down a promotion, you don't get another shot. I'm pretty much fucked with Coopers if I say no." He got up from the bed and walked slowly over to the kitchenette where he had been packing pots and pans.

"My dad would hire you in a heartbeat. He thinks the world of you."

He no longer looked confused. He stared at Kayla like she had insulted him. "I don't think that would be a good idea for anyone."

"It wouldn't be forever." As she said those words she wondered if Oscar's wife had told him the same thing when he turned down his big opportunity.

"Okay," he said.

He reached into the packing carton and pulled out his electric fry pan. He returned it to the oven range drawer.

"Barry?" Kayla watched him from the bed as he retrieved his plastic salad spinner from the carton and placed it back on the counter. "Can we talk about this, Barry?"

He shrugged, his expression grim. Resigned. "What is there to talk about? What are my choices? Move to New York without you? I don't want to do that. Call off the wedding? I don't want to do that. Do you?"

"God, Barry. No." Kayla stood up from the bed. She wanted to wrap her arms around him. Wanted him to hold her. But he was so cold. So analytical. She just stood there, uncertain what to say or do.

"Okay then. Good. We're having a baby, Kayla. It's not just us anymore. Do I want to work in West Plains for the rest of my life? No. Do I want to work for your father? No. But I don't want to lose you. It looks like I don't have a choice." He surveyed his shabby apartment, hands on his hips. "So let's get this stuff unpacked."

Kayla walked over to him and wrapped her arms around his neck. "I love you, Barry." An unexpected sob convulsed her. "Dammit! Why am I crying? This baby is already fucking with me." She held him tighter and she was sobbing and laughing at the same time.

Barry gently massaged her shoulders. "How about some takeout tacos before we get started?"

Kayla kissed him hard and long. "Are you sure, Barry? I mean about staying here. I don't want you to be miserable."

"You can't get rid of me that easily. I like my job. I love you. And I'm going to love our baby. The first of many." He smiled. Finally.

Kayla kissed him again and whispered in his ear. "One at a time, okay? And let's pray we don't have twins."

They made love for an hour and then they lay together, Kayla resting her head in the crook of Barry's arm. She fell asleep but awoke when Barry scooched his arm out from under her head.

"Trying to escape?" she asked, her voice sleepy.

"I'm hungry." He jumped up from the bed and grabbed the takeout bag from the table and brought it back to the bed. He grabbed one of the crispy chicken tacos and took a bite. "Needs sour cream."

"You're going to mess your bed up," Kayla said. She was lying on her back studying the flaking paint on the ceiling.

Barry took a tub of the sour cream and dumped it on her belly. "Not as long as you don't move." He dipped the taco into the puddle of sour cream. He took a bite and the taco shell crumbled. "Oops."

Bits of taco shell dotted Kayla's breasts and belly. "Nice move, Ace."

Barry grinned. "Don't move." He bent over and nibbled the taco pieces off her breasts and licked up the sour cream.

Kayla pressed his head toward her pussy. "Make sure you get it all."

"I'll do my best, but I think we better take a shower before we leave. You know. Just to be sure."

In the shower, Kayla sighed as Barry soaped her back. Everything was happening so fast.

"Are you worried about tomorrow?" Barry asked.

"No. Not the ceremony. Just all the other stuff. Although the reception might be interesting." She giggled.

"What's so funny?"

"My mom's made a seating chart. Her family doesn't play well with the Stonemasons."

She explained the graduation party fight that Clayton had instigated.

"It sounds like Clayton was a lot different from your father. Were they close?"

Kayla closed her eyes and let the warm shower rinse off the soap. "My father loved Clayton, but they weren't close. He said Clayton wanted to get away from Maple Springs but something always came up. The war ended, their mom died, he met a girl. Something held him back. Dad said he wished . . ."

Barry turned off the shower and handed Kayla a towel. "Wished what?" he asked.

"That Clayton had escaped." Escaped. Those had been her dad's words. Dancer, her mother, Oscar, Clayton—they all wanted to leave town, pursue bigger dreams, but something held them back. They all probably thought that they would have another chance somewhere down the line. But they hadn't.

She dropped the towel to the floor and wrapped her arms around Barry. "I love you, Barry. Let's go to New York."

CHAPTER 16

Noon

ANITA

The break room, where Anita normally ate her lunch, stank. Someone had tried to heat a foil-wrapped burrito in the microwave. The air was rancid from fried electrical wiring and burnt jalapeños. Anita grabbed her container from the refrigerator, which had its own set of unpleasant food odors from long-forgotten meals no one had thrown out. She walked across the Small Parts compound to Shipping.

This department was all old white guys who brought sandwiches for lunch. Their microwave looked like it had never been used. Most of the men ate outside under the awning where they were allowed to smoke. It was cool and quiet in the break room. Anita settled in at the picnic table with the latest Harlan Coben novel, which she hoped would distract her from the meagerness of her yogurt and apple lunch.

She had been starving herself all week. She wanted to look her absolute best for Ted's party. Not for Ted—he would have even loved the mousy Anita—but for all those guys and girls who had ignored her in high school. Anita loved her new look—the boobs, the platinum hair, the slender waistline, the snug-fitting jeans and tops. She knew she was hot. After this party, so would everyone else.

"Is that a good book?"

Anita looked up, startled. Her father-in-law, lunch pail in hand, hovered over her table.

"Zeke!" she said. She jumped up from the table and hugged him. "Don't sneak up on me when I'm reading a thriller. I almost had a heart attack."

She hadn't seen Zeke since she had the boob job. He was a devoted grandfather and took the kids on outings regularly, but Anita always arranged it so that he picked them up from Johnnie's place. Anita wanted to tell herself that she did that because it was more convenient for Zeke, but the truth was she was afraid of what Zeke would think of her transformation.

It had only been a few months, but he looked different. He always had such a military bearing. Perfect posture, work pants clean and pressed. Nothing out of place. But today he looked pale, tired. His gray hair, usually trimmed like he had just come from the barber, was longer, tickling his ears and running over his shirt collar.

"Mind if I join you?" he asked.

"Of course not. I'm the one trespassing."

"I like your hair," he said. He tried to maintain eye contact, but he had definitely noticed her chest. "What are you doing over here in the geezer lunchroom?" He set his lunch pail down and slid onto the bench across from her.

"You guys don't stink the place up with tacos and tamales," she said. She dog-eared the page she was reading and set the book down. "And it's quiet so I can read."

Zeke picked up the book and read the blurb on the cover. "'*Tell No One* is suspense at its finest.' What's it about?"

"A man whose wife disappears without a trace. He thinks she's dead and then eight years later he gets a mysterious email that makes him think she's still alive." Too late, Anita remembered that Zeke's wife had also disappeared mysteriously. But not without a trace.

"Interesting," Zeke said. He set the book back on the table. "Daniel looked great in his little league game this week."

"He was thrilled you showed up. Thanks. Kristi made a macramé bracelet for you at her day camp. She can't wait to give it to you."

Zeke smiled broadly. The news seemed to rejuvenate him. He lost some of his paleness. "Could I take them to the fair next weekend? You know, like I did last year with Daniel."

Anita smiled, relieved. She was afraid he was going to say something about Wayne. "They would love that, Zeke. Daniel had a great time last year. Kristi will be thrilled to be included."

"Saturday morning, then? I'll pick them up at nine at your place, before it gets too hot?" He stood up. "I'll leave you to your book. I need a smoke." He backed away from the table, but he kept his eyes on Anita, like he still had something he wanted to discuss. "Wayne says you guys are working things out. None of my business, but I hope that's true. He needs you."

Anita nodded slightly to acknowledge she had heard him and hoped her face didn't reveal how she felt. "I'll have the kids ready by nine. They'll be excited." Anita smiled thinly and opened her novel to the earmarked page. She tried to read, but she'd lost interest in the story.

CHAPTER 17

12:15 PM

DANCER

Dancer drove out of the parking lot and followed an ice truck down to the loading dock. The river was wild. White-capped swirls splashed over the edge of the loading dock.

Another beefy guy with a clipboard waved him into a spot at the railing. "Just leave it running. We'll get it unloaded. Mr. Landis is waiting for you on the upper deck." He pointed to the boat.

Barrel-chested Ted Landis was standing on the deck of *The Spirit of St. Joseph* in a white polo and khaki shorts, hands on his hips, surveying the activity taking place on shore. Last month when the boat had been towed to the water park from Cape Girardeau, the local paper had run a front-page story on Landis's big riverboat project. How he had purchased the 1880s vintage boat from a salvage company and spent two years and a small fortune having it made river worthy.

The riverboat strained at the ropes that kept it tethered to the dock. Dancer walked cautiously up the ramp. He crossed the main deck and climbed a spiral staircase to the top deck. As he stepped out on to the deck, Landis turned away from the railing. "Dancer. Welcome." He walked over, his hand extended.

The last time the two men had been that close, Landis had been left gasping for air on Dancer's patio. Landis was bigger than Dancer remembered. He'd probably put on thirty pounds, but he had spread it evenly, so he looked more husky than fat.

Dancer probably didn't look like he would be much of a match for Landis now. With his post-Clayton weight loss, his cargo shorts sagged and his T-shirt was no longer tight across his chest.

"Boat looks great," Dancer said. He could feel the deck roll beneath his feet. He had to shift his weight to maintain his balance. "The river's rough today."

Landis stood ramrod straight, his feet planted. He was used to the roll. He waved off Dancer's observation. "The storms up north are just about flushed out. It'll be calm by tonight." He marched over to a large table. "Let me show you something."

On the table was a three-dimensional mock-up of the Caledonia River from Landis Landing to Maple Springs. "This is the grand plan." He leaned over the table and put his hand on the tiny steamboat. "First phase is the casino. If everything goes right, it will throw off the cash to finance the rest of the project. Eventually, if I can persuade the Army Corps to dredge the river up here," he pointed to a spot north of where the boat was docked, "I'll have the riverboat cruise from here to Maple Springs and back."

"River's high enough now, you could probably make it. That's a pretty short cruise," Dancer said. It was only about five miles from the Landing to Maple Springs as the crow flies, but the river had a winding path.

Landis nodded, smiling. "We're going to crawl up that river. Keep the customers on the boat, gambling. It'll take at least ninety minutes, roundtrip. But that's for later." He moved on down the board. "We'll build a luxury hotel right here." He pointed to a spot on the river about where the bandstand had been assembled. "We're talking to Hyatt. They're for sure interested if we can get the permits. They can build one of their luxury timeshare resorts next door. Leverage their resources."

As always, Landis was playing every angle: use county commissioners to threaten reluctant landowners; convince the Army Corps to dredge the river for a cruise to nowhere; persuade zoning boards in three counties to approve his projects.

"Lots of politics involved," Dancer said.

"It's the name of the game," Landis said. "Gotta be a politician to get anything accomplished these days."

"Never thought of the Caledonia River as a luxury destination," Dancer said.

"That's because you've lived here all your life. You take it for granted. People love to live on water: lakes, oceans, rivers. It don't matter."

Dancer pointed to the map. Just beyond the timeshare building were dozens of sugar-cube size blocks. "Houses?"

"Yep. Minimum of three thousand square feet, and three acre lots. Every one of them with river access. Those will go for seven-fifty to a million, easy."

"Where are you going to find all those rich folks? This is hillbilly country."

Landis smiled smugly, like Dancer was following his script. "They'll find us. But this isn't just for the well-off. On the east side of the river we'll build one of the largest campgrounds in the state. There will be a swimming area, a marina, and areas especially designated for fishing." He swept his hand all along the eastern border of the river.

He had set it up so the rich folks were on one side of the river and the regular folks would be on the other.

"What's this building?" Dancer pointed to a domino-sized block just north of the campground.

"Factory outlet stores. Gap, Land's End, all the popular brands."

"Won't that take business away from your mall?"

The smug smile again. "Nope. I'll make sure we don't put in stores that compete with our tenants. They'll complement each other. Make this a destination for affordable shopping. But those are all later phases. Next month we're breaking ground on the golf course."

Dancer stared at the board. Beyond the luxury houses there was a large splash of green, and on closer inspection, he could see there was a golf course laid out. It appeared to run right up to the gorge where Dancer lived.

"Jim told you I bought the house?" Landis asked.

Dancer nodded. "Yeah. He told me."

"That's a great location." He paused. "Damn shame about Clayton. I'm sorry."

They both stared at the board.

After a moment, when it was clear Dancer wasn't going to respond, Landis said, "I want to make Clayton's place our clubhouse for the golf course. Great location. Fantastic view. We'll have to expand it, but we're not tearing it down."

Dancer had been hearing about Ted Landis's plans his whole life. He was tired of the man and his ideas. He just wanted to get paid and leave. But first he had to do what Jim had refused to do. He pointed at a spot just south of Clayton's A-Frame. "You don't have a golf hole here at the bend in the river, where the basket ladies live. Why can't they stay put?"

Landis scoffed. "They're a little too, uh, countercultural. With their skinny-dipping and their pot-smoking. That scrawny gal—Phoebe—she's a troublemaker." He reached on to the board and repositioned the tiny steamboat so it was lined up with the dock. "I learned early in the game, you let someone like that slide, it will come back to bite you in the ass every time. I'll give them a fair price for their property. I'm bringing in the county commissioners to help me persuade them."

Dancer should have known when he brought it up that it was pointless. There was no sense wasting his breath on the ladies' lost cause. He turned away from the board and looked out at the parking lot, where a band was doing a sound check.

"Who's playing tonight?" he asked.

"You mean the mystery band?" Ted grinned, relieved he no longer had to talk about the basket ladies. "I'll tell you, but you have to promise not to share it with all your friends. It's the Confederate Pirates."

"Never heard of them," Dancer said, but he had. That was the group Wayne said he had a tryout with before he went to Iraq.

"They're up and comers. Just got a recording deal and they're going on tour this fall."

Dancer wondered if Wayne knew they were playing here tonight. "I guess we ought to settle up. I need to get back to the house. You want to inspect the jukeboxes?"

Ted was already walking away. "Nah. I trust you." He moved into the stateroom, which was a combination office and bedroom, sat down at his desk, and pulled out his check ledger. "Make the check out to . . . ?" he asked.

"American Jukebox, LLC. We're still in business," Dancer said, more sourly than he intended.

Landis detached the check and handed it to Dancer. "You sound annoyed. What's wrong?"

"Jim never should have sold those boxes to you."

Landis's brow creased. "Why not?"

"They're worth twice what you offered. Jim should have known better."

"What do you think they're worth?" he asked.

"Two thousand. Those are top of the line Seeburgs in primo condition."

Landis picked up his pen again and looked quizzically at Dancer. "So four thousand dollars instead of two?"

"Yeah," Dancer said.

"Okay, then." Landis wrote another check. "Here's another two thousand. Didn't mean to take advantage."

"Thank you," Dancer said, but he didn't mean it. He knew Landis's generosity would come with strings attached.

"I have a proposition you might be interested in," Landis said, on cue. "I think it would be a good fit for your skill set. Let me show you." He walked back to the project board, his face animated like a kid playing with his electric train.

Dancer wasn't interested in anything Landis could offer him, but he was curious to hear what Landis thought his skill set was.

"See these houses here?" He pointed to the smaller dominoes—just north of the hotel development project.

"The luxury homes?" Dancer asked.

"Exactly. I'll need to furnish multiple model units and same goes for all the other building projects I'll be undertaking."

Dancer stood silent, refusing to be Landis's straight man again.

"You know that lady you picked up the sconces from?"

Dancer shrugged. "Johnnie Brown? Yeah, I know her."

"I'm her biggest customer. Her stuff gives the models a much more authentic feel."

Dancer nodded.

Landis frowned at Dancer's refusal to contribute to the conversation. "Her business and Clayton's ain't that different. Both dealing in old stuff that people want today. So I was thinking, I could take over Clayton's jukebox business—I know Jim wants to close it all down, but I could keep it running. You could help me do that, and also be my point man for dealing with Johnnie."

There must be something to Clayton's business if Ted Landis was willing to take it off their hands. Dancer wanted nothing to do with that deal or anything else Ted Landis was working on. "Didn't think you needed point men," he said.

"I don't normally, but this is a little complicated. I'm dating Johnnie's daughter."

Ted Landis was dating Wayne's wife? That kid couldn't catch a break. "I thought she was married," Dancer said.

"That's over. He just hasn't come to accept it yet. He will. Just a matter of time."

"I don't get it."

"Johnnie doesn't know about us. But when she finds out, she ain't going to be happy. I get that. But we still need to do business. I have a lot of places that need to be furnished. Johnnie does good work, I want to keep using her. You could be my buffer. Everyone likes you, Dancer."

The way he said that, there wasn't any doubt Ted Landis wasn't including himself in that everyone.

Dancer looked at the checks in his hand. "Here." He handed the second check back to Landis. "Jim made the deal with you. Not up to me to renegotiate."

"So you don't want to keep Clayton's business alive? Probably the one thing he ever did on his own that wasn't fucked up."

Dancer could feel his cheeks warming, but Ted was way ahead of him. His face was florid.

"We aren't closing that business," Dancer said.

Landis smirked. "You have a gift for fucking things up too, don't you? That hasn't changed in forty years."

Dancer smiled coldly at Landis and stepped closer. "Last time you talked to me like that, you almost blew your lunch." He grabbed Landis by his shirt front. "One more word and I'll throw you over that fucking railing."

From the look on Landis's face, he didn't think it was an idle threat. Dancer let go and walked across the deck to the stairway. Landis didn't say a word.

Five minutes later, Dancer was back in his truck heading for Zelda's Tattoo Parlor.

CHAPTER 18

12:25 PM

WAYNE

Zelda pressed an oval-shaped piece of white paper on Wayne's chest and wet it with a damp cloth.

"What's that?" he asked.

"It's a decal of your tattoo," she said. She pulled the paper off and Wayne could see the outline of the tiger.

"So you just fill it in, like a coloring book." His words sounded slurred. Zelda's potion had given him a mellow vibe and numbed his tongue.

Zelda picked up what looked like a fountain pen with a cord attached. It hummed when she flicked a switch on the side of it. "Not a good idea to insult your artist when she's holdin' a weapon."

She pressed the needle into his skin and scraped it across a section of his chest. "Fuck! That hurts!" Wayne screamed. He wanted to twist himself out of Zelda's chair, but that would have made his rib hurt even worse. He gripped the side of the table and squeezed as hard as he could.

Zelda stopped etching and wiped his chest with a damp rag. "Just relax, Wayne. Tell me about Anita. How long have you two been married?"

Over the next hour, between inkings, Wayne told Zelda about his life with Anita from high school right up until he arrived home unexpectedly from Iraq.

Zelda sponged his chest again and then stood back to study

her handiwork. "Almost done. Lookin' good," she said. "You didn't tell your wife you were coming home?"

"No. Sonny's death fucked me up. I wasn't thinking straight. We didn't get any notice. It was just, 'Okay guys, pack your bags, we're shipping out.' When I got to Fort Hood I called her, and she told me not to come home. Said we needed to move on."

"Damn. That's one cold bitch."

"She's just confused. That woman she's been hanging out with is messing with her head. Turning her against me."

Zelda opened a bottle of a clear liquid and poured a few drops on to a soft white cloth, which she rubbed into his chest. It smelled like fingernail polish remover. "We're almost ready for you to take a look."

Wayne started to sit up, but Zelda put a firm hand on his shoulder. "Not yet, Wayne." She took a cool cloth and gently wiped his face and neck and then swabbed all of his chest. She brushed her lips over his nipples and down to his bellybutton. "Why do you want to be with a girl who disrespects you?"

Wayne closed his eyes and now it was Sonny, running his hands all over Wayne's body. "Oh, Sonny."

A brilliant lightning flash illuminated the dark room and a crack of thunder like a tree splitting rattled the tattoo parlor.

Wayne opened his eyes with a start. Had he said Sonny's name out loud? Or was he still dreaming?

"It's okay, Wayne." She was staring at him with a sad, wistful look. She said something about being gay, but the rumble of rain pelting the tin roof drowned out her words.

"I'm not gay," Wayne said. His voice croaked like he'd been asleep for hours.

"That's just a word, darlin'. You can't help who you love."

Wayne started to roll over on his side away from Zelda but was immediately jolted with a sharp pain in his back. He fell back on to the recliner and covered his face with his hands. "I want to love Anita. I want her to love me. I want things to be normal again."

Zelda sighed. "Normal's overrated," she said. "And boring." She handed him her makeup mirror so he could see the tattoo. "Rad," she said. "This is totally rad. Do you like it?"

The skin was red and raw but the tiger looked just like Sonny's tattoo. Serene and powerful. Lethal.

Zelda grabbed a roller of clear surgical tape from her workbench. "Raise your arms, Wayne."

"Wh-what are you gonna do?"

"We need to cover the tat so it doesn't get infected. You can take it off tomorrow. Hold on to the mirror." She stood in front of him, so close he could smell her Juicy Fruit gum. She started the taping in the back, reaching her arms around Wayne and sticking the tape to his shoulder blade. The tape made a rippy, ratchety sound as she unwound it.

"Be careful," Wayne said.

"Don't worry. I won't hurt your rib. Just breathe normal." She wrapped it around him three times. When she was done, she cut the tape and gently pressed the end of it on to his chest to make sure it stuck. She leaned into him and kissed him on the forehead. "All done."

Another thunder and lightning combination rocked the building and Wayne flinched and dropped her makeup mirror, shattering it on the concrete floor.

He looked at Zelda with alarm. She smiled. "It's just glass, darlin'. It don't mean nothing."

Above the din of the rain pelting the roof, there was the sound of someone pounding on the front door.

"Wayne! Zelda! Are you in there?"

Dancer had returned.

CHAPTER 19

12:30 PM

JIM

Jim had a one o'clock appointment with Ted Landis at King Arthur's Pub. The pub on the east end of Landis Mall and Applebee's on the west end had been a lethal one-two punch to the town's restaurants. Within a year, only the Main Street Diner was still in business.

The mall was a mile east of the city limits on US 60 and a mile west of Stonemason Chevrolet. It was a far more convenient location for Jim than a lunch-hour drive back into Maple Springs. Jim favored Applebee's, but Landis had proposed they meet at King Arthur's, where his granddaughter was the hostess.

Jim changed to a fresh white shirt and debated whether to wear his blue blazer. It had gotten tighter in recent weeks and made him look heavy. He decided to skip the blazer. Ted never wore a jacket or tie. Most of the time he looked like he had just walked in off the golf course.

It was only 12:30, but Jim didn't want to be late. Landis's support for his renovation plan would make everything easier. Gillespie was wrong—Landis would be excited about the plan to rejuvenate downtown. It was good business for everyone. What was the saying? A rising tide floats all boats.

Those storm clouds he had spotted on the southern horizon had rolled in. It was dark enough that the headlights on his Cadillac activated when he drove out of the dealership.

King Arthur's was a popular Friday lunch destination and all the parking spaces near the restaurant had been taken. When Jim stepped out of his car it was noticeably cooler and the air had an ominous tingle, as though it were charged with electricity. He trekked across the parking lot clutching his rolled-up plan. A sudden burst of wind almost ripped the paper from his hand as a jagged streak of lightning lit up the southern sky. Several seconds later he heard the distant rumble. The storm was hitting well south of them, probably in Arkansas.

By the time he made it to the entrance his renovation plan needed its own renovation. It had been whipsawed by the wind and was now a floppy horseshoe with the edges frayed. As he waited to give his name to the hostess, he tried to straighten it out, but only succeeded in crumpling it more. A real developer, like Landis, would have carried his plans in a tube for protection. Jim Stonemason was still an amateur, but that was about to change.

"Dining alone today?" the young woman asked as she returned to the podium.

Jim stared at her, dumbstruck. It was Candy Landis, the girl who had starred in all of his high school fantasies. Beautiful Candy, with the smile that drove Jim to despair knowing that to her he was just Clayton's studious, not-so-little brother. She could have had any boy in high school, so of course she chose Clayton—unable or unwilling to resist his cool indifference.

But it couldn't be. Candy had to be in her fifties now.

"Sir? Table for one?" she asked again.

Jim, finally remembering he needed to speak, said, "You must be Candy's daughter."

Her smile wattage increased. "I am. Did you know my mother?"

"My brother Clayton dated your mother in high school. I'm

Jim Stonemason. I have a one o'clock reservation with your grandfather."

Cindy's eyes lit up with recognition. "Oh yes. Hello, Mr. Stonemason." She looked down at her schematic of the tables. "Mr. Landis is not here yet, but I'll seat you in his booth. He usually gets here early for his appointments."

She picked up a menu and Jim followed her across the restaurant to a corner booth that looked out on the parking lot.

"Where does your mother live now?" Jim asked.

"Lake Forest. That's a suburb just north of Chicago. She has her own real estate agency."

"I'll bet she's great at that," he said. It wasn't a throwaway line. Candy had real charm. She succeeded at almost everything she tried.

"My mother *is* a great businesswoman. She built a business and raised me all on her own. No help from anyone." She said it with a smile, but there was an edge to her voice.

Clayton had probably been Candy's only failure. They had dated all through high school and she talked all the time about their plans to marry after college. But Clayton dropped out of Southwest Missouri State and then drew number 14 in the draft lottery. He could have avoided the draft by returning to school, but he refused.

Instead he ran from Candy Landis to Trudy Bennett, and from Maple Springs to Vietnam. Vietnam broke him and Trudy was never able to fix him. Of all the Stonemasons, Jim had been the one who could have easily left town and made his mark somewhere else. But he loved Maple Springs. He was proud of the life he had built there. For Clayton and Dancer, the town had too many bad memories. If Clayton had married Candy instead of running off to Vietnam, his life would have been better. As much as Jim loved Trudy, he wished Clayton had let Candy marry him. With Candy, Clayton would have escaped. He would have survived.

Jim slid into the booth and took the offered menu. "Say hello to your mom for me," he said.

Cindy winked—just like Candy always did. "I'll do that, Mr. Stonemason. Y'all have a good lunch now. I'm sure Grandpa will be here soon."

But he wasn't. Jim had tried to ignore the bread they brought to the table. But the hot fresh dough smell tortured him and twenty minutes later he had finished the last of the dinner rolls. He stared at his phone, debating whether to call. Could Landis have forgotten? He had that gala event tonight; maybe Jim had the date wrong. But no. He was certain they had agreed on the eighteenth.

Jim was about to call when he spotted Ted Landis weaving his way through the maze of tables. Landis stopped at one and shook hands with the mayor. They chatted for a minute and then Ted moved on, not acting like a man who was a half hour late for his appointment. As he approached the booth Jim tried to slip out to shake hands, but Landis waved him back. "Don't get up." He slipped into the other side of the booth. Jim settled back down, not sure whether to reach across the table for a handshake or not. He decided to let Landis make the first move.

Landis picked up the menu. "I'm starving. Sorry I'm late. Got held up at the boat."

"Everything on track? Is the weather going to be a problem for your event?" The sky, which had been charcoal gray when Jim arrived, had lightened. There were patches of blue in the west and north.

Landis waved for the waitress, who had been waiting for his

signal. "I'll have the cobb salad and an ice tea. What are you having, Jim?"

Jim knew he should be ordering salads too, but he hated them. And he was still hungry. "I'll have the Little John Burger with seasoned fries."

Landis scowled as he glanced out the window. "Weather's blowing over. Won't be a factor tonight."

The waitress returned almost immediately with their orders, as though the kitchen had been expecting them. Landis started cutting up his salad. "You said you had a business deal you wanted to discuss?"

Jim knew Landis wasn't much for small talk, but the abruptness surprised him. Jim eyed the Little John Burger—two patties with a layer of bacon, onion, and blue cheese. He wanted that burger, but he knew he couldn't eat and talk. He moved his plate to the side and leaned forward. "First bit of news—GM has awarded me a Saturn franchise."

Landis had a forkful of salad halfway to his mouth. He stopped and put the fork back in the bowl. "That's awesome. That franchise will be a game-changer. I heard they weren't interested in giving them to the established dealers. How'd you pull it off?"

A good start. Landis was clearly impressed.

"I convinced them I had a plan that would work. I have a good relationship with GM." Jim didn't want to explain Kayla's role. Landis wouldn't understand.

"Where you locating?" Landis asked.

A perfect segue for Jim's next item. He looked longingly at his untouched burger. He popped a seasoned fry in his mouth, which made him crave the burger even more. "I'm taking over the Crutchfield property. Building a state-of-the-art showroom there—"

"What!" Landis slammed his fist on the table. "You can't be serious. You're putting the Saturn dealership on fucking Main Street?"

Jim reflexively leaned back in the booth. Landis had pounded the table, but it was like he had gut punched him. He took a ragged breath. "It will be a perfect anchor for the west end."

Landis's eyes went wide and his whole head seemed to expand. "Jimmy. Main Street is dead. You can't put that dealership in a graveyard. How much are they paying you to take that white elephant?"

Jim no longer wanted to talk about his deal with the city. "I just have to pay the back taxes," he said.

Landis hung his head, acting as if that were the stupidest thing he had ever heard. "No! No, no, no, no, no. Fuck the taxes. If you take over that property they need to pay *you*. Don't buy that property."

"I've already signed the papers."

Landis waved his hand. "Don't matter. There ain't a contract written I couldn't get you out of." He offered his charm smile. "Look. I have the perfect place for that dealership. You can be part of my river project. I'll make you a super sweet deal. This is just the kind of business I'm looking for."

Jim looked over at his crumpled plan for the rebirth of Main Street. Maybe if Landis saw it, he'd understand. He unrolled it on the table, almost knocking over Landis's extra cup of blue cheese dressing. "This is part of my plan for rebuilding Main Street. See, here we—"

"Rebuilding Main Street?!" Landis shoved the document aside. His voice boomed across the restaurant. Several tables ceased their conversations and looked over at them. "Are you out of your fucking mind?"

A vein in Jim's head throbbed and he was out of breath

again, as if he had just run a hundred-yard dash. Landis was a bully and Jim had dealt with bullies all his life.

"No," he said, rolling his document back up. "I'm not out of my mind. A healthy, vibrant Maple Springs would be good for you too. Good for your river project. Two plus two will equal five." Even though the restaurant was cool, he could feel a bead of sweat on his upper lip.

Landis leaned across the table, his teeth clenched. "Two plus two will always equal four," he hissed. "I had the plan that would have saved Main Street and those myopic, self-righteous hypocrites told me to go to hell. Now they're sorry, but it's too goddamn late for them." His meaty fists were clenched and he looked like he wanted to punch someone. "I'd expect that kind of simpleminded thinking from your old man, or that hard-ass brother of yours, but not from you, Jimmy."

A lightning flash lit up the restaurant, followed immediately by a crack of thunder that sounded like it came from the parking lot. The restaurant went dark. Exclamations of shock were followed by a collective groan from the diners. But before Jim could say anything, the power returned.

Jim felt physically ill. How could he have been so naive? Landis was never going to forgive the merchants who had rejected his project to honor his ex-wife. Building that mall had been a personal vendetta. He would never support Jim's project.

They both looked out at the parking lot as another windblast rattled the windows. "Do you think you'll have to cancel the boat thing?" Jim asked. No point in talking any further about his project.

Landis grunted dismissively. "We ain't on the ocean. The goddamn boat's sitting in five feet of water. Fucker's not going anywhere." He pressed his lips together tightly. Jim guessed he was trying to conjure up Good Cop Ted. He was right.

"I'm sorry I'm sounding like such a hard ass," Landis said, with the patented Landis smile. It looked better on Candy. "I respect you, Jim. You're one of the smart businessmen in this town. Landing a Saturn dealership is brilliant." He stared out the window at the clouds, as if he could will them to disappear. "Think about this: I'll buy that Crutchfield property from you for a hundred grand. That's an instant hundred K profit for you. Then I'll sell you a piece of property on the river just out of town that will be perfect for Saturn. I'll give you a smoking deal. It'll be a win-win."

A win for Ted, maybe. But what about the town? Jim picked up his burger and took a bite. It was cold and unappealing. He wolfed it down anyway as Ted talked on about his plans for the Caledonia River and how the Saturn dealership would fit right in.

As Ted finally wrapped up his spiel a shaft of light broke through the clouds, illuminating their table. Maybe Landis really did have magical powers.

Jim looked at his watch. It was past 1:30. He stood up. "I need to get back. Give Kayla some help. She's having her wedding reception in the showroom tomorrow."

Ted stood up too. "Give her my best. After the wedding let's talk some more. I'll show you that property. You'll see. It's perfect for you."

Jim nodded—noncommittally, he hoped. He pulled a twenty from his wallet, but Ted held up his hand.

"I've got this, Jimmy. My treat."

CHAPTER 20

1:30 PM

WAYNE

Zelda opened the door and tried to give Dancer a welcoming hug, but he wasn't having any of it. Maybe because he had gotten soaked to the skin walking from the truck to her porch. Hard to tell with Dancer, as grumpy seemed to be his default position. But when she tried to show him Wayne's new tattoo, whatever attitude he had got a whole lot worse.

"Wayne, go to the truck," Dancer said. His eyes were cold. Wayne imagined it was the kind of look he had when someone dared to challenge him back in the day.

Rain was coming down in sheets. It didn't make any sense to leave now. "Let's wait a minute. The storm will let up," Wayne said.

Dancer didn't take his eyes off Zelda. "Get in the truck. I have a few things to discuss with your friend."

"Thought she was your friend."

"Y'all don't have to fight over me. We can all be friends," Zelda said. She had a lot less attitude with Dancer on the scene.

Dancer finally stopped staring at Zelda long enough to give Wayne a look that convinced him it was pointless to try and reason with the man. He stepped down from the porch into a wall of rain and couldn't have gotten any more soaked if he'd jumped in the river. He climbed up into the cab and waited for Dancer. Whatever Zelda had given him for the pain had started to wear off. His tattooed chest stung like a bad sunburn and his back throbbed. His soaked fatigues felt as though they weighed a hundred pounds. He slipped off his shirt.

Dancer returned a minute later. Zelda didn't walk him out. He climbed up into the cab, handed Wayne his wedding ring, and gave him that "what a fool you are" look. He started the engine and steered the truck back onto the highway.

"I thought you weren't going to be taken by some hillbilly fortune-teller," he said.

"I didn't get taken," Wayne said, but he had the feeling he was probably wrong.

"You gave her a thousand-dollar ring for a hundred-dollar tat."

"She was just holding the ring until I brought her the cash." Wayne hoped Zelda hadn't told Dancer about the hundred dollars Wayne had paid her in addition to the ring.

Dancer laughed, but his face stayed grouchy. "She'd have hocked that ring by tomorrow. Zelda doesn't finance."

"There's a faster wiper speed," Wayne said.

Dancer was hunched over the steering wheel trying to see the road as rain sheeted the windshield like they were driving through a car wash. He flicked to the higher speed, but it was still hard to see.

"Want me to drive?" Wayne asked. They were sputtering along in first gear about five miles per hour. It would take them hours to get back to Dancer's place at this speed.

"No. Don't ask again."

"Why you in such a good mood?"

"Dealing with dipshits," Dancer said.

"Landis give you a hard time?" He pretended Dancer wasn't referring to him.

"I can't stand being in the same room with that man. Never

have." He looked at Wayne. It was different than his earlier looks. Like he was trying to read him.

"What?" Wayne asked.

"Found out something that might be of interest to you. The mystery band is that pirate group you were talking about."

"The Confederate Pirates? They're playing the riverboat?"

"Landis has a big bandstand set up in the parking lot. They aren't on the boat—they're playing for all those folks who aren't important enough to get on."

"Hot damn!" Wayne clapped his hands together and then winced. "We gotta go to that party."

"You can barely walk." Dancer had that disgusted look on his face. The rain stopped suddenly and Dancer pressed the accelerator until he was back to driving at typical old man speed.

"Not partying," Wayne said. "Just want to check in with the band. Let them know I'm available again."

Dancer looked at his watch and then pulled a wad of bills from his shorts pocket. "Take a hundred out of here."

"You're still paying me?" Wayne had figured after the fiasco at the Madman's place, Dancer would back out of the arrangement. Wayne would have.

Dancer smiled, like Wayne had just told him something funny. "I'm paying for the use of your truck and that lift gate. I need to get one of those."

"Are you going to keep running the jukebox business?"

Dancer colored slightly and his grip on the steering wheel tightened. "I sure as hell ain't letting Jim sell it to that son-of-a-bitch Landis."

"Cool. Anytime you need my help, you got it. Hey! That's Lucy's car."

Up ahead on the side of the road was a ten-year-old rust-red Subaru station wagon.

Dancer slowed down and squinted at the car. "You're right. That's their wagon." He pulled to a stop. "I'll check things out, make sure they're okay. Stay in the truck."

Dancer walked to the window of the basket ladies' car and peered in. Then he walked over to the edge of the road and looked down the embankment that sloped all the way to the river. He shrugged and came back to the truck. "No sign of them. But there are a couple of old lawn jockeys and a St. Louis Cardinals birdbath in the back."

"A Cardinals birdbath?" Wayne asked.

"Yeah, the baseball team. It has the team logo on the base."

"I know. Anita's old lady has had that in her junkyard for years, just waiting for some sucker to buy it. What do they need that shit for?" Wayne asked.

Dancer pulled himself up into the truck and started the engine. "Beats me." He pulled on to the highway. "They must have broke down. I'm guessing they hitched a ride back to their place."

"That looks like Lucy up ahead," Wayne said.

They rounded a sharp curve and were starting to climb up toward the top of the ridge of the gorge. Lucy was trudging slowly up the hill. She turned at the sound of Wayne's truck and started waving. Wayne rolled his window down and waved back.

"Hey! Soldier boy," Lucy said, clapping her hands together.

Lucy was wearing cut-off jeans shorts and a white T-shirt. Her pink hair dripped like she had just stepped out of the shower. Her T-shirt clung to her large breasts, her nipples poking through the sheer fabric.

"You want a ride, ma'am?" Wayne asked, grinning.

Lucy ran her hands through the tangled strands of her hair, squeegeeing out water and pushing the hair off her face so she could see. She squinted up at Wayne. "How come you're driving, Dancer?" she asked.

Wayne opened the door and grimaced as he climbed down from the truck. "Had a little problem and got a rib busted," he said.

Lucy, without a trace of embarrassment, pulled off her wet T-shirt and twisted it to wring out the water, then tugged it back on. Wayne stared at her, not sure what to do or say.

She smiled at him. "Haven't you seen breasts before, Wayne?"

He could feel his face coloring.

The first time Wayne saw Anita's bare breasts, he had been pleased he'd finally made it to second base, but it wasn't as exciting as he had expected. Lucy's boobs, nice as they were, didn't do anything for him either.

"What's wrong with your car?" Dancer asked.

"I think it had a heart attack," Lucy said. "We need to replace it. Can Jim help us?"

Wayne reached out to help her into the cab, then winced as his rib gave a twinge. He withdrew his arm.

Lucy stared at him the same way Zelda had. Like she could see right through him. "Who'd you pick a fight with?" she asked.

"A couple of security badasses were treating me like a soccer ball, but old Dancer here gave them a serious attitude adjustment. That one dude"—he looked over at Dancer, who as usual wasn't smiling—"he's probably still trying to figure out what hit him. You should have seen him in action, Lucy. Pop! One punch and the asshole went down like a sack of rocks."

"Get in the truck, Lucy," Dancer said.

Back to his pure grumpy mode again.

"Can we go back to get the lawn jockeys?" Lucy asked.

"You sprucing up your place?" Dancer asked.

Lucy blushed. "They're for a configuration I'm doing with two of our baskets for a new client. It's supposed to be ironic." She shrugged. "We need the money."

Lucy pulled herself up into the cab and settled into the club seat. Wayne pulled himself back into the cab, trying not to stress his rib, which was throbbing.

"Hey, you got a tiger tattoo!" Lucy said.

"How do you like it? Got it this morning."

"Very cool," Lucy said as she leaned forward to study the art. "Who did the inking?"

"Zelda," Wayne said. "She has a place—"

"Zelda's awesome!" Lucy squealed. "She did my cherubs. Want to see them?" She unsnapped her jeans shorts and started to slide them down.

"I've seen them," Wayne said, laughing.

"You have?" Lucy looked confused.

"You showed the bartender at Jake's for a free round."

Lucy giggled and pulled her shorts back on. "Those cherubs have almost paid for themselves," she said.

Dancer drove past the Subaru and did a U-turn, coming up and parking behind it. "Want me to call Jimmy's place and have them tow it to the dealership?"

"That would be great," Lucy said. She leaned forward to look out the front window. The storm clouds had moved off to the northwest and the sun was shining brightly again. "It looks like the party is on!"

Dancer quickly loaded the lawn boys and the bird bath in the back of the truck. As they headed back to Lucy's cottage, she tapped Wayne on the shoulder. "Do you want to go to that party tonight?" Before Wayne could answer, she added, "I need a ride. I can get home on my own."

Wayne hitched his shoulders. "Okay," he said.

"We need to get there early so we can get on the boat," Lucy said. "Pick me up at 5:30?"

She was just like Anita. Every time you agreed to something, she asked for something more. Maybe all women were like that. Maybe that's why it was so easy to be with Sonny. No demands.

As they started back up the hill, the birdbath fell into one of the lawn jockeys. "Don't break our lawn jockeys," Lucy said. "Johnnie doesn't have any more like that. Hey, I got some juicy gossip from Johnnie, Dancer."

Dancer didn't say anything. He looked like he didn't want to hear, but Lucy couldn't see his face.

"Her daughter's fucking Ted Landis. Johnnie's not happy about it."

It took a moment for Wayne to even comprehend what those words meant. Anita was fucking Ted Landis? Could that be possible?

Wayne's cheeks burned. Johnnie wouldn't make up a story like that. Was he the last to know? How could Anita be with that guy? Was money that important to her? It must be, because that jerk was fat and ugly. And old. At least thirty years older than her.

Dancer didn't look surprised, but his face never revealed much, except when he was annoyed. "I know a thing or two about rumors," he said. "Most of them are a little truth and a lot of bullshit."

He steered the truck slowly down the access road from the highway to the basket ladies' house.

"Stay in the truck, Wayne," Dancer said. "You don't want to keep stressing that rib."

He jumped down from the cab and held the seat forward so

Lucy could get out. He lifted out the two lawn jockeys, Lucy grabbed the birdbath, and they carried them to the screened porch.

Anita with Ted Landis? It didn't seem possible. Wayne wouldn't believe it until he saw them together. Until he heard it from Anita. She owed him that much.

A few moments later, Dancer and Lucy reappeared and walked back to the truck together.

Lucy came over to his window. "I can find another ride for tonight, Wayne. You shouldn't be driving with that rib all busted up."

Obviously Dancer had talked to her. But he didn't need the old man's help this time. "No. It's cool. I'll be back at 5:30 to pick you up."

He would find Anita tonight and they would sort this out, one way or another. Zelda was right—Anita had disrespected him, and it was up to Wayne to set things straight.

CHAPTER 21

2:15 PM

DANCER

Dancer pulled into his driveway and parked next to Clayton's old Ford. "I could get used to this comfort," he said as he handed the truck keys to Wayne. "Want to trade?"

Wayne tried to smile as he climbed down cautiously from the cab, but he couldn't hide his pain. Dancer had broken a few ribs in his day and he knew there weren't many ways you could move your body that didn't hurt. At least for the first few days.

"I don't think plum metallic is your color," Wayne said as he walked slowly around to the driver's side. "But I could bring the truck back on Monday and help you move the rest of your stuff. Whole lot easier with a liftgate."

Dancer considered the proposition. Today was shot and tomorrow he had Kayla's wedding. Might as well put off the rest of the move until after the weekend. "Okay. Good idea. Does a hundred dollars a day work for you?" he asked.

Wayne nodded. "What time you want me?"

"Nine o'clock will be fine." Dancer paused for a moment. "Why don't you forget about the party tonight? Give that rib some time to heal."

Wayne shook his head. "I know what you're thinking, but I ain't going to make any trouble. I need to see Curt—he's the head of the Pirates. I want him to know I'm back and available."

"You could call him," Dancer said.

"I don't have his number. And I don't have a cellphone. Better I go see him."

Dancer didn't believe him. But he knew he wouldn't be able to talk him out of going. "Don't take the gun. Okay?"

Wayne gave him a wave of dismissal and pulled himself up into the driver's seat. "Don't worry. I learned my lesson. I'll just pick up Lucy and be a perfect gentleman. Don't plan to even see Anita." He started the engine and then looked down at Dancer again. "Did you tell Lucy Anita's my wife?"

"I thought she should know." Dancer didn't want to get involved—it wasn't his business—but he had to give Lucy the heads-up on that situation.

"Did you know she was hooking up with Landis?" Wayne asked.

"Remember what I said about rumors," Dancer said. A caution, not an answer. "Talk to your woman. But not tonight." He stepped away from the truck as Wayne backed out of the driveway. He hadn't exactly been honest with the kid, but honesty wasn't always the best policy. Especially when women were involved.

As Wayne drove away down the ridge road, Trudy Bennett appeared, heading up the ridge in her mail jeep. She pulled into the driveway and jumped out with a handful of mail.

"Dancer!" She skipped over and hugged him. Something she used to do all the time when she and Clayton were dating. That had been decades ago, but for Dancer it brought memories flooding back of those happier times.

"Now that's my kind of mail delivery," he said. "Good to see you, Trudy."

A rumble of thunder seemed to come out of nowhere. A moment before the sky had been almost clear, but now a mountain range of bruise-yellow clouds had formed on the southern horizon, closer than they had been earlier. The air was unnaturally still. It made Dancer shiver even though the temperature was still above eighty.

Trudy handed him his mail. A couple of bills, the August issue of *Jukebox Monthly*, and Dancer's social security check.

"Do you know that guy in the purple truck?" she asked. She looked back over her shoulder, but Wayne had rounded the bend and was out of sight. It was clear from her expression that her opinion of Wayne wasn't any better than Wayne's opinion of her.

"He's helping me move," Dancer said. "Don't really know him."

She frowned when she spotted the "Sold" sign in the front yard. "You sold Clayton's house?"

Trudy and Clayton had split well before Clayton bought the A-frame with some long-forgotten girlfriend. But just in the way she said his name, Dancer could tell he still meant something to her. She had looked ragged at his funeral, as bad as Paula. They had both loved his son at one time. Maybe they still did. Too bad Clayton couldn't do something with all that love.

"Jim sold it," Dancer said. "I'm moving over to their place."

"What about Clayton's jukebox business?" she asked.

"I want to keep running it. Not sure Jim and I are on the same page, but we'll see."

She looked as if she wanted to say something more.

"What's on your mind, Trudy?"

A jagged streak of lightning followed almost immediately by a crack of thunder—much louder than before—made them both turn and stare at the southern ridge. With the thunder and lightning and the charged air, it felt like they were in the middle of a storm, but the sun was still shining bright and there was no rain.

Trudy glanced at her phone and frowned. "A line of tornados spotted south of West Plains. They're putting us on alert."

West Plains was twenty miles south.

"The post office is on alert?" Dancer asked.

Trudy grinned. "No, I needed something to do in my spinsterhood, so last year I became an EMT with the fire department. They're just giving us a heads up. Don't worry. We get these notices all the time."

"Spinsterhood? What are you? Thirty-five?"

"Fifty this fall. It doesn't matter. All the good ones are gone," she said.

Her dark brown eyes were shiny with tears as she looked at Dancer. For the moment neither spoke, but they were both thinking about Clayton.

"Did you have something you wanted to ask me?" Dancer asked.

Trudy scuffed the ground with her toe, like a nervous kid. "Did you know I had a date with Clayton a few weeks before . . . the accident?"

"No. But there was a lot going on with Clayton I didn't know about."

"It wasn't really a *date* date," Trudy said. "We just went out to Miller's Quarry with a six-pack and drank a few beers. Talked about the old days. He was glad you were in his life, Dancer. I mean, he didn't say it in so many words, but I could tell when he talked about how you guys were a team working on his business. He wanted to make you proud."

Dancer swallowed hard. He needed to believe her. "I was proud of him," he said softly. "I hope he knew that."

Trudy wiped a tear from the corner of her eye. "I believe he did," she said.

"Remember when he came home from Vietnam?" Dancer

asked. "I thought . . ." This was stupid. He didn't need to open old wounds. He pressed his lips together.

"What, Dancer?"

"I thought when you two got back together, he was finally going to get out of this place."

Trudy rubbed her hands like she was cold. "I wanted us to leave. Start fresh somewhere new. But Clayton didn't want to start over. Going to Vietnam when he didn't have to, that was supposed to be Clayton's great escape, but it didn't work out like he planned. He wasn't a fighter like you, but he wasn't a runner either. He wanted to succeed in his hometown. Show everyone. You. The town. His brother. I know what folks are saying, but he didn't kill himself. Clayton wasn't a quitter."

Dancer wanted to wrap his arms around Trudy and hug her for dear life. She spoke the truth. How could anyone have thought otherwise? He felt like a weight had been lifted off his chest. Jim was wrong. So was Landis.

He would keep Clayton's business alive.

"Are you coming to the wedding tomorrow?" Dancer asked.

Trudy frowned. "I don't think so. Too many sad memories." Another flash of lightning followed by an ominous rumble. "I better get a move on it. I'm supposed to go to that big riverboat party tonight."

Dancer recalled Wayne's angry words about Trudy's bad influence on his wife. Wayne had somehow convinced himself that Trudy was the reason Anita was leaving him. Maybe he had changed that opinion now that he knew about Landis. Whatever Wayne thought, it was another situation where Dancer was helpless to do anything but worry.

"Be careful, Trudy," he said.

She smiled at him, surprised, but appreciative of his concern. "Of course. I'm always careful." She hugged him again and brushed a kiss on his cheek. "I don't want to hear any more of this I'm-getting-old talk. Okay?"

"Be careful," Dancer said again as he watched her truck disappear around the bend.

CHAPTER 22

3:00 PM

JIM

The Maple Springs emergency care clinic where Paula worked had been opened by Lutheran General Hospital in West Plains five years ago so that folks in Maple Springs didn't have to make the twenty-mile drive to the hospital for every minor emergency. It was a great success. Dr. Manickavel was the primary care physician and she hired Paula and two other unemployed nurses from Maple Springs to help her. Jim had been pleased to have his obsessive-compulsive wife devoting at least some of her time to projects she actually got paid for.

The clinic was located on the east end of Main Street, three storefronts down from the Maple Springs Diner. The courthouse, the post office, Barclay's Bank, and the diner were all clustered together and because of them, that end of the street did not have the ravaged, abandoned look of West Main Street where Jim was planning to locate his Saturn dealership.

Jim had a burning sensation in his gut. Landis's dismissal of his plan and his wolfing down of the Little John Burger were probably jointly responsible for his gastric distress. Maybe he could get an antacid from Dr. Manickavel.

While East Main showed more life than West Main, it was not thriving. When the mall had started sucking away customers, the town council had reacted by getting rid of all the Main Street parking meters. It was an impotent, ineffective gesture. Free parking wouldn't bring customers back. There were just two cars parked on the block and one of them was Dr. Manickavel's.

As Jim walked toward the clinic, he had a vague sense something was different. Then it hit him. It wasn't blistering hot anymore. It was almost cool, comfortable, like a late fall day. Probably a perfect day for the Landis riverboat promotion. That man had all the luck.

Paula and Kuzhali were talking in the reception area. Dr. Manickavel—"Doctor K" to most of her patients—was meticulous in her appearance. White lab coat crisp like it was fresh from the laundry, dark hair pinned up, nails polished. But more than her appearance, it was her voice that inspired confidence. She had the clipped British accent with that Indian lilt that made her sound, at least to Jim, like she knew what she was talking about. She had been good for Paula. She was unflappable and direct and not bothered in the least by Paula's bluntness. They were both no-bullshit women.

There were no customers, or, as Paula was always correcting him, "patients" in sight.

"Where are all the customers?" Jim asked as he pulled the door shut.

Paula gave him the look but didn't correct him. That was a good sign.

"Hello, James," Dr. Manickavel said. "It's been slow today. A couple of kids with bad sunburns, a few routine physicals, and a young homeless man who I think just wanted to enjoy our air conditioning."

Paula smiled and Jim's guard went up.

"Jim," she said, and he could tell by the way she tried to look natural that something bad was coming. "I have some lab reports I need to file. It will only take a few minutes. Why don't you let Dr. K give you a mini-physical while you wait? It's been over a year."

"I think that's a grand idea, Paula," Dr. Manickavel said, as if the suggestion were a total surprise to her.

Jim was more upset that they could believe he was so blind to their plotting than he was at the actual prospect of having a physical. But he was upset about that, too. It felt like everyone he had encountered today wanted to tell him how he should live his life.

Everyone except Kayla.

"Just basic stuff, James," the doctor said. "Height, weight, BP. That kind of thing."

Paula looked like she wanted to jump in with her two cents, but she restrained herself.

Jim raised his hands in surrender. "Fine. Where do I go?"

It was the usual bait and switch. Those women would have made great car salesmen. Once she had him in the patient room, Paula handed him a gown and told him to strip down to his boxers. "The doctor will be right in," she said, smiling at him like he was just another customer.

"Don't forget to do your filing," Jim said. He would bet a hundred dollars there wasn't any.

Doctor Manickavel entered, studying her clipboard. She frowned. "You have not had a complete physical in over three years. At your age, you should have an annual checkup."

"Absolutely," Jim said. He sounded earnest. "I will definitely put that on my calendar."

Dr. Manickavel was temporarily disarmed. She had expected Jim to be resistant. But he had learned in the sales game it was much better to sound agreeable, even when you didn't agree.

She had him step on the digital scales. He weighed 283.

She checked his height: six foot two. She took a tape measure and wrapped it around his hips, waist, and chest. Finally she wrapped the blood pressure cuff around his arm. She did it all without the editorial comment he usually got from the doctors or nurses. For that Jim was grateful.

Dr. Manickavel entered the numbers into her tablet computer and her frown, which was her normal countenance, deepened. "Your BMI is 37.0, which classifies you as obese. According to the HEMRI optimal weight calculator, you should weigh 183.2, which makes you about a hundred pounds overweight."

She was wasting no time on bedside manner. Jim started to say something, but she held up her hand. "Your weight is a concern, obviously. You know that as well as I do. But I am much more concerned about your blood pressure. 190 over 100 is dangerously high. We need to bring that down. You are at serious risk for a heart attack."

Jim felt a tightening in his chest. He wondered if worrying about having a heart attack could cause a heart attack. "So, cut back on salt, right?" he said. The doctor had stopped talking so it seemed like he should say something.

She shrugged. "Sure, that will help. But you need to come into West Plains and have a complete physical. Blood work, EKG, stress test, prostate exam. It's time, James."

He grabbed his shirt from the hanger and started buttoning it. "Okay," he said. "After the wedding, I'll make an appointment with you."

She stared hard at him. "You're a lot like your father, you know."

Jim frowned at her. Clayton, athletic and stubborn, had always been told he was just like his father and he hated it. Jim, a clumsy, overweight kid, would have loved for someone to tell him he was just like his father. Now, after all these years, someone finally had, but Dr. Manickavel obviously didn't mean it in a good way.

"How's that?" he asked.

"You tell people what they want to hear so they'll shut up and leave you alone."

Jim belched and hot stomach acid burned the back of his throat. "Do you have a Tums? I ate my lunch too fast."

Dr. Manickavel frowned. "Those aren't recommended—"

Paula knocked and then opened the office door. "Sorry to interrupt. There have been reports of tornados south of West Plains and the hospital wants all emergency personnel to return to the hospital."

Dr. Manickavel slipped the tablet computer into her briefcase. "So you'll make that appointment next week, James?"

He obviously wasn't going to get a Tums now. "Yes, I promise. Early next week, after the smoke clears from the wedding."

Dr. Manickavel looked at him skeptically. "Good." She turned to Paula. "I'll see you Monday. Enjoy the wedding. Sorry I can't make it."

The doctor wasn't one for long goodbyes, even when there wasn't an emergency.

Jim grabbed his pants and dressed quickly. He hustled out of the exam room. Paula was waiting for him in the reception area. "I'll take you home," he said, "and then I'm driving over to the lot to help Kayla and Barry get ready for the reception. I don't want them staying there all evening with this weather situation the way it is."

"I'll go with you."

Jim looked at her to see if she were kidding. Paula hadn't been to Stonemason Chevrolet since Kayla started working there. She had wanted Kayla to go to college, but Kayla knew what she wanted and she was as stubborn as her mother. Paula had stopped complaining and gave up pushing college, but Jim knew she was still unhappy with Kayla's decision.

"Really?" he asked her, trying not to sound too incredulous. She looked absolutely sincere.

"You're not very good at setting up," she said. She tried to look serious, but the corners of her mouth had turned up. This time she was kidding.

CHAPTER 23

4:00 PM

WAYNE

The lot for Crestview Manor was nearly empty when Wayne pulled in. Zeke's shift wouldn't be over for another half hour, and Wayne thought about taking his parking spot but decided against it and parked in the visitor's section close to the highway.

He was halfway across the lot when the lightning struck. A jagged streak to the south, blindingly bright, followed by a deep rumble that ended with an earsplitting crack. For a moment he was back in Iraq standing with Sonny on the banks of the Tigris as the cruise missiles and B2 bombers pounded Baghdad. Even forty miles from the carnage, Wayne had been terrified. And ashamed that he was grateful they were safe in the backwater of Zubayidiyah helping build a useless bridge. Better than blowing things up, Sonny had assured him. He had been right, but being right hadn't saved him.

Wayne sprinted toward the front door as if he were under attack. The weird thing was the sun was still shining. He jerked his head around as another bolt of lightning brightened the sky. His foot caught the concrete parking berm in front of Zeke's apartment. He fell hard, his face smashing into Zeke's welcome mat.

There was a searing pain in his chest and it felt like his tattoo was being rubbed off with sandpaper. But that was almost immediately forgotten as the dull ache from his broken rib came alive with a nauseating intensity.

"Fuck!" he screamed. "Fuck! Fuck! Fuck!" He pounded the worn rubber mat with his fist, which caused his ribcage to compress, and the pain redlined. He squeezed his eyes shut trying to block it out. He lay on the mat sobbing and wishing he could start this fucked up day all over again. Or just skip it completely.

Slowly, he got to his feet. He unlocked the apartment and walked through the kitchen to the bathroom.

He peeled off his fatigues and turned on the shower to hot. He looked at himself in the medicine cabinet mirror. He felt worse than he looked, and he looked like shit. His tiger tattoo, still wrapped tightly in the surgical tape, was barely visible under the layer of blood and mucus that had oozed from the artwork. He needed something to dull the pain.

While the room filled with steam, he opened the medicine cabinet, but he wasn't optimistic. Painkillers, like air conditioning and cable TV, were unnecessary luxury items for Zeke. The cabinet was almost empty. Toothpaste (but no shaving cream—that was another of those luxury items), razor blades, a tube of Preparation H, and a jar of Vaseline. He didn't even have aspirin. Wayne pulled open the top drawer of the vanity. Pushed to the back of the otherwise empty drawer was a prescription bottle.

OxyContin. Fifty tablets and it had been issued on June 30, four weeks before Wayne returned from Iraq. The prescription had been filled by a West Plains pharmacy. Dr. Steinberg was the issuing doctor.

Who was Steinberg? What kind of doctor was he? Why did Zeke need oxy and why was he having his prescription filled in West Plains?

Wayne twisted off the cap. The bottle was half empty. He shook two pills into his palm and swallowed them quickly. He turned down the water temperature until he could stand it and stepped into the shower. He closed his eyes and draped his arms over the shower head as the hot water pelted his scalp.

Zeke must be having some serious pain for him to be taking oxy. He had been wounded in Vietnam, shot in the thigh. It caused him to limp slightly, and he said it bothered him more when it got hot. He never complained, never even took an aspirin. But this had been the hottest summer in years and maybe it had finally gotten to him.

Wayne hated to admit it, but his father had never believed in him. He didn't think playing in a band was a real job. He thought Wayne was wasting his time trying to make it as a musician. Maybe Zeke hated the guitar because it had been Wayne's mother who had given him that first guitar. In Wayne's memory, his mother had always been encouraging. Just like Sonny. Sonny had been way more interested in his music than Anita.

But both his mother and Sonny had been unhappy with their lives. They had both deserted him. His mother gave up her family to panhandle on street corners, so she must have badly wanted to escape. For what? Spiritual fulfillment? Wayne would never know.

And Sonny. Wayne had been in denial. He didn't want to believe Sonny killed himself. But when he looked at Sonny's action on that day it was obvious. His manic happiness after being miserable for two weeks. The boat engine disabled. Telling Wayne to go take a nap while he swam. Sonny hated his life so much he gave it up. He chose nothingness over Wayne.

Now Anita wanted out too. He didn't love Anita. He wanted to, but he knew, deep down, that he didn't. Never had.

But he was tired of being the loser. He'd lost his mom to that creepy guru. Sonny had chosen death. Now Anita was giving up on him. For what? Security? Landis was old enough to be her grandfather.

If he could get another chance with the C-Pirates, that would change things. Anita would see that he could provide for her and the kids. He was not a loser. Maybe that was what Sonny had been trying to tell him in that dream. He could be a jukebox hero.

He turned off the shower and quickly toweled off. He swallowed another oxy and wrapped four more in a tissue for later—just in case.

He needed to make a good impression on the C-Pirates and with Anita. His clothes were still in a pile next to his duffel where he had dumped them this morning. He grabbed his Wrangler boot-cut jeans, the black cowboy shirt with mother of pearl buttons Anita had given him for his birthday last year, his black leather belt with the silver buckle, and the black and cordovan ostrich-skin boots he picked up at Fort Hood before he shipped out. He tugged on the jeans. When he had left for Iraq it had been a struggle to get them buttoned, but now they snapped easily. He looked at himself in the hall mirror. No more muffin-top and when he sucked in his gut he had the faint outline of a six-pack. Too bad the tattoo wasn't healed. Anita would love the tiger tat.

The shirt was wrinkled but it didn't smell that bad. Zeke's ironing board was set up in his bedroom—he ironed his work shirt every morning. Wayne plugged in the iron and sprayed the shirt with starch to give it a fresher scent.

While he waited for the iron to warm up, he picked up the boots. Putting them on was going to hurt. The oxy had given him a good buzz, but those boots had never been worn. Wayne popped another oxy and washed it down with a shot of Zeke's cheap house-brand whiskey. While he waited for the oxy to kick in, he stuffed his clothes back in the duffel. At the bottom of the pile in a canvas drawstring bag were the four ammo magazines Sonny had purchased when he bought the Sig.

Sonny paid twice what he should have for that gun, but he was so proud of it. As he loaded the magazines, he had lectured Wayne on the details. "This is the official sidearm of the Swiss Army," he said. "It takes a 9 mil parabellum cartridge and has a muzzle velocity of twelve hundred feet per second. Seven rounds in the magazine. Those snakes better watch out."

He never even got a chance to fire it.

Wayne wiped away a tear that had slipped down his cheek. The oxy was fucking him up good. He gripped the right boot by the top straps and yanked it on. It hurt, but he powered through, forcing his arch through the tight opening. He repeated the process with the left. His brow beaded with sweat. The boots were new-boot tight. When he walked, he had a slight hitch in his stride—sort of like his old man. It made him look more like a cowboy.

Wayne licked his finger and touched the iron, like Zeke always did, to make sure it was hot enough. He worked the iron around the mother-of-pearl buttons, then ironed the other side and the cuffs. That was enough. With the muscle he'd added in basic training, the shirt would be snug enough that he didn't need to iron the whole thing.

He slipped it on. It fit great. Anita would be surprised and impressed. He considered leaving it half un-buttoned so the tiger would be visible, but the tattoo wasn't ready for viewing, and besides, that was too gay.

"I'm not a fag," he whispered. But when he said those words it made him think of Sonny and he wanted to take them back.

Zeke walked in as Wayne was buttoning his shirt. Zeke's uniform was sweat-stained and his face had a fine layer of grit, like he had darkened himself for a combat mission. Maybe it was just Wayne's oxy imagination at work, but his father looked tired. Even with the grit, his face seemed gray, faded. His cheeks were hollowed out and his pants sagged. He'd lost weight. A lot of weight. How had Wayne not noticed?

"Where the hell you going, all gussied up?" Zeke asked, checking out Wayne like he was conducting barracks inspection.

"Riverboat. Got to pick up some friends on the way."

Zeke's face grew puzzled and he ran his hand through his hair. It was longer than normal. "Thought you were getting with Anita tonight," he said.

"I am. Later tonight," Wayne said. "You need a haircut." His father always got it cut every three weeks.

Zeke scowled. "Riv closed his shop. Couldn't compete with that fucking Bo-Rics at the mall. I think I'll just shave it all off. Save the money."

Something was wrong. Zeke wasn't taking oxy for some thirty-year-old war wound. Playing a wild hunch, Wayne asked, "When do you start chemo?"

"Who told you that?" Zeke walked over to the kitchen sink and washed his hands, splashing water on his face to rinse off the grime. "Jesus. There ain't no secrets in this motherfucking town." He wiped his hands and face with a dishtowel. Then he waved his finger at Wayne. "I ain't taking that fucking poison."

Wayne had a tight feeling in his gut. He had wanted his father to tell him he didn't need chemo because he wasn't sick. "If you need chemo, why aren't you taking it?" Wayne asked. "You got insurance. The company will pay for it, right?"

Zeke smiled sadly and shrugged with un-Zeke-like resignation. He nodded toward the whiskey bottle on the counter. "Priming yourself for your big date?" He filled two juice glasses and handed one to Wayne. "Have a drink with your old man before you take off."

It was almost five o'clock, but if Lucy was anything like Anita, she wouldn't be ready at five thirty. He took the glass from his father and raised it. "Oorah!" he said.

Zeke's face got all squirrelly. "Didn't they teach you anything in the goddamn reserves? Oorah is jarhead shit. We're regular army, son. Hooah!" He raised his glass and gulped it down like Wayne might steal it from him.

Wayne took a large sip. It burned his throat and he had to take a few deep breaths before he could finish the glass. "What kind of cancer, Dad?"

"Pancreas. Stage four. There really ain't no point in chemo. My doctor agrees. I got three months, maybe six if I'm lucky. Or unlucky, I guess. Fuck of a thing, huh?"

Wayne felt as though there was no air left in the room. His face and lips were numb. "You're still working?" His voice sounded hollow, like someone else was talking.

Zeke shrugged again and looked embarrassed. "What else am I going to do? Play golf? Take a goddamn cruise? I go fishing on weekends. Watch the Cardinals games. I can go to the Legion if I'm desperate for company. Which I'm not." He poured himself another glass and offered the bottle, but Wayne waved him off.

"I got to roll, Dad." He didn't mean it the way it sounded. Like he was too busy to hang around. It was just that with the oxy and the whiskey he was already feeling half drunk and half stoned. Another drink and he might not make it to the truck.

Zeke put the bottle away. "I saw Anita today. She looked good. I'm taking the kids to the fair next weekend. I hope you're serious about fixing things with her. She's good for you, Wayne.

I didn't used to think that, but she's grown up." He looked down at his shoes. "Want to go fishing Sunday?"

When he was a kid—before his mom left—they went fishing almost every summer weekend. Back then he and Zeke did stuff together all the time: drove to St. Louis for a Cardinals game, canoed on the Caledonia, bowled at the Legion hall where you had to set up your own pins. But after she abandoned them, it all stopped.

Wayne had always hated fishing.

"Sure," he said. "Sunday's good. But I don't have any gear."

Zeke smiled. "I got plenty. I'll loan you mine. Drive careful, son."

Wayne thought about hugging his father, but Zeke turned away quickly and marched into his bedroom before Wayne could make a move. Instead, he started for the front door, but stopped when he noticed the drawstring sack of ammo next to his duffel. His Sig was still in the glove box, unloaded. Dancer had been right, pointing an unloaded gun at someone was a good way to get killed. He didn't figure he'd need the gun, but the army had taught him to prepare for the unexpected. Everything that had happened today had been unexpected, and there was no reason to believe that was going to change. He grabbed the ammo.

CHAPTER 24

4:05 PM

KAYLA

One of the things Kayla loved about Barry was that he never insisted on taking charge of all the so-called guy things like driving. He drove his father's ten-year-old Beemer, not because he was one of those foreign car snobs, but because it helped him remember his father as he had been—a good-natured ad exec for Leo Burnett, the lead manager on the BMW account. His father had early onset Alzheimer's and now he was a good-natured stranger who didn't recognize his son or the wife who devoted her life to his care.

Kayla and Barry had spent the afternoon in bed making love and napping. When Kayla woke up at three-thirty she insisted they take her Camaro instead of Barry's car so they could make it back to the dealership by four as Stu Collins had insisted.

They had no chance of making it in time if Barry drove. He was too cautious. He obeyed all the speed limit signs when everyone in moonshine country knew that those signs were merely suggestions.

They would have made it on time if Barry hadn't brushed his teeth for five minutes. Kayla covered the twenty miles on US 60 in less than fifteen minutes and they pulled into the dealership lot at 4:05. The storm clouds that had massed on the southern horizon like an army ready to invade had kept their distance and the sun was shining brightly. Stu Collins stood under the Stonemason sign, where Kayla had stood in the morning seeking relief from the blistering heat. Now there was no need. The temperature had dropped dramatically.

"What the hell you doing on point, Stu?" Kayla asked as she parked the Camaro in her father's parking space. Stu never took point. He considered that a job for the newbies.

"Just enjoying this fall weather and waiting for you." Stu walked over to the car and shook Barry's hand as he slipped out of the Camaro. "You're a brave man, Barry—letting Kayla drive. How many tickets she have to talk her way out of? I swear she knows the name of every highway patrol officer from here to the Arkansas border."

Barry smiled good-naturedly. "She's a great driver. No encounters with law enforcement. What's with this weather? It feels like October."

"You scare all the customers away, Stu?" Kayla asked. There were no cars parked in front of the showroom.

Stu shrugged. "I think the whole county is on their way to the riverboat party. Come on. I'll show you the dos and don'ts of making a Chevy showroom into a hillbilly wedding hoedown." He winked at Barry. "You'll need plenty of spit buckets for all those Red Man chewers and a gun check for the mobsters."

"Chill, Stu." Kayla looked at Barry and rolled her eyes.

Stu bounded up the showroom steps and stood at the entrance waiting for them like a Walmart greeter. "Right this way, folks." He pulled open the door with a flourish.

"Surprise!" A raucous cheer exploded from inside the showroom. It appeared that the entire Stonemason Chevrolet team—new and used car salesmen, bookkeepers, customer service reps, mechanics and custodians—had crammed into the space.

It no longer resembled a showroom. The new 2004 display cars that normally occupied the prime real estate had been replaced with highboys and dining tables all covered in elegant white linen. All the setup work had been done.

"We couldn't let you and Barry work so hard the night before your wedding," Stu said, draping a meaty arm on Kayla's shoulder.

Kayla had a lump in her throat. "It's beautiful, Stu." She brushed his cheek with a kiss. "Thank you."

Barry stared at the scene, mouth agape. "This is awesome."

Karl Kompe, the inventory parts manager, yelled from across the room where he was manning a beer tap. "Take all the credit, Stu. Typical salesman."

Karl weighed at least three hundred pounds and, with his Fu Manchu mustache and ponytailed red hair, still looked like the badass biker dude he had been in his twenties. He had served three years in the Chillicothe Correctional Center for dealing pot and had worked for Jim Stonemason for the last ten. Clean and sober for all those years, he was always the designated bartender and bouncer at company functions.

Paul Habner, the dean of used cars, walked over and wrapped his arms around Kayla in a gentle fatherly embrace. "We're so happy for you." He bowed slightly to Barry. "Congratulations, son. I'm sure I don't have to tell you how special this young lady is." Habner was older than most of the salesmen and with his wire-rim glasses and immaculately groomed white hair, he looked like Hollywood's notion of a Wall Street banker.

Stu Collins put his fingers in his mouth and whistled sharply. "All right, gang. You've all done a great job of getting this place set up." He turned and addressed Kayla and Barry. "We know we have to be on our best behavior tomorrow—meaning a lot of these misfits can't really be themselves—so we thought we'd have a special happy hour for y'all tonight."

Stu's announcement was greeted with a mixture of cheers

and catcalls. Fernando Lopez, one of the mechanics and a former Golden Gloves boxer, wrapped Stu in a headlock. "Who you calling a misfit, you new-car pussy."

Collins extricated himself. "Might want to go a little lighter on the cologne tomorrow, Pancho." He tried to regain control of the crowd. "We're all set up over in the service department. Karl, you need any help moving the tap over there?"

"Hah! You think I'd let any of these rednecks touch the keg?" The keg was set up on a vertical lift cart, which Kompe started rolling toward the door.

Kayla turned to Stu. "Did you tell Jim you were doing this?"

Stu's face tightened. "Not exactly. I tried to, but he was always working on the secret Saturn project so I didn't get a chance."

"You know about Saturn?" Kayla asked.

"I'm a salesman. I have to know these things. Why do you think I'm being so nice to you? I'm hoping you'll hire me for the new place. Where you building it?"

"Does everyone know?"

Stu looked at her with faux indignation. "What? You think I gossip like an old lady?"

"Kind of, yeah," she said and laughed. She took Barry by the hand and they all walked next door to the service department.

Jim Stonemason had always insisted that the service department be as clean as the showroom. He wanted to make sure the customers who returned with their cars would feel comfortable and confident. They had a long table set up on the runway where customers normally drove their car in for service. The table was filled with the usual mix of wings, nachos, pork rinds, chips and salsa, and a bushel of tamales that had been specially prepared by Maria from bookkeeping. For drinks, there was Kompe's beer tap and two enormous thermos jugs of ice tea and lemonade.

Kayla and Barry mingled, greeting everyone. Barry brought her an ice tea, which brought catcalls and derisive laughter from most of the salesmen. "Not drinking any more, Kayla? See how marriage changes you? Probably gave up cursing too."

Kayla giggled. "You guys are all assholes, you know that, right?"

"That's why you love us."

Barry was enjoying himself. He leaned over and whispered in her ear, "This really is like a family."

Kayla kissed him hard, which brought more catcalls and whoops.

"What's going on here?" Jim Stonemason's unmistakable booming voice silenced the crowd. He stood at the entrance to the service ramp with Paula by his side, a worried look on her face as Jim managed to glare at the entire collective throng of partygoers. His jaw was set in the way Kayla instantly recognized as serious bad news.

He marched down the aisle past the nachos and wings and dips and up to Kompe's keg. He picked up a red Solo cup of Bud and held it aloft. "How dare you have a party for the bride and groom and not invite the parents of the bride!"

Loud cheers. Stu Collins looked like a man who had just been pardoned by the governor. Sweat beaded his forehead, and all the color had drained from his face.

Jim marched over to Kayla and hugged her like he hadn't in years.

"Did you know about this, Dad?"

He shrugged. "Of course. You think these guys could plan something like this without me knowing about it?"

CHAPTER 25

4:30 PM

DANCER

Russell was missing. Dancer had filled his food bowl out on the deck and whistled sharply. That was usually all it took. Russell would often be gone for hours, tagging along with Ozzie. The younger dog would romp in the river while Russell would doze under the willow tree on the bank. But Russell never missed a meal.

Dancer had been calling him for ten minutes and was now officially worried. The sky had a freakish yellow cast like something from another planet, and the air had an eerie feel that made Dancer's skin prickle. The wind raced through the gorge in fierce bursts, roiling the river and flexing the pines that lined the ridge. The sound of thunder rumbled down the valley.

In the silence between the gusts and the thunder, Dancer heard a dog barking. But it wasn't Russell's slow-cadenced throaty tenor. It was higher pitched, more snarly. That had to be Ozzie. That dog could bark for hours if something had his attention.

Dancer started down the river trail. He remembered all the times he had gone down this path with Clayton in the last ten years. Dancer hadn't been there for Clayton or Jim while the boys were growing up. He had wasted more than a decade trying to drink away the memories of the accident that destroyed his reputation. Then when he finally got his act together and rejoined his family, Dede died. Those river walks with Clayton had been one of the best things in his life.

It started to rain. No warning drops, just sheets of rain, drenching him. The footing, already difficult, would now be treacherous. It was foolish to trek down to the river in these conditions, but Clayton loved that dog and Dancer couldn't let something happen to him.

He forged ahead, slipping and sliding down the trail, but pushing the pace nonetheless. He could hear the raging current of the swollen river well before he saw it. Know-it-all Ted Landis was confident the river had flushed out all the storms. But he was wrong. The water was more out of control than it had been ten hours ago.

Beyond the tree line, the trail sloped gently toward the riverbed. The soil was rocky and dotted with scrub bushes and doomed saplings. Dancer grabbed hold of one of the saplings and started to back his way down the short embankment, like a mountain climber descending with a guide rope. He worked his way down, grabbing one sapling after another. Ten feet from the riverbed, the tree he was holding un-rooted itself and Dancer toppled backwards, skidding down the bank headfirst on his back. He hit a rock with the back of his head and his bifocals catapulted off his face. Lights flashed in the corners of his eyes.

"Fuck! Goddammit, Russell!" He lay there cursing and waited for the ground to stop spinning. The torrential rain eased to a gentle misting and then stopped altogether. He rolled onto his side and then on to his knees, but it took a few more seconds for the dizziness to pass. He finally got to his feet and retrieved his glasses. One of the lenses had popped out, which sent him into another cursing tirade. He almost wished something had happened to that damn dog to justify all the misery he was putting himself through. He didn't want to think about climbing back up that muddy trail without his glasses.

He felt the back of his head. It was tender to the touch and there was a lump forming. His hair was matted with mud and rain, but no blood. The pain was dull, not shooting like when he caught a punch to his nose or jaw. He felt like he had been drugged.

Ozzie's staccato barks brought him back to reality. The trail that normally flanked the river was now completely under water. Dancer walked along the edge of the swollen river and headed around the bend toward the basket ladies' cottage.

A floating tangle of uprooted trees, pieces of washed-away docks, and garbage had formed an island in the middle of the raging Caledonia. Perched shakily on a large log was a whimpering, bedraggled Russell.

Ozzie stood rigid, like a sentry, next to the shed where Phoebe and Lucy stowed their lawn chairs. As Dancer approached him, he stopped barking. He looked at Dancer curiously, as though he were trying to figure out if this old man could save his friend.

Phoebe emerged from the shed with a tow rope, wearing the leotard she always wore for her yoga workout. She pointed at Russell. "He got caught out there with Ozzie, but Ozzie swam back," she said, shouting to be heard over the river.

"He's afraid of the water," Dancer said. Russell didn't like to even get his head wet. The river was continuing to rise. Soon the shaky island of debris would be swept downstream. Dancer looked at the rope Phoebe was clutching. "What are you thinking?"

"That junk is all hung up on a sandbar. It's not that deep. I can wade out to Russell and put the leash on him. I'll guide him back. He can dog paddle, can't he?" she asked.

Dancer admired her guts, but she'd never get Russell off the island by herself. "If Russell freaks out, he could pull you off the sandbar. You're not heavy enough. That current is powerful."

Phoebe frowned and her forehead furrowed. "We have to do something," she said.

Dancer felt guilty about all the times he had made fun of her complaining nature. When the chips were down, she had guts to spare. And no drama.

"I've got more ballast. You hold on to the end of the tow rope and when I hook him up, pull him in."

Phoebe squinted at him, her frown intensifying. "You're bleeding," she said. "Your elbows. They're both bloody."

He hadn't noticed. "I slipped coming down the bank. That's mostly water. I'm okay."

"I don't like your plan. You're not a very good swimmer," she said.

"Don't plan on swimming. Walk out, walk back."

Phoebe sucked on her bottom lip. Her eyebrows peaked. "Hold on." She disappeared into the shed and returned with a much longer tow rope. "Clip both ends to your shorts and I'll hold the middle of the line so if you fall off that ridge I can drag you back in."

Dancer nodded. "I'm not planning to fall, but that's a good plan." He clicked the hooks into the belt loop in the back of his shorts and handed the rope to Phoebe. His head throbbed. His vision was blurry, which made him feel vaguely nauseous. "When you pull Russell in, hold on to him. I don't want him dragging me off the sandbar."

They walked to the edge of the river. The ridge that led out to the island of debris was about three feet wide. It wasn't really a sandbar. The surface was rocky and irregular.

Dancer stepped into the river, tensing his whole body, anticipating icy water. It was cold, but bearable.

He relaxed and raised his right foot to take a step. The current pushed his foot downstream and his left foot slipped out from under him. He fell sideways into the river. Pain shot through the back of his head and the light flashes in the corners of his eyes returned.

Phoebe helped him to his feet. "Are you okay?"

Dancer gritted his teeth. He tried to smile. "I need more weight. I've got to keep my feet on the ground." He bent down and grabbed a handful of small stones from the riverbank. He filled the front and back pockets of his cargo shorts.

Phoebe watched him, a studious look on her face.

Russell had spotted Dancer and crawled toward him, as far as he could. He was in his down position, whimpering and pulsing, like he was planning to fly across the river.

"Hold on, Russell. Be there in a minute," Dancer called.

He waded back into the water, this time with a shuffle step, keeping both feet in contact with the riverbed. His progress was excruciatingly slow. He kept his eyes focused on Russell. He tried not to look down at the swirling water. It took him almost five minutes to cover the first fifteen feet. The river was above his knees and getting deeper with every step. He was still at least twenty-five feet from Russell. Every muscle in his body was tensed as he struggled to maintain his balance. His heart pounded like he had run a mile uphill. His vaunted cardio conditioning was failing him.

Inch by inch, he shuffled closer. Halfway to the island, he ran into a large rock when he tried to shuffle his foot forward. He had to take several short sidesteps, upstream, against the current to get around it. He was no longer on a direct path to Russell.

"You're doing great, Dancer," Phoebe shouted.

Dancer had never experienced the upbeat, encouraging

version of Phoebe. He was grateful for her help. When he was ten feet from the logjam, the rocky riverbed turned mushy and sloped downwards. He curled his toes as though he could grip the surface through his shoes. The water was up to his chest, the current severe. He strained to maintain his footing. A stumble would send him down the river. His thighs burned and his calf muscles were starting to cramp, but then the riverbed leveled out and the footing improved. Several seconds later he grabbed hold of a long, smooth log. Russell was perched at the other end, fifteen feet away.

"Stay, Russell!" Dancer shouted. He held up his hand like a stop sign. For once, the dog obeyed him. Dancer worked his way down the log, hand over hand. When he was five feet away he paused to catch his breath. He was cold, but he was sweating. His heart pounded and his head throbbed. Everything looked slightly out of focus. He hoisted himself up on to the log, straddling it like a bull rider.

Russell started scrabbling towards him. Dancer reached back and unhooked one end of the tow rope. "Down, Russell," he said. Russell hunkered, his whole body quivering. Dancer reached out and hooked the tow rope to his collar.

"Pull, Phoebe!" Dancer yelled. He grabbed hold of Russell's collar and tried to lift him off the log, but he couldn't budge him. The dog weighed over sixty pounds.

Phoebe pulled the line taut, but Russell dug himself in. He wasn't coming off that log without a fight. As Phoebe tugged on the rope, the log wobbled. The current and the tugs on the tow rope were breaking it loose from the pile. Dancer released his grip on Russell's collar and grabbed hold of the log to keep from slipping off. He held his breath. The log stopped bobbing. At least for the moment. He needed to get better leverage.

"Don't pull again till I give you the signal!" he shouted. Phoebe's okay was barely audible over the roar of the river.

Dancer sat up higher on the log, squeezing it with his knees. He was just about to reach over to grab the loose fur around Russell's neck when a bolt of lightning struck one of the pine trees on the ridge, electrifying the sky. Russell yelped and jumped off the log.

"Pull him in!" Dancer shouted. His command was unnecessary. As soon as Russell hit the water he started dog paddling and Phoebe dragged him to shore. It had taken Dancer fifteen minutes to make it out to Russell and the dog made it back in less than thirty seconds.

Phoebe pulled him out of the water, hooked him with the other tow rope, and tied it to the dock. "Okay, Dancer. Your turn."

Dancer raised his hand and gave her the OK sign. He was too tired to yell. That was a great idea she had, using the other rope to tie up Russell. Dancer shimmied his way back down the log to the sandbar. The log wobbled but didn't break free.

Maybe because he knew what to expect, it was easier going back. Dancer was over halfway to shore when a pine tree came barreling around the bend in the river. The trunk barely missed Dancer, but the network of branches caught the tow rope and yanked him off the sandbar.

"Dancer!" Phoebe yelled. She quickly let out the rope, but there was nothing she could do. In seconds she ran out of slack and the rope was ripped from her hands. She ran down the riverbank, shouting at Dancer, "Unhook! Unhook!"

Dancer was being dragged down the river, bouncing from his back to his side to his belly. He flailed at the rope hooked to his shorts but couldn't reach it. Then the belt loop ripped off.

He was no longer being dragged by the tree, but now he was careening headfirst into the rapids. The current whipped him toward the shore and he flailed at the stumps and outcroppings and reeds, trying to grab hold of anything. He got a grip with his good hand on the branch of a fallen willow and with all his strength torqued himself into an upright position, his feet pointed and scissoring like a ballet dancer as he stretched to touch bottom. But the current was too strong and it swept his legs out from under him. Dancer clung to the branch, his body extended feetfirst downriver. He willed himself to not let go, but the river's will was stronger. One by one his fingers were pried loose.

Dancer's forehead struck a submerged rock as the swirling waters spun him facedown. A log rocketed past, filleting his legs with its rough bark and flipping him on to his back. Dancer gasped for air. There was no time to think about the pain. He tried to flutter kick and slap the water with his hands, but his arms and legs refused to move. The stones in his pockets were dragging him down. His strength was gone.

He could hear Russell barking on the shore.

Clayton's dog was safe.

Not perfect, but good enough, Dancer thought as his head slipped below the surface.

CHAPTER 26

5:00 PM

ANITA

When Anita arrived home from work just after four, there were two FedEx packages waiting for her. Fortunately, the driver had been able to push them through the mail slot on her door. They had to be from Ted. Last week he had handed her a catalogue from Peter Hahn and asked her to pick out a "special blouse" to wear to the riverboat party. Ted had lavished attention on her, opening doors, taking her to fancy restaurants, telling her she was beautiful (something no one had ever told her), even asking about her day or what book she was reading. But he had never given her gifts before. Maybe he was moving things to the next level or maybe it was just because of his party.

He was so excited about that party. He wanted everything to be perfect. Anita knew there was nothing in her wardrobe close to perfect, so she had agreed to choose something. Ted told her he didn't care how much it cost, but Anita didn't believe him. Ted cared about money. So she didn't select the most expensive (a four-hundred-dollar print from St. Emilie) or the cheapest (which was still over a hundred dollars) and went with the one from some designer named Uta Raasch. It cost two fifty, which was two hundred dollars more than she had ever spent on a blouse.

The larger package, a soft plastic envelope, had to be the blouse. She opened it as soon as she walked in the door. She had never owned anything silk. The blouse felt so deliciously smooth that Anita wanted to try it on immediately. But she knew better. After eight hours of testing engine small parts, her body was coated with oil and sweat. The other package looked like it might be a jewelry box. Anita was afraid to open it. What if it was a ring?

The weekend before Wayne returned, Ted had taken her to Branson to hear Reba McEntire at the Starlite Theater. On the drive over, he talked to her about his plans. Not just the riverboat casino. He had plans for a golf course and shopping malls and luxury homes. Even a campground. Enough projects for the next forty years. The man thought he was going to live forever. He kept saying "we" and "us" as though he were counting on Anita to be by his side for that whole ride.

Trudy would be there by five. The woman was never late, so Anita rushed through her shower.

On their Branson weekend, Ted had dropped Anita off at the Tanger Outlet Mall while he met some developer for lunch. At the Ralph Lauren factory store, Anita had found a pair of Tompkins skinny white jeans that fit her perfectly. She had been saving them for this day.

She closed her eyes as she slipped on the blouse. She was a size eight, but with her new breasts, some of her old blouses were too snug around her chest. This fit perfectly. At least, if she didn't button the top two buttons. She opened her eyes and checked herself out in the mirror. She almost gasped. She had never been beautiful. Her nose was too wide, and her eyes, chin, and cheekbones—the features everyone always noticed on beautiful women—were remarkably forgettable. But as she stared at herself in the mirror, she was . . . striking. The light blue was perfect for her fair skin, and the silk fabric draped over her breasts sensually. She looked hot, but not in a cheap way.

She applied her makeup and lip gloss and then looked through her jewelry box for earrings. It was all bling, selected to distract folks from her plainness. Trudy would say that was evidence of her lack of self-esteem. Anita closed the box. None of her jewelry was worthy of this new outfit. "Less is more," Trudy had told her. Of course, Trudy didn't even wear makeup.

Anita checked the front drive to make sure Trudy hadn't arrived before picking up the second FedEx package. She ripped off the wrapper to reveal a jewelry box, as she had guessed. From some place called Angara, "The Jeweler of the Internet," according to the card that came with the box.

Blue sapphire teardrop earrings set in white gold. Anita had never owned anything so beautiful. They were far more exquisite than anything Bernie Campbell had ever displayed in his doomed little jewelry store on Main Street.

She had just put them on when she heard Trudy knocking on the door. When she opened the door, the look on Trudy's face was priceless.

"Wow," Trudy said. "I think I have the wrong address."

Anita knew she was grinning like an idiot. She couldn't help herself. "Do you like?" She tilted her head to the side so Trudy could see the earrings.

"Wow," she said again. "Are those real sapphires?"

"I don't know. You want to see the box?"

Trudy shook her head. "You look lovely, Anita. Beautiful. You should have warned me. I would have worn my fancy cutoffs." Trudy was wearing jean shorts and a white peasant blouse that showed off her flat stomach.

Anita laughed. Trudy always looked hot. "I would kill for your abs."

A lightning bolt lit up the northern sky, followed by a drumroll of thunder. Trudy glanced back over her shoulder. "Looks like the storm has missed us. The warnings were all coming from the south."

"I hope so," Anita said. "I better get an umbrella just in case. Come on in."

She pulled two umbrellas from the hall closet. She handed the pink one to Trudy. "You can borrow Kristi's Barbie umbrella."

"No thanks. I'm not wearing a fancy silk blouse. I'll drip dry."

The doorbell rang. Trudy looked at Anita. "Wayne?" she mouthed.

Anita opened the door. A man in a dark suit stood on her stoop. Behind him, a black limo idled next to Trudy's car.

"Mr. Landis has sent a car for you, miss. And your friend. He said the traffic is really bad and he doesn't want you ladies to be late."

"Wow," Trudy said. "That man is serious."

Anita looked at her. "Is that okay?"

"Hell yes. I haven't been in a limo since my mom's funeral. Let's go."

CHAPTER 27

5:30 PM

WAYNE

If it hadn't been for her pink hair, Wayne might not have re-cognized Lucy when she walked out to his truck. She had on a black cocktail dress and heels and carried a little black purse. Wayne grabbed his step stool and eased himself down. He did it out of habit, expecting pain, but felt nothing but a warm buzz from the oxy.

"You look very nice, ma'am," he said.

Lucy air-kissed him. "How do you like my costume? I'm going as a lady." She glanced down at Wayne's ostrich skins. "Cool boots."

"Didn't know it was a costume party," Wayne said.

"They're all costume parties, Cowboy."

"Is Phoebe still mad at you?" Wayne asked.

"She can't stay mad at me. I'm too cute." Lucy batted her eyes playfully. "She hasn't come back from the river, actually. Her afternoon yoga workout. Maybe she's chilling out with some extra meditation or plotting how to kill Ted Landis."

Wayne swung the truck around and started back up the long driveway to Ridge Road, the Dodge bouncing and splashing through the muddy potholes that pockmarked the driveway. "You folks need to resurface this sucker."

Lucy shrugged. "No money." She pulled down the window visor and bared her teeth as she looked at herself in the mirror. "Do I have spinach in my teeth?"

Wayne turned to look at her and the truck dipped into a huge pothole. Dirty rainwater splashed the windshield and he lurched forward, almost smacking his face on the steering wheel.

"Fuck!" The jolt sent pain waves through his gut. The oxy buzz wasn't enough. He glared at Lucy. "You look fine," he said, his teeth gritted.

Lucy smiled at him, unfazed by his annoyance. "Did you get caught in that storm on the way over?"

Until he drove through the flooded underpass at Rigby Road, Wayne hadn't even noticed that he was driving through a torrential rainstorm. He had been thinking about Zeke. He would never have a chance to show his dad that he was wrong about his son. Never have a chance to make Zeke proud. Ever since his mother had run off, he and Zeke had been at odds. Like two wounded animals living together but never there for each other. Both dealing with their pain. Or not dealing with it.

"Roads are flooded a bunch of places, but that's the cool thing about this truck. I don't have to worry about a little flooding."

The rains had stopped almost as quickly as they had started. The sky was still dark in the north but had brightened considerably to the south.

"You gambling or dancing tonight?" Lucy asked.

"Neither. Did I tell you that the C-Pirates are your mystery band? Not Kenny Chesney."

"The C whats?"

"The Confederate Pirates. They're touring with Brad Paisley this fall. I'm going to be their lead guitar player."

"For real?" Lucy asked. "That's awesome."

Wayne flushed. He hadn't meant to say that. "I mean, I hope to play with them. They wanted me last year, but I got called up. I think they'll give me another shot. I need to talk to Curt—he's the leader."

Wayne turned on to the ridge road. Behind them, a rumble of thunder rolled through the ink black sky. To the south the sky was clear and the sun was peeking through the wispy clouds in the west.

"Is that storm headed our way?" Lucy asked. "I can't tell."

Wayne shrugged. "I hope not. I don't want to get these new boots muddy."

CHAPTER 28

5:35 PM

KAYLA

Stu Collins had stopped the tap at 5:30, which was the signal that the party was over. "Don't want any drunks on the road. Save it for the riverboat," he said.

Barry, who was not normally comfortable drawing attention to himself, tried to give a final thank you toast, but he couldn't make himself heard over the noise. Jim wrapped an arm around his shoulder.

"Hey!" he shouted and the room went instantly quiet. "Listen up. My future son-in-law has something to say."

Barry, blushing, raised his beer cup. "Kayla and I want to thank everyone for helping us out. Hope to see you all tomorrow, so be careful on that riverboat. Have a great evening. We'll finish the clean up here."

"Hey gang, give it up for Barry," Stu yelled. "For a big-city bean-counter, he ain't bad." The crowd joined Stu in a rousing ovation.

Kayla's stomach was churning. So many different emotions coursing through her hormone-saturated body. She loved this group and hated leaving them. She had never worked anywhere else, but she knew no other place would be like this. This was a family. Her family.

Karl Kompe wheeled the beer tap back to his truck, while the mechanics and the salesmen put away all the chairs and tables. The office ladies quickly swept up the few remaining food items.

Someone handed the remains of the cake to Paula. Kayla and Barry wouldn't have much to do to get the place buttoned down.

Jim and Paula stood in the middle of the service center. Kayla did a double take. They were actually holding hands. First her mom had shown up at the dealership for the first time in years, and now this public display of affection. She had seen no visible affection between her parents since Clayton had died. There would never be a better time to tell her father their plans.

Barry walked back from the service bay door where he had been saying a final goodbye to the last group to leave.

"I'm telling Dad now. Before I lose my nerve," she said.

Barry nodded, his face tight.

Kayla waved to her parents and tried to look natural. "Hey, Dad. Let's go to the showroom. There's something I want to talk with you about."

Jim nodded, instantly in businessman mode. "Just the two of us?"

Kayla took Barry's hand and started to walk toward the showroom. "No. This is a family thing." She caught her mother's eye. Paula nodded her encouragement.

"Do you want a piece of cake, Jim?" she asked.

Kayla winced. Paula never offered him sweets. His guard would be up now. But he just sighed and looked at the cake longingly.

"I don't think your doctor friend would approve. I've got the physical coming up. Remember?"

They headed to the showroom. Puddles dotted the parking lot. There had been a crazy thunderstorm right after Jim and Paula had arrived, but it had moved on, leaving a wedge of blue sky to the south, while turning the northern sky inky black. They arranged themselves in comfy chairs around a marble coffee table stacked with glossy brochures of Corvettes, Camaros, and Silverados.

Kayla decided that this news was best delivered like ripping off a Band-Aid. "Dad, Barry is being promoted and after the wedding we're moving to New York. I can't tell you how much I appreciate the Saturn opportunity, but I can't take it." Her lips had started to tremble and Barry reached over and squeezed her hand. "I love you, Dad. I hope you understand." She bit down hard on her lip, hoping the pain would keep her from breaking down.

Jim stared at her. At first she wasn't sure whether he had heard her or not. Paula had sat down next to him and was gently rubbing his back. He nodded at Kayla, like the words had finally made it to his brain. Then he smiled. It wasn't his salesman smile. It was genuine.

"You will love New York." He hugged Kayla. He turned to Barry, his hand extended. "Congratulations."

Kayla's heart was bursting with conflicting emotions. Love was winning.

An explosive crack of thunder rattled the windows in the showroom.

"We better get home, Jim," Paula said. She turned to Barry. "Stay at our place tonight. You don't need to go all the way back to West Plains."

Kayla saw Barry's hesitation.

"Good idea," Jim said.

Her father seemed so mellow. She wondered if her mother had told him about the baby. "We'll come over as soon as we finish cleaning up. Another fifteen minutes," she said.

CHAPTER 29

5:46 PM

JIM

The reality of Kayla's announcement didn't start to register with Jim until he pulled out of the dealership lot. His daughter was leaving town. Immediately. If she were like so many of those other young people who had fled Maple Springs, chances were she would never return, except for obligatory visits on the holidays, which would have to be split with Barry's family in Chicago. She had been the most important part of Jim's life for twenty years and next week when he returned to work, she wouldn't be there.

It physically hurt him to consider that emptiness. Doctor Manickavel was worried about him having a heart attack. This felt like something else—a broken heart.

"Jim? Are you okay?"

Slowly he registered what Paula had asked. By the concerned look on her face, it might not have been her first time. He relaxed his hold on the steering wheel. "Sorry. Thinking about Kayla."

Paula reached over the console and rubbed his neck. "You handled that really well. I'm proud of you."

They exited US 60 and as Jim drove north on Town Line Road, a gust rocked the Cadillac. Jim gripped the steering wheel tightly with both hands to keep the car from being pushed off the road. Behind them the sun was still shining, but ahead and to the west the sky had turned midnight blue. It started to rain hard. Jim turned the windshield wipers to the fastest speed, but it wasn't enough. Even though he had slowed the car to a crawl he could barely see beyond the hood of the car.

"Damn," Paula said. "It's like a hurricane. I hope the kids don't get caught in this. They should just stay put until it blows over." She pulled out her phone. "Should I call them?"

Jim was leaning forward, trying to make out the road ahead. Their house was less than two miles from the highway. There was no light or stop sign at their intersection and he didn't want to miss the turn. "They're smart enough to figure that out. Help me look for our street." The wind was howling. He had to shout for Paula to hear him.

Paula gave him a funny look. "It's right up there," she said, pointing unhelpfully down the road. "It's just past the Baptist Church. Which you have passed at least ten thousand times."

Jim squinted harder, a death grip on the steering wheel. Finally, through the waterfall of rain, he spotted the church. He turned right past the Baptist cemetery and two minutes later they were in their driveway. Jim pushed the button on the garage door opener but the garage didn't open. The house was dark. "Power lines must be down," he said.

The rain beat angrily on the hood of the Cadillac. Jim reclined his seat so he was staring up at the sky roof. "Might as well wait until it blows over," he said.

Paula leaned over the console and grinned at him. "Did you say you wanted a blowjob?" Leaning into him, with one hand she unbuckled his belt and pulled down his zipper. "See. I still have the moves."

Jim smiled and stroked the back of her head. "I never doubted you."

CHAPTER 30

5:51 PM

ANITA

Anita pulled the bottle of champagne from the ice bucket and refilled her glass. "Are you sure you don't want to have some, Trudy? Looks like we're in this car for a while."

The only paved road to Landis Landing was County Road UU. Paved was a generous characterization. The access road to the riverboat was five miles from the highway and traffic was bumper-to-bumper for nearly a half mile. Maybe no one liked Ted, but everyone wanted to go to his party.

"No thanks," Trudy said. "I'm pacing myself. I might get called for EMT duty." She looked out her window at the traffic and sipped her bottled water. "So glad we're not stuck in my shitty Corolla." She sank back into the leather seat. "This is what I call luxury." She stretched out her legs. Her feet were still a foot from the facing seat. "Even you have enough leg room," she said.

"Do you think the driver can hear us?" Anita whispered. There was a plexiglass screen separating the driver from the passenger compartment, with a window in the middle that he could slide open and close.

"Are you worried? I haven't said anything bad about your boyfriend."

Anita refilled her glass and leaned in closer to Trudy. "I think Ted wants to marry me."

Trudy took another sip of her water. She had a serene, I've-got-a-secret look. Anita had expected a more dramatic reaction. Trudy was never shy about expressing her opinions.

"What do you want?" Trudy asked.

Anita shrugged. "I don't know." She reached for the champagne, but Trudy laid a hand gently on her arm.

"Slow down. You don't want to be shit-faced before you even get to the boat. Do you love Ted?"

Anita opened her palms in a how-would-I-know gesture. "I've never been in love. I know he loves me." She looked at Trudy, her brow troubled. "How come you're being so polite? I expected you to tell me I was crazy."

Trudy looked out her window. "I know. Yesterday I probably would have. I had a visit with Clayton's dad and it's got me thinking about Clayton—and a lot of things."

"Did you love Clayton?"

"I did. It wasn't enough. At least, I didn't think it was enough. When things were good, we were good for each other. But when they were bad, we were both miserable. I didn't think we should live like that. I was young. I thought I had all the time in the world. I figured both of us would be better off if we found someone more 'compatible.'" She air quoted the word. Her expression was even more serious than when she had tried to talk Anita out of getting the boob job. "Compatibility is such a bullshit concept. Neither of us found someone compatible." She spat out the word. "Maybe Clayton was doomed no matter what I did. But we could have had five good years. Maybe more. If I could go back and do it all again, even if I knew that in the end we would fail, I'd take the chance. Bad love is better than no love." She sighed and buried her face in her hands. "Oh my God. I sound like one of those sappy Lifetime movies."

Anita poured herself another glass of champagne. "So this

morning you think Ted's too old for me and now you think I should marry him?"

"I don't know." Trudy shrugged. "He obviously loves you. You look happy. Are you?"

Anita took another sip of champagne and then held the glass aloft, watching the bubbles effervesce. "Yeah, I guess so. Not like high school girl giddy happy, but I enjoy being with him. I never had someone who really loved me before. It's a nice feeling."

"Well that's something," Trudy said.

The limo had stopped. "Yeah, it's something," Anita said. She stared out the side window at the sun as it tried to break through the clouds. "But is it enough?"

A highway patrol car in the westbound lane drove past them with its lights flashing. It did a quick U-turn and pulled up next to the limo. A moment later, the driver slid open the plexiglass window and said, "Ladies, make sure you're buckled up. We're moving out."

The patrol car took off heading east in the westbound lane, blasting its siren and flashing its lights. The limo followed in its wake. They whizzed past the jammed traffic and took the service road access down to the water park. In less than three minutes they were in front of the riverboat.

"God. We're like celebrities," Trudy said. "All we need is the red carpet."

Anita was checking herself in her compact mirror. "Do I look okay?"

"You look great. Take a deep breath and don't trip getting out."

A beaming Ted Landis stood by the gangway to the boat. He quickstepped over to the car and opened the passenger door.

Anita climbed carefully out. Ted grabbed each of her hands

with his. He took a step back like he was trying to take her all in. His eye-closing smile was so real it almost hurt Anita to look at him. She would never be able to live up to his fantasy of who she was.

"You look lovely," Ted said. "Do you like the earrings?" He kept her at arms' length, waiting for her answer.

She broke free of his courtly handholding. She kissed him on the lips with feeling, but not so much that he would be embarrassed. "I love them, Ted! Thank you so much." She turned to Trudy, who stood grinning beside her. "This is my friend, Trudy."

"How do you do, Mr. Landis," Trudy said, extending her hand. "Thanks for the ride."

Ted gripped Trudy's hand with both hands. He gave her his professional smile. "Call me Ted. It's my pleasure, Trudy. Anita talks about you all the time."

Trudy arched her eyebrows. "Really?"

Before Anita could say anything, a man with a cellphone wearing a Landis Development polo shirt came up and said, "Sheriff needs to talk to you."

Frowning, Ted grabbed the phone. "Patrick, how y'all doing," he asked, affecting the drawl he only used on people who didn't really know him.

His face morphed from faux cheerful to something close to angry. "We ain't seeing that down here," Ted said. He had a forced smile on his face. "Hell, the sun's shining so bright I might have to put on another layer of sunscreen." He winked at Anita and Trudy. There was blue sky to the south, but storm clouds were rolling in from the north. The sun was definitely not shining on them.

"The river's fine," Landis said, his teeth gritted. "That storm water's almost flushed out. Another hour it'll be calm as a duck pond." His face was creased with displeasure as he listened. "There ain't no reason for that. Boat's practically sitting on the bottom. It can't go anywhere." Whatever the sheriff was proposing, Ted was having none of it. "Not doing that, Patrick. If the situation down here changes, I'll be sure to let you know." He handed the phone back to his employee. "He's a Nervous Nellie. Always has been. Let me know if he calls again." He turned back to Anita and Trudy, the affable host again. "Let's get on board, ladies, and have some refreshments. Do you like lobster, Trudy?"

The line to board the boat started at the edge of the parking lot, but Ted walked them to the rear ramp, where two burly men in sunglasses stood guard as a large black woman pushed a catering cart up the loading ramp.

Ted winked at Anita. "VIP entrance," he said.

The river was higher than Anita had ever seen it. The wind from the north was roiling the water and the deck was rolling.

"Whoa!" Trudy staggered as she stepped on to the deck, reflexively grabbing Ted's arm.

"Give it some time," he said. "You'll get your sea legs. Follow me." He led them over to a table in the corner and pulled out a chair. "Have a seat, Trudy." As she sat down he said, "Do you mind if I borrow Anita for a few moments? We'll be right back."

Trudy clutched the table like she was afraid it might slide away. "No. Not at all. Take your time."

Ted signaled to a tall black man in the center of the room who looked like he was in charge of the servers.

The man walked with authority over to their table. "Yes sir, Mr. Landis."

"Morris, will you make sure that Miss Trudy is taken care of? Whatever she wants."

Morris bowed slightly. "Of course." He leaned in toward Trudy. "Would you like to start with a beverage? A Bloody Mary or perhaps a Mimosa?"

Trudy smiled nervously, like she was going to get sick. "Maybe just a coke for now?"

Ted turned toward Anita. "I have something I want to show you."

Anita gave Trudy a quick eyebrow raise but Trudy was too seasick to notice. She followed Ted up the spiral stairs to the top deck. In the center of the deck was a large board that looked like a toy train set up, but instead of a toy train there was a toy riverboat.

"This is the Landis Caledonia River Gorge Development. It's the biggest project I've ever undertaken. The capstone of my career. Golf course, luxury homes, campgrounds, condos, shopping malls, and of course the riverboat casino." He talked for ten minutes, his face lit up like a kid at Christmas. All the good things that would come with the project: jobs, new roads, more choices for the people. Then his voice got lower like he was praying. He looked at her. His eyes were shiny.

"Anita, I know a lot of people who don't know me think I'm just another money-grubbing developer. I understand that. This project should make a pot load of money. But I hope you believe me that it isn't about the money. I already got more than I need. This is a chance to build something that will endure. It's going to take a lot of hard work. I need your help. I'm not looking for some arm-candy trophy. You know that I love you, Anita. You are a beautiful, talented woman, and I know I'm a big old ugly guy who doesn't deserve you, but . . ." He stopped and plucked a little box from his development board—it looked like another of his luxury home cubes, but it was a ring box. He opened it to show her a diamond ring. It was beautiful. Understated, but elegant. "I know I don't have any right to ask this, but will you marry me, Anita?"

Anita stared at the ring and then at Ted. He had an expression on his face she'd never seen before. He was nervous. Maybe even frightened. Afraid Anita would say no. She remembered her mother's caution and Trudy's regrets and what all this would mean to her kids and to Wayne. So many things to consider.

She slipped the ring into her front jeans pocket and kissed him gently on the lips. "Yes," she said. "I will marry you, Ted. You can put the ring on me tonight, after the party."

And as if he orchestrated it, a sheet of lightning lit up the northern sky and the loud crack of thunder brought an exclamation from the crowd outside still waiting to board.

Tears leaked from Ted's eyes. He swiped them away with the back of his hand. His smile lit up his face. But it wasn't his eye-closing grin of pure adoration.

It was the confident smile of a victor.

CHAPTER 31

5:56 PM

WAYNE

Wayne had taken the exit to Siloam Springs, just like Dancer had earlier in the day, but now the rutted, worn-out road was packed with folks trying to get to the riverboat. He had to drive even slower than Dancer had.

He drummed his fingers on the steering wheel. "It's going to take over an hour to get there."

"The drink specials end at seven," Lucy said. "I shouldn't have spent so much time squeezing into this damn dress." She sighed and glanced at her phone, her brow creased with a look of annoyance. "How can there not be cell service here?"

Phoebe had called her five minutes after they left, but before Lucy could answer, they lost cell service. She had tried every few minutes since then, without success.

"There's a cell tower near the water park," Wayne said. "You'll be able to call her there."

Lucy held the phone up to the windshield. "Shit. Nothing." She had lost her smile and her sunny disposition. "Can I try yours?"

"Don't have a cellphone," Wayne said.

"Oh. My. God. You're as bad as Phoebe," Lucy said.

The traffic started moving again. Wayne tapped the gas. "Why are you so hung up on calling her back? She'll just yell at you for going to the party."

"Phoebe never calls," Lucy said. "Never. I'm worried."

Wayne's oxy buzz was fading. He had wanted to get to the bandstand before the C-Pirates started playing. He reached into his shirt pocket where he had stashed the four extra oxys.

"You poppin' pills, Cowboy?" Lucy asked.

"Aspirin," he said. "For the rib."

"Uh huh," she said, plainly unconvinced.

They made it to Siloam Springs. Zelda's Tattoo Parlor was dark. Wayne wondered if Zelda was headed for the riverboat too. He didn't really want to run into her. Not after Dancer had repossessed Wayne's wedding ring from her.

"How much did Zelda charge you for your cherubs?" Wayne asked.

"You want some of your own?" She raised her eyebrows, trying to leer. "Cherubs would be a nice complement to the tiger. What body part you planning to ink?"

"Fuck you," Wayne said.

Lucy reached over and patted his knee. "I'm just having fun. Trying to kill this long boring drive. Zelda charged me a hundred dollars."

Fuck. Dancer had been right about the price. "Yeah, me too," Wayne said.

They were approaching the Siloam Springs four corners. "Can you really drive this beast through water?" Lucy asked.

"Damn straight. I got four-wheel drive, with thirty-seven-inch nitro trail—"

Lucy held up her hand. "I know a shortcut. Turn left here. Take 173 toward the river."

"There's no road down there," Wayne said.

Lucy leaned forward in her seat and pointed to the intersection. "A trail runs along the river. It's rough and it might be a little underwater, but it goes all the way to Cape Girardeau."

Highway 173 was empty. Wayne made it to the bridge in

five minutes. There was a Missouri Recreation Department sign marking the Caledonia River Trail. An arrow to the right indicated 12.5 miles to Peace Valley and an arrow to the left for Maple Springs, 12.3 miles away. The river had overflowed its banks. The trail was underwater.

"It doesn't look too deep," Lucy said. "Can your truck handle it, Wayne?" He was no longer Cowboy. He was in charge. At least for the moment.

The sun had broken through the western clouds, illuminating the river and the trail. It didn't look like the water was over a foot deep. Wayne slowly turned right and eased the truck onto the submerged trail. With the huge tires, the water was well below the axle. He pressed down slightly on the accelerator and the truck rumbled along. The trail felt smoother than the crowded county road they had just left.

"The river looks crazier than it did this morning," Lucy said.

Wayne drove cautiously, keeping his eye out for rocks, fallen trees, and any junk the current might have deposited along the banks. As they rounded a bend in the river they could hear the riverboat crowd, and up ahead they could see the top of the Jesse James water slide.

"Fuck," Wayne said. "The place is fenced off." He stopped the truck. Thirty yards ahead there was a battered chain-link fence that went right down to the river, blocking their path. It had probably been built by the water park owners.

"What are we gonna do?" Lucy asked.

"We can't go around the fence," Wayne said. "That would dump us in the deep water. We could walk from here."

"I can't walk in this dress with these heels," Lucy said.

"Hike up the dress and carry your shoes," Wayne said.

"No panties," Lucy said.

Wayne looked at her and sighed.

"I didn't want the panty line."

He scanned the terrain. "I'll drive straight up the hill. Maybe there's a break in the fence," he said. "Buckle up."

He wound his way through the trees, doing his best to avoid the stumps and large rocks. He felt a stabbing pain every time the truck dipped or bounced.

Beyond the trees, he heard the sound of a truck engine snorting as the driver downshifted. "There's a road up there. Must be to the service entrance." Wayne waited until he heard the truck pass, then rumbled another forty yards up the hill and crested the raised shoulder onto a dusty, rutted service road.

The gate into the park was closed and there was a kid in a neon yellow vest guarding the entrance. When he spotted Wayne's truck, he got up from his lawn chair and stood in the middle of the road in front of the gate.

Lucy tugged on Wayne's sleeve. "That kid was at Jake's the other night."

"Don't remember him. What's his name?"

"Tom or Timmy. Something generic. He was a horny little boy. You were too drunk to notice anybody. I know how to handle him."

"Okay." Wayne stopped the truck three feet from the gate.

Lucy opened her door and climbed down. "Hi, Tommy!"

"My name's Chuck," the boy said.

"That's what I meant. Chuck. Remember me? Jake's last night?"

"Yeah, I remember you. You showed the bartender your tattoos."

"Could you let us in, Chuck? We took this shortcut 'cause I really *really* have to pee." Lucy offered him her most playful smile.

"I'm not supposed to let anyone come in this way. What kind of tats you got?" he asked.

"Cherubs," Lucy said. "Didn't I show you?"

"Nah. Just showed the bartender. I saw your thong though. It was pink."

"Jesus, Lucy. Get in the truck," Wayne said. "We'll find another way in."

Lucy ignored him. "Guess what, Chuck? I'm not wearing the thong tonight." She turned sideways and patted her pantyline-free butt. "If you open the gate and let us in, I'll show you the cherubs."

"No way. You show first."

"Are you a man of your word, Chuck?" Lucy asked as she gripped the hem of her dress.

"Ye-ye-yeah. I promise."

Lucy looked up at Wayne in the truck and winked. She faced Chuck and tugged her dress over her hips. Chuck's eyes went wide. His mouth hung open until Lucy pulled her dress back down. "Okay, open the gate, Chuck."

The boy's face was almost as pink as Lucy's hair. He grinned foolishly as he pushed the gate open, waving them through.

Lucy gave him a little finger wave as they drove by. "Nice to know there are still boys who keep their word."

"A real stand-up guy," Wayne said. He drove the truck up to the loading zone.

There was a long line of folks waiting to get onto the riverboat. At the stern, a crew from Budweiser was loading beer kegs. There were at least a dozen more Landis employees between their truck and the customer parking lot up the hill beyond the bandstand.

"This should be close enough," Wayne said. He parked next to one of the Budweiser trucks.

"Let's go to the big top tent next to the bandstand," Lucy said. "That's where they're serving the drinks."

Wayne didn't argue. More than likely, that's where Curt would be hanging out.

The big tent was buzzing with activity. As they approached the entrance, Lucy pulled out her phone again. "Hey. I've got a signal." She held the phone to her ear, frowning. "Phoebe, it's Lucy. Call me back when you get this message. Okay? I mean it. Love ya."

Something made Wayne turn and look upriver, to the north. The sky had turned black. He had the sensation something awful was hurtling down the river out of control. He stood there, his body trembling, like he had a chill.

Lucy took him by the hand and tugged him toward the entrance. "A storm is coming. Let's go inside and get some of those dollar drafts."

The tent was circular with side panels attached except for an opening that fronted on the river. Lucy nudged Wayne as they walked in past the security guards. "Are you ready to be saved?"

"Huh?" That girl was sometimes hard to follow.

"This is a revival tent. Baptist used it last month over in Pomona."

"You go to revivals?" Wayne asked. He couldn't tell if she was teasing him or serious.

She stared wide-eyed into his eyes, as though she were trying to hypnotize him. "I'm very spiritual. But right now I'm mostly thirsty."

Food booths were set up inside the perimeter of the tent— burgers, hot dogs, nachos, BBQ sandwiches. It was a bar food extravaganza. In the center of the tent was a large circular bar where the dollar drafts were being dispensed. Folks were lined up three deep.

"Rednecks love cheap beer," Wayne said.

"Me too. I'm from Seattle," Lucy said. "We don't have enough sun to get red necks. Stay here, I'll get you a Bud."

Lucy slipped through the beer crowd and was back with two drafts in less than a minute. "Is that guy signing autographs over by the nacho wagon one of your band buddies? He looks like General Custer."

Wayne turned around. It was Curt. She was right: with his long, flowing blond hair and horseshoe mustache and trail hat, he did look like Custer. "Yep. That's Curt."

Now that he found him, Wayne wasn't certain what he should do. He hadn't counted on him being surrounded by a big crowd of fans. What if Curt blew him off?

"What are you waiting for?" Lucy said. "Let's go. I want to meet your buddy."

"Well, we aren't exactly—"

Lucy weaved her way through the throng surrounding the band leader. The girl did not believe in waiting in line. "Hey Custer! Do you want a beer?"

Curt looked up from the poster he was signing and grinned when he saw Lucy holding up her Bud draft. With the beer, the bubblegum hair, and the form-fitting cocktail dress, she had his attention. "Awesome." He reached for the cup. "Thanks, babe."

Wayne walked up behind Lucy, trying not to look embarrassed.

"Wayne! My man!" Curt slipped off the barstool and offered a fist bump like they were old pals. "You made it back from the war. Great to see you, dude!"

Wayne could tell he was grinning like some hayseed. This couldn't have worked out better if he had planned it. "Congrats on the Paisley tour," he said. "I'd love a chance to—"

Curt had turned away to sign a playbill from a buxom girl in a Confederate Pirates T-shirt. "Here you go, honey." The girl squealed like he'd handed her a hundred dollar bill and kissed him on the lips.

Curt winked at Wayne. "I love this job." He took a big gulp of beer and wiped his mouth with the back of his hand. "Why didn't you return my calls? I was starting to think you didn't make it back."

"You called?"

"Hell yes. I wanted you play with us on the tour. Your old lady said she'd give you the message."

Wayne sputtered. "Bu . . . but I didn't—"

Curt grinned. "It's okay. Worked out for the best. Daryl Putney fell in our laps when the Rock Men broke up. That dude was fucking trained at Juilliard. He's tight with Paisley. We're in solid now."

Another girl was tugging on Curt's sleeve. "I gotta go," he said. "We need to catch up one of these days. After the tour, for sure." He turned away and started signing again.

Wayne felt sick.

"Wow," Lucy said. "Your ex didn't tell you the guy called?"

"I need to get out of here." He moved toward the entrance.

"You're not leaving, are you, Wayne? We just got here. Wait up. I can't walk that fast."

He could hear Lucy clip-clopping, trying to catch up to him. He stopped. "I just need to get something out of the truck."

Lucy frowned at him, her face screwed up with concern. "Don't do anything crazy, Wayne."

He waved her off. "Why not?" he said, but not so she could hear him.

CHAPTER 32

6:08:10 PM

DANCER

Fire! There is frost on the ground and the cold seeps into Dancer's bare feet as he stands by the water pump between the hay barn and the farmhouse. Flames peek from the upstairs bedroom windows and tease the edges of the roof. His eyes sting.

His mother and the hired hand work the pump. The water gushes into the milking pails, which are handed from one woman to another down the line to their men who swarm around the burning house.

His daddy sprints across the top of the front porch roof and empties his buckets through the window. Over and over again he runs from pump to porch to roof and back.

Dancer can feel the heat of the flames, but still he shivers. His feet are numb. He wants his daddy to put out this fire right now so he can burrow back into his cozy bed. His daddy can do anything.

The flames reach the roof. When the embers leap from the farmhouse to the barn, his mom stops pumping. She walks over and picks up Dancer. Her cheeks are shiny.

The hired man grabs his daddy before he climbs the ladder again. The barn explodes. Flames light up the sky like its daytime. His daddy slips to his knees and punches the hard, cold ground over and over and over again. His hands turn bloody, but no one tries to stop him.

6:08:12 PM

Dancer's mom takes sick. Her skin is so pale you can see through it. She sleeps all day. His grandpa and uncle drive down from Festus in a fancy black car with running boards. The two men and his dad carry his mom to the car.

You be a good boy, she says. *Obey your dad.*

When are you coming home? he asks.

Soon, she says.

6:08:13 PM

Dancer's dad says they're going on a special trip.

Where? He asks.

St. Louis. Your grandpa sent us tickets to see the Cardinals play.

Why? he asks.

You ask too many questions, he says. But then he smiles and Dancer feels better because his dad never smiles anymore.

The stadium has more people than Dancer has seen in his whole life. They sit in the balcony right above the catcher. When the Cardinals pitcher walks on to the field, the crowd stands and cheers.

That's Dizzy Dean, his father says. *Best pitcher in the major leagues.*

Dizzy comes to bat and the roar of the crowd is so loud it makes the boy's teeth ache. He hits a foul ball. It rises up and up and up—almost to the puffy clouds that hover over the park—then descends toward Dancer. He tries to catch the ball, but the man in front of him grabs it. It splats against the man's palm and falls to the ground. An usher hands the ball to Dancer.

Here, kid. Special delivery from Dizzy Dean.

6:08:14 PM

His dad stops the car in front of Grandpa's house.

Are we going to see Mom now? Dancer asks.

His dad's face is tight. Like when the farm burned.

Your mom passed, son.

He takes a hand off the wheel as though he wants to wrap it around Dancer, but he doesn't.

Dancer picks up the baseball in his lap. He starts to rub it just like Dizzy Dean.

I know, he says.

6:08:15 PM

Clem the Moonshiner is waiting for Dancer on his porch. His face has that familiar tightness. Dancer knows his father is dead even before he tells him about the accident.

6:08:16 PM

The crowd is so loud he can't hear himself breathe. The catcher signals for a fastball, the manager perches on the top of the dugout steps, unlit cigar clenched in his teeth, Dede stands with her hands in front of her face, and Clayton jumps up and down on his seat waving his cotton candy like it is a flag.

Strike threeee! the ump croaks as he punches the air with his left fist.

Dede is in the aisle with Clayton and he lifts them both over the rail. Clayton clings to his dad's neck with cotton-candy sticky hands as they parade around the field. The crowd chants Dancer's name.

6:08:18 PM

Dancer tugs off his work boots on the back porch and carefully opens the door.

Jimmy's asleep in his crib. Clayton is sprawled facedown, his feet sticking out of the untucked bedsheet, his baseball uniform wadded up on the floor next to his ball and glove.

He has promised Clayton he would play in the Father and Son game.

He tucks in the covers and pulls the sheet up around Clayton's shoulders. He strokes his son's hair, then picks up the baseball and glove and hangs his head.

You promised, Dancer.

Dede stands in the doorway wrapped up tight in her terrycloth bathrobe.

I know.

If you keep this up, you'll lose us.

I hate that place.

You don't have to work there.

We need the money.

I could get a job. Help Joyce with her husband's projects.

You want to work for Landis?

Dede smirks. *Are you jealous of Ted Landis?*

Maybe.

You shouldn't be. Dede unbelts her bathrobe. She is naked. *You're the only man I want.*

6:08:22 PM

Dancer opens the bedroom door. Joyce Landis is kneeling on the bed, naked, her breasts jiggling over the facedown body she straddles. She screams and tries to cover herself as she runs for the bathroom.

As Dancer backs out of the room he looks into the sleepy blue eyes of Dede as she raises her head to see why Joyce has run off.

6:08:23 PM

Three sheets of steel left to slice. Dancer inches his finger toward the cutting line.

A half million dollars for one finger that he'd never miss. Why not do it?

Two sheets. He closes his eyes but he can still see Joyce Landis rubbing her tits all over Dede's body. He can feel the force of the guillotine as it rips through the steel. His finger is a quarter inch away.

He locks the last sheet in the frame. As he slides his finger across the cutting line, he feels Clayton's cotton-candy sticky fingers clinging to his neck. He pulls his finger back. The foreman shouts his name and his left hand slips forward on the oily surface as his foot hits the activation pedal. Blood splatters his goggles, and he collapses to the floor.

6:08:24 PM

Dancer splashes water on his face. He looks gaunt and hospital pale in the mirror. In the dining room, the crystal globe Joyce gave Dede is still on the hutch on its satin pillow, next to the framed picture of him and Clayton celebrating the perfect game.

Dancer's hand aches again.

The steaks sizzle as Dede pulls them out of the broiler. His stomach rumbles with anticipation. He clutches his fork with his maimed hand and stabs at the steak. A jolt of pain surges up from his phantom fingers all the way to his shoulder. *Fuck!* he yells as the fork torques out of his hand and clatters onto the plate.

The boys stare at him. They finish their meal quickly and escape to their bedroom. As Dede clears the table, Dancer takes the bottle of Jack Daniels and retreats to the porch.

6:08:26 PM

Dede is dabbing Clayton's face with a washcloth. There is a split in Clayton's lower lip, and his right cheek is turning an ugly yellowish purple.

What happened? Dancer asks.

Clayton stares at him like he is the one who has beaten him. Dede's mouth twists sourly. *He was in a fight.*

I can see that. What happened, Clayton?

Let it go, Dede pleads.

A boy said you chopped off your fingers on purpose.

The look on Clayton's face is worse than losing his mother, his father, or his fingers.

6:08:30 PM

Jimmy and Dancer sit on one side of Dede's bed, Clayton on the other. Dede holds Jimmy and Clayton's hands. *Talk to me,* she says.

Jimmy leans closer. *I've lost another five pounds, Mom. Almost under two hundred now.*

Dede smiles faintly. *Did you get your grades?*

Jimmy nods. *Yesterday. I did okay.*

Clayton punches him in the shoulder. *Kid made Dean's List.*

Are you treating Trudy, right, Clayton?

She got a job working at the post office.

I like Trudy, Dede says. *She reminds me of me.* She winks at Clayton. *When I was young and pretty.*

Clayton's eyes water. He bites his lip.

Dede wraps her arms around her sons. *Look at us. One big happy family again.* She smiles.

Jimmy kisses her on the forehead and sits back in his chair as she releases his hand.

Dede wraps both her hands around Clayton's. She closes her eyes.

Clayton bows his head. *I'm sorry I was such a jerk for so long, Mom. You were right about school, and the war, and you're right about Trudy. And Dad. I'm sorry.* His voice breaks. He buries his head in her lap.

We love you, Clayton. She sighs and looks at Dancer. *I want to rest for a while.*

The boys file out as Dede drifts back into sleep. Dancer closes the drapes and sits back in his chair. He's not ready. He prays. *Just give me one more day, God. Don't take her today.* His prayer ends with a sob.

Don't cry. Dede is sitting up in her bed. Her eyes are bright. *Hold me, Dancer.*

He wraps his arms around her. *I love you, Dede.*

She presses her lips against his. She sighs and lets go.

6:08:30 PM

Dancer picks up three jukes at the auction in Licking. A good price. Clayton will be pleased. In the driveway, Jim's Cadillac is parked where Clayton's truck should be. Jim and Paula and someone he doesn't know are sitting in Clayton's deck chairs. Jim stands up and walks towards him. His face has that awful familiar tightness.

Dancer sinks to his knees and pounds the deck with his fist. Over and over and over again. No one tries to stop him.

6:08:34 PM

Dancer stops struggling and drifts peacefully below the surface. Clayton calls his name.

The church is crowded and hot. The pew uncomfortable.

Dede squeezes his hand as Clayton, with a cocky, bemused half smile reads to him:

Those who trust in the Lord will renew their strength; they will soar on wings like eagles; they will run and not become weary, they will walk and not faint.

CHAPTER 33

6:09 PM

KAYLA

Kayla stood at the top of the Service Department ramp waiting for Barry to return. He had carted all but one of the bags of garbage to the dumpster while she closed down the department, making sure all the doors were locked and the power switches off.

The lot was a mess. The swirling winds stirred up the highway litter. Discarded cups, fast food containers, and plastic bags whipped through the aisles of cars, plastering windshields and hiding behind tires. A Starbucks cup bounced up the ramp and flip-flopped into the service department waiting area. Kayla pulled down the service bay door and locked it before any more refuse could blow in.

The winds were gusting stronger and the sky had turned so dark that the highway lights had gone on. The rain would arrive soon. She picked up the last garbage bag—it was mostly paper plates and beer cups—and pulled open the glass walk-in door. She stepped outside. It was a struggle to close the door behind her. They needed to leave now.

The gritty wind stung her cheeks and made her eyes water. She struggled to hold on to the garbage bag. Barry stumbled around the corner of the building, looking like he had been in a brawl. His shirt was ripped open. His pants were stained with motor oil. He bent over, trying to catch his breath.

"Don't . . ." Barry said.

The rest of his warning was lost in the wind. Kayla turned the corner and the wind ripped the garbage bag from her hands. Plates and cups exploded across the employee parking lot. The gust almost knocked her to the ground. She retreated to the front side of the building. Barry grabbed her around the waist.

The dark clouds, which an hour ago had been on the distant horizon, were upon them. Kayla gasped as a jagged bolt of lightning backlit the sky over Landis Mall, a mile up the highway. The thunder that followed was muted by the roar of the wind. A strange white fog rolled in, obscuring Kayla's view of the mall.

A rat-a-tat sound like popcorn popping began. "Ouch! That stings." Kayla covered her face with her hands.

"It's hail," Barry said.

BB-sized hailstones pelted the hoods of the cars in the used car lot.

Barry yelled into her ear, "We better go to the basement! Wait this out."

"There is no basement," Kayla yelled. "The parts storeroom. It's reinforced block. Follow me!" Bent over and turning her face away from the wind, she scurried back to the walk-in door. Icy pellets stung her cheeks as she fumbled with the ring of keys.

Barry stood behind her to block the onslaught of hail. On her third try she found the right key. As she turned the knob, the wind slammed the door open, blowing over the magazine rack in the waiting area and knocking the parts catalog off the service counter.

"Dad's going to freak out when he sees all that hail damage," Kayla said.

"I've never been in a storm like this," Barry said. He leaned hard into the door to get it closed. "That damn wind knocked me over. I fell onto the oil slick next to the dumpster."

Kayla giggled. "You look like you fell into the dumpster.

Don't let Dad hear you call it an oil slick. That's just a little run-off from the rain."

The wind rattled the service bay door.

"Where is this parts storeroom?" Barry asked.

Kayla flicked the light switch by the door, but no lights went on. "Shit. Power's out."

The only light source for the cavernous service center was from the glass entrance door. "If it gets much darker out we won't be able to see anything in here," Barry said. "This place is like a cave." He up righted the magazine rack, which had fallen across the yellow-highlighted pedestrian pathway.

"The parts room is behind the service counter," Kayla said. "Damn. It's dark in here."

She tiptoed, trying to remember how the place was configured. The warehouse was the domain of the parts manager, Karl Kompe. He sat at a terminal for eight hours a day, managing the inventory and directing two parts pullers. He operated from an over-sized leather swivel chair.

"Barry, where are you?"

"Right behind you."

The glass door rattled and someone yelled, "Help! We need help!"

Kayla grabbed Barry's hand. "Come on." They hugged the counter back to the walk-in door. A boy was shining a flashlight through the glass and pounding on it while the girl next to him screamed hysterically. "Help! Let us in! I don't want to die!"

Barry opened the door and the children literally blew through the entrance. "Are you hurt?" he asked as the girl, a freckled redhead with pigtails, fell to her knees. The boy knelt beside her and tried to hold her, but she pushed him away.

"Oh my God! Oh my God! Oh my God!" She looked to be about fourteen and was clutching a small instrument case. The boy looked older, but not much. They were dressed in white shirts and dark slacks, like Mormons or some kind of religious folks.

Kayla knelt beside the girl. "It's okay. You're safe here." The door was banging. The wind came in fierce bursts. "My name's Kayla. What's your name?"

"She's Amy," the boy said. "My name's Greg. We were on our way to band practice when that wind almost whipped me off the highway."

"Hey. You have a flashlight," Barry said. "That's great because our hideout lacks lighting."

Amy got back to her feet and tucked her white shirt back into her black slacks.

"My dad always makes sure we have a flashlight in the car," Greg said.

Kayla led them back to the storeroom while Barry worked on closing the door again. With the flashlight, Kayla could see that they there were two more chairs in Kompe's office, probably for his parts pullers. "Have a seat. Hopefully this storm will soon be over."

"It's not just a storm. It's a tornado," the boy said.

"You don't know that, Greg," Amy said.

"Do too. I saw it. It's heading for the mall."

"Just because you're in science club doesn't mean you know everything about the weather."

Kayla hoped they wouldn't be trapped too long with these kids. She plopped herself down in Kompe's chair.

There were voices outside again. Several.

Barry shouted, "Hey, Kayla! I could use that light."

She walked back to the entrance. Barry and a small middle-aged man were pushing the door shut, while three women in various states of dishevelment watched.

Barry made sure the door was latched and then turned toward Kayla and the new arrivals. "Kayla, this is Charlie and Dorthea and Edith and . . ." he paused and smiled. "I'm sorry. I've forgotten your name."

"Gladys. Gladys Lansing. From Pomona. We're sisters. I'm the youngest."

"We were on our way to Applebee's," Charlie said. He looked disgusted. "I told you it was a damn fool notion to go out on a night like this."

Kayla wasn't sure which of the women he was directing his comments to.

"Oh, Charlie. It's nobody's fault," Edith said. "Is it okay for us to stay here for a while? Charlie doesn't like to drive in the rain."

"Rain! Goddamn it, woman. That's a hurricane. You see any other idiots out there driving on a night like this?"

Kayla led the group back to the storeroom. While the new folks argued, she went back to check on Barry, who had waited to see if anyone else showed up. He stood with his nose pressed against the door, looking down the highway at Landis Mall. He turned around and even in the fading light, Kayla could see the fear in his eyes.

"Look down there," he said. He pointed toward the mall.

A tall swirling white spiral seemed to have descended from the heavens. It appeared to hover over Landis Mall like some alien spacecraft. The lights from the mall flickered and then went out. The spiral turned from white to gray to mud brown.

Kayla gripped Barry's hand.

There was a screech of metal on metal, a fingernail-on-the-blackboard kind of sound only a thousand times louder. It was followed by a crash. The Stonemason Chevrolet neon sign ripped from its moorings and toppled across the eastbound lane of US 60.

"Oh my God," Kayla said, her voice barely a whisper.

"There's a car coming," Barry said.

Out of the swirling fog that was advancing in front of the tornado, a vehicle emerged. The driver, racing to outrun the storm, didn't see the sign blocking the highway until it was too late. Even with the roar of the wind, they could hear the screech of tires. The car skidded off the highway into the drainage ditch. A minute later, a man crawled out of the car.

Barry opened the door. "Hey! Over here!" His words were swallowed by the wind, which now howled like an out-of-control freight train. The funnel cloud couldn't be more than a half mile away. The man waved his arms frantically. "Hurry!" Barry shouted.

The man leaned back into the vehicle.

"He's got kids!" Barry said. The driver was hunched over with one child under his arm like a sack of potatoes, while he clutched an infant in the other. He was limping and his face was bloody.

"I'm going to help him," Barry said.

Before Kayla could protest Barry was off, sprinting through the parking lot like a broken-field runner. Barry was built low to the ground. He was strong and had great balance from gymnastics.

He grabbed the older kid, a boy about five, from the man and started back. The man, in obvious pain, followed him.

The children were uninjured, but the man had a deep gash over his eye. As he handed his baby to Kayla, he collapsed.

"My wife," he moaned. "She's hurt. She can't walk."

Barry looked at Kayla. "I'll get her," he yelled and was out the door again before she could say anything.

The tornado had reached the bend in the highway. The

giant Electronics King of Joplin billboard disappeared into the cloud.

Kayla hugged her belly. "He'll never make it on his own," she said. Barry was right. It wasn't just the two of them anymore. She had to think about the baby and what she thought at that moment wasn't that she had to protect the baby at all costs. What she thought was that they were a family and they had to look out for each other. She handed the baby back to the man and ran after Barry.

Kayla hadn't run in months, and even though she had only gained five pounds, her body felt different—bloated, and her balance was all off. Now, with the wind against them, it was like she was in one of those nightmares where she tries to run, but her legs won't move. She got down on her knees and crawled on her belly like a boot camp trainee.

By the time she reached them, Barry had pulled the woman from the car, but he couldn't carry her out of the drainage ditch by himself. The woman was barely conscious and her left leg from the knee down was a bloody mess. When he saw Kayla, Barry's face screwed up with concern, and he started to say something but stopped. It was too late for a debate.

"Grab her other arm," he yelled as he wrapped the woman's left arm around his shoulder.

With Kayla on the woman's uninjured side, they climbed out of the ditch and started back across the parking lot. Now the wind pushed them toward the building and it was easier for Kayla to stay on her feet.

They passed the first line of used cars—the eye-catching Corvettes and Camaros—and had just reached the row of pickup trucks that had been taken in trade during the week when a metal strut from the Stonemason sign pinwheeled across the lot.

It struck Barry in the knee. They all went down together. Barry screamed in pain as he tried to get to his feet.

The swirling funnel cloud reached the employee parking lot at the edge of the property. There was no time left.

"Take her, Kayla. I can't walk." Barry started to crawl toward the entrance.

Kayla grabbed the woman by the hands and, using the fireman's carry she'd learned in gym class, lifted her onto her back. With a primal scream, she sprinted across the lot. The service door opened. The little boy who Barry had rescued was holding the baby while Greg bandaged the driver's head. Kayla laid the woman next to her husband and said, "I have to help Barry."

Greg looked at her with alarm. "You can't—"

Kayla was back out the door before he could finish his protest. Whatever the boy had to say, she wasn't interested. Against the wind again, she went to her belly and slithered the thirty yards to where she had left Barry. He wasn't there.

She was in the storm now. She screamed for Barry but she couldn't even hear herself. It was as though a fire hose of grit was being blasted at her. Her eyes burned and she crawled blindly. Her hand touched the sole of a shoe. Barry was trying to drag himself to the row of used cars.

Her eyes flooded with tears. Ten yards in front of them was a GMC Suburban. She grabbed Barry by the belt and, scooting on her hands and knees, hauled him to the side of the van. She grasped the passenger door handle for leverage and with her feet she shoved him under the van as the swirl enveloped them.

She clung to the door handle. Her arms felt like they were being pulled from the sockets. The pain was excruciating and she wanted to let go, to let the storm take her away, but she couldn't do that. She had to keep fighting for the baby. For the family. The wind whipped her like a flag, her feet flying above her head. Joining the freight train roar of the wind was the crashing sound of vehicles smashing into other vehicles.

Kayla closed her eyes tightly and waited for the end. The Suburban jolted backwards, wrenching the door handle from her grasp. But the wind spared her. She fell to the ground next to the van. She quickly rolled under it. She gouged her back on the undercarriage as she wedged her body next to Barry. He wasn't moving. The rear axle had snapped and the back of the vehicle had collapsed, pinning his legs.

Kayla stared out at the carnage. She was too numb to feel anything. The car lot looked like a demolition derby in Hell. Oscar's S-10 had flipped over and landed nose first in the aisle, three feet from where she had been hanging on to the door handle. That was why she hadn't been blown away. Oscar's little truck had created a wind barrier.

She scooched closer to Barry and reached for his hand. It was cold, lifeless.

The demolition derby continued. The crashing percussion of steel smashing into steel and glass exploding added to the cacophony of the storm. It built to a crescendo that could only end one way. Something loud and heavy crushed the hood of the GMC. The front end collapsed and Kayla was squeezed between the undercarriage and the pavement. She couldn't move and it felt as if the whole weight of the GMC was pressing down on her.

She gasped for air and squeezed Barry's hand. "I love you, Barry. We're here. We're all here."

He squeezed back.

CHAPTER 34

6:10 PM

WAYNE

Wayne sat in his truck staring at the riverboat. The wind was whipping out of the north, creating surf-like waves on the river. The boat, tethered to shore, rocked up and back, banging into the dock bumpers. A girl in a tank top and cutoffs staggered out to the lower deck and threw up over the rail.

To the northwest, jagged bolts of lightning fired from the black storm clouds punishing Maple Springs. Sonny's Sig and the four ammo magazines were on the console next to Wayne. He had been sitting in the truck for ten minutes trying to find the courage to pick up the Sig. To load it. To shoot himself.

First his mother. Then Sonny. Now Anita. Everyone he had tried to love had rejected him. Whatever it was that was wrong with him, whatever it was that he lacked, it was too late to fix it now. Anita didn't care enough to give him a lousy phone message. A message that might have changed his life. From the rearview he could see the bandstand. Roadies were crawling all over the stage making last minute adjustments to the sound gear. He could have been up there playing tonight with the C-Pirates. It could have been Wayne Mesirow on tour with Brad Paisley.

But it wasn't, and it wouldn't be. Ever.

His broken rib throbbed. He was so tired. His whole body ached with weariness.

Hearing that news from Curt had sucked the life out of him. But he was still alive. Still in pain. He knew how to end

it, but he was scared. It was clear to Wayne now that Sonny
had meticulously planned his death, but in the end he had lost
his nerve. Asked Wayne to save him. That was the good thing
about a bullet. It would be over in an instant. There would be no
chance for him to change his mind.

He took the last two oxys and washed them down with the
beer Lucy had given him. He grabbed an ammo magazine and
slipped it into the handle of the Sig. It made a reassuring click
as it snapped into position. But when he tried to raise the gun
to his temple, his hand shook violently. He couldn't hold the
gun steady enough. Once the oxy kicked in he would have more
control. He rested the gun in his lap and tried to breathe calmly.

A black Crown Vic with Howell County Sheriff printed on the
door raced down the service road and skidded to a stop in front
of the riverboat just beyond Wayne's truck. Wayne hid the Sig
under the seat and stashed the other three ammo magazines in
the console. He recognized the driver. Patrick Quinlan had been
the county sheriff for as long as Wayne could remember. He had
stopped Wayne once for speeding on US 63, a few weeks after he
had bought his truck. Quinlan was interested in the Dodge Ram
and asked Wayne a bunch of questions about how it handled, gas
mileage, off-road capability. He never got around to writing him
a ticket. Didn't even give him a warning.

Gray-haired and trim, he reminded Wayne of Zeke. He
carried himself like a professional soldier. Now he walked over
to the security guards who were checking the folks lined up
to get on the boat. One of the guards, a black dude built like
a weightlifter, stepped away from the line to confer with him.
The sheriff pointed upriver. Sheriff Quinlan was notoriously
unflappable, but it was clear from his expression and the way he
gestured that he was agitated.

The guard nodded and yelled something to the other guard,

who held up his hand and stopped the line. There was a steady north wind now and the dark clouds were getting closer. Sheriff Quinlan walked back to his car and pulled out the communications handset.

"Attention! Attention!" His voice blared from the speaker on top of his patrol car. "This event is closed!"

There was a collective cry of protest from those waiting to get on the boat.

"A category three tornado has hit east of Maple Springs and is heading this way. You need to leave the area immediately. Do not drive north. I repeat. Do not drive north." The sheriff conferred with the beefy guard again, then drove over to the big top tent and repeated his announcement.

Ted Landis emerged from the main cabin of the riverboat, his brow furrowed. The security guard walked up the ramp and said something to him. Landis looked up the river and hung his head. A look of resignation, not resistance. He pointed to the parking lot. The security guard said something into his walkie-talkie and almost immediately a dozen or so men and women in Landis Development polo shirts were in motion. Landis had mobilized his crew to direct cars out of the lot.

He turned and walked back into the main room. Minutes later folks started filing off the boat. Landis came out, hand in hand with Anita. That Trudy woman was by their side. A black limo pulled up next to the riverboat. Wayne closed his eyes as Anita leaned over to kiss Ted. When he opened them again, Landis had disappeared back into the main cabin. Anita and her friend were walking toward the limo.

Anita looked happy. It saddened Wayne to think he would never see her or Daniel or Kristi again. They were better off without him, but he needed to explain things to Anita. This wasn't on her.

He ejected the magazine from the Sig and checked the chamber to make sure it was empty. He stuck the gun in the back pocket of his jeans. He slipped out of the truck painlessly. The oxy magic was working again. Trudy, who looked seasick, hustled ahead of Anita and slipped through the door held open by the driver.

Anita stopped to glance back at the boat.

"Anita!" Wayne shouted.

She spun around. "Wayne? What are you doing here?"

"Can we talk?" he asked.

"Not tonight," Anita said. She started to walk again.

Wayne cut her off. "Please." He grabbed the sleeve of her blouse.

"Ma'am?" The limo driver had started to walk toward them. "Is there a problem?"

The driver looked too much like one of the Madman's security guards. Wayne wasn't playing that scene again. He yanked out the gun and pointed it at the driver's head. "Get the fuck back in your car and drive away, asshole."

Unlike at the mall this morning, no one in the crowd noticed Wayne holding a gun. Everyone was intent on getting to their cars. The security guards were all focused on directing the crowd, trying to maintain an orderly evacuation.

The limo driver threw up his hands. "Easy. No problem here, son. They ain't paying me to be a hero." He turned and jogged back to his limo without looking back.

"Please, Anita. Just a minute." He beckoned toward his truck.

Anita's eyes were wide. "What are you doing with that gun, Wayne? We need to get out of here. Did you hear the sheriff? There's a tornado coming."

Just as she spoke, the wind gusted and the poles holding the front end of the big top tent ripped loose. The tent flap billowed like it was trying to fly away. The crowd in and around the tent screamed. The orderly evacuation gave way to a full-fledged panic.

"The gun's not loaded. I'm not going to hurt anyone. I just need to talk to you, Anita. Please."

Her face softened. She wasn't afraid of him. That was good. "Okay," she whispered.

He opened the passenger door and she climbed up. Wayne winced as he pulled himself into the driver's seat. The oxy buzz was fading. He held up the Sig so she could see it had no magazine. "See, it's empty. I would never hurt you, Anita."

With the wind howling, it was noisy even in the truck. It would be impossible to have a quiet conversation. There were so many things he wanted to say to Anita, but there wasn't time.

A small willow branch smashed into the windshield. "Damn!" Anita yelled. "The storm's getting worse. What do you want, Wayne?"

He slipped the wedding ring off his finger and held it out for her to take. "I'm going away, Anita."

Anita shook her head. "I'm sorry, Wayne. I haven't been fair to you. We do need to talk. But not tonight. Keep the ring."

Wayne took a ragged breath. "Please tell the kids I love them." He wanted to say more. Something more profound that would let his children know that he did love them. But he couldn't make his brain work. He was exhausted. Why was it so hard to die?

"You can tell the kids yourself. Tomorrow. We need to get out of here now, Wayne. Stop acting crazy. You're scaring me."

Wayne smiled. "You don't scare that easily." Wind whipped the truck. The storm would be there soon. It was time to go. He grabbed her hand and pressed the ring into her palm and made her hand into a fist. He jumped down from the truck and opened her door. "You're a good mother, Anita. Now get outta here. Your limo's waiting."

Anita stepped down from the truck. The wind was whipping fiercely. It was difficult to stand. She started toward the limo, but then stopped. "No," she shouted, the wind plastering her hair against her face. She stared defiantly at him, her jaw set. "Come with me, Wayne. You can see the kids tonight."

Trudy had stepped out of the limo and was waving at her. "Anita! Let's go!"

Wayne stepped away from Anita and slammed her door shut. "Get out of here. Now!"

Anita looked at him and then the limo and her face was screwed up like she was going to cry, but Anita was not a crier. She turned and ran toward the limo.

Wayne climbed back into the truck and grabbed the magazine and clicked it into the handle. His hand was steady now. He could do this. He waited for the limo to pull away and then he started to raise the gun.

"Hey, Cowboy!" A girl was waving her arms and running toward his truck. Barefoot. Bubblegum-colored hair.

Lucy.

Wayne lowered the gun as she ran up to the driver side window. "What the hell, Wayne! You taking off without me?"

He swallowed hard and tried to think of something to say to her.

Lucy didn't wait for him to answer. "Phoebe called me back. There's been an accident. Dancer got swept down the river trying to rescue his dog."

"What? Is Dancer okay?" Wayne asked.

"They don't know. Can't get searchers in there with that tornado coming. Let's go to West Plains. We can go back as soon as it's clear."

Not again. He couldn't leave Dancer out there.

Lucy hopped up on the bully step and tugged on Wayne's sleeve. "You can't go up there now, Wayne. The sheriff said that storm is coming this way."

"Step off, Lucy. Get yourself a ride to safety. I'm going north. I don't want company."

She frowned but jumped down. Wayne wheeled the truck around. The wind was fierce now, and leaves and grit plastered his windshield. He looked in his rearview. Lucy stared at him for a moment and then shook her head and started running toward the parking lot.

Security guards were directing cars to exit on the service road as well as the main access road. When Wayne pulled out of the loading area the road was packed. He pulled off the road and headed toward the river. Scrub brush scraped the sides of his truck as he plunged down the hill. The river trail was empty, but the wind was rippling the water, and waves splashed the truck hood and windshield.

Dancer swept away? The river was wild, but Dancer was one tough dude. He could survive. He might be holed up somewhere, maybe just off the trail. He would see the lights of the truck. Wayne could save him.

The wind was roaring. He couldn't hear his own voice. His head ached and his back throbbed. He rounded a bend in the river and ahead of him he saw the funnel cloud. It was black, not white like he expected. It was east of the river and heading straight for him. He pressed down on the accelerator and shifted into third gear. If he was fast enough, he could pass west of the storm before the tornado reached the river.

Waves splashed the cab like he was driving a powerboat. The trail was rough and the truck rocked wildly. His head bounced against the window and the headrest. He gripped the steering wheel as tightly as he could and tried to brace himself, but his back and broken ribs were taking a pounding.

The tornado reached the opposite bank. The river was being sucked up into the waterspout and the trail was no longer submerged. Wayne floored it. Swirling water hit his truck from above and buried the windshield. The truck whipped hard to the left like he had run into a buzz saw. He yanked hard on the wheel, pulling back to the right. A torrent of water pounded the truck. The engine died.

The truck slipped off the trail into the river, listing to the passenger side. Wayne pushed open the driver's door and tumbled into the water.

"Don't fight the current," Sonny had said. "Play along with it. It's a seduction."

Wayne let the current take him downstream. He tacked toward the shoreline. The storm now seemed to be in front of him and moving away. Up ahead a toppled willow leaned low over the riverbank. Wayne aimed his body toward it, closing fast. Twenty feet. Ten feet. Five feet. He reached as high as he could and grabbed the branch. He screamed as his back twisted from the sudden stop. He pulled himself up and threw his leg over. With his knees straddling the branch he shimmied to the base of the tree.

He slipped off into the muck. He crawled on his belly into the scrub brush that lined the riverbank.

"Thanks, Sonny," he said. He realized he could hear himself again. The wind had stopped. He had beat the storm. He got to his feet and started walking up the trail. Now he had to find Dancer.

CHAPTER 35
6:16 PM

JIM

The tornado warning sirens went off at 6:08, just as the rain stopped. Jim unlocked the front door. With the help of the penlight Paula carried in her purse, they made their way down to the dark, windowless basement, filled with the detritus of twenty-five years of marriage: old furniture, clothes, Kayla's toys, boxes of Paula's paperbacks, and stacks of Jim's *National Geographic* magazines. Jim found two rickety folding lawn chairs. They had just settled in for a long wait when the all clear siren sounded.

"Must have been a false alarm," Jim said. He flashed Paula's light around the basement. "I guess I need to clean this place up." He was grateful for the dark so he didn't have to look at her expression.

"Pffft. That'll be simple. Just rent a dumpster. There's nothing here worth saving."

He leaned over and squeezed Paula's knee. "You were more fun in the car."

Paula elbowed him. "Bring up that box." She pointed at a pink cardboard toy chest.

"Why?"

"Kayla's art projects. We need candles. Remember her candle-making phase?"

They settled down on the living room sofa that looked out

onto their front lawn and in the distance, the Caledonia River Gorge.

"Who should I burn?" Jim asked. "Felix the Cat or this family of owls?"

Paula was digging through the toy chest. "Look." She pulled a threadbare cocker spaniel puppet out of the chest and slipped it on her hand. "Remember Cosmo?" She made a barking sound as Cosmo stared at her. "And Zorro?" On her other hand she had a black rabbit puppet. "Hi Cosmo," her rabbit puppet said in a squeaky falsetto. Cosmo tried to nip at Zorro, but Zorro was too fast. "Bad doggy, Cosmo," the puppet squeaked.

"Kayla always wanted a puppy," Jim said. "I shouldn't have been such a hardass."

A wave of disappointment and regret swept over him. He had been so busy building his business. A dog, a cat, even a bunny was too much of a distraction. He sank down onto the sofa. Sunlight was filtering through the puffy mountain-like clouds on the western horizon. He didn't need to light any candles. They still had an hour of daylight.

Paula sat down on the couch next to him and stroked his cheek with Cosmo. "You can make it up to her by spoiling your grandchild."

There was something in the way she said it that made Jim think it wasn't just a throwaway line. He stared at Paula, trying to read her face. "What?"

Paula slipped off the puppets and took his hands in hers. "Kayla's pregnant."

Jim swallowed hard and his eyes welled with tears. How foolish he had been.

"Look at me. Crying like a big baby." He swiped his face with his sleeve. "When were you planning to tell me?"

Paula wiped a tear from his cheek. "You're a good man. A good husband. A great father. You need to let go of Clayton."

Jim looked at her, his face wrinkled with confusion. "What do you mean, let go?"

"He's gone, Jim. All your life, you've been trying to prove to yourself that you're as good as your brother."

Jim's face burned. "I guess you'd know better than anyone."

"Yes, I would. I loved Clayton a long time ago for a short while. And I've cared about him for years. But he was a very troubled boy and he never grew up. I don't say this to be cruel, but he was not half the man you are. Don't end up like him. Don't kill yourself."

"Clayton didn't—"

"Just stop it, Jim. Your brother didn't lose control of his car on a perfectly clear day and drive straight into a tree. You know as well as I do that the one thing Clayton could do better than anyone was drive a goddamn car. He killed himself. He was tormented and he wasn't tough enough to keep fighting. He didn't have your strength."

Jim covered his face in his hands. He started to sob, his chest convulsing. "He always looked out for me. Protected me—his fat little brother." He took a ragged breath and tried to continue but his lips were trembling.

"I know, Jim." Paula brushed the tears from his cheeks. "I know."

"When Dad left, Clayton was angry. Said he hated him, but it wasn't hate." Jim's voice broke. He wiped the snot from his face and took several shallow breaths. He swallowed hard. "He never showed people he was hurting. Not even me. When Dad returned after all those years and they became partners, I was jealous. I wanted that. I was selfish and blind. I should have helped Clayton, Paula. Supported him. Not just with money. I should have been there for him." He buried his face in Paula's chest. "Why didn't I help him?"

Paula put her hands on his shoulders and held him at arm's length. "Look at me, Jim. You were the rock. Dancer spent all his time with Clayton because he was trying to make amends. The whole family depended on you. Clayton loved you more than he loved himself."

"I miss him so much."

Paula wrapped her arms around him. "I know. But you have to let him go. I don't want to lose you."

Jim snuffed. "You're not going to lose me."

"You're killing yourself. You have a great business. A wonderful daughter, you're about to become a grandfather, and you even have a damn good wife. Who gives blowjobs. Do you really need another dealership? Or to be the savior of this goddamn town?"

Jim rubbed his face. He had been working hard all his life. Why? Was Paula right? Did he just want to prove he was as good as his brother?

He loved his daughter. He hated to admit it, even to himself, but he had always thought Paula loved Clayton more than him. Maybe he was wrong about that. Maybe he was wrong about a lot of things.

He held his head in his hands staring down at the floor. In her renovation project, Paula had ripped out the carpeting and replaced it with a stylish parquet floor.

"Floor looks great. Never really noticed it before," he said. "You're right. I don't need to do Saturn." The sun broke through the clouds and reflected brightly off the polished floor, blinding him. Jim closed his eyes. "If Ted Landis wants to destroy Main Street, I guess Main Street needs to fight its own battle."

Paula rested her head on his shoulder. "You'll be a fantastic grandfather. Spoil the kid rotten."

"I hear that grandparent stuff takes a lot of work." Jim patted his belly. "I better get myself in better shape. Maybe I should start running with you in the mornings."

Paula looked at him skeptically. "First you need to see the doctor. And change your diet."

He held up his hand to stave off another fitness lecture. "When's the baby—" His cellphone buzzed. He pulled it from his pocket. It was Stu Collins. On the other end of the line, the sound of sirens wailing and loud static drowned out Stu's voice.

"Say again," Jim said. Something was wrong. He heard the sound of a door closing and then the siren sound was much fainter, but the connection was worse, cutting out every other word. Then nothing. The connection was lost.

Jim looked over at Paula, his lips trembling.

"What's wrong?"

"I think he said a tornado hit the mall and that the car lot was wrecked? We need to call Kayla."

He stared at his phone, his hand shaking. He couldn't press the keys.

"Give it to me, Jim." Paula took the phone from him. She was incredibly cool. In control. She put the phone to her ear and listened. "Kayla, call us immediately. We're worried about you. Let us know you're safe."

They sat on the sofa staring out at the ridge. The sun had broken through the clouds and it was a majestic, beautiful evening. Every few minutes, Jim tried to call Stu, but there was no answer.

Just before seven, as the sun started to dip below the ridge, the house phone rang.

Jim looked at Paula. "The phone lines aren't down?" He picked up the receiver. "Hello?"

"Hello, James. This is Dr. Manickavel."

Her voice sounded strained. Jim felt his guts tighten. His mouth went dry. "Yes," he said. His whole body felt numb. He knew in his heart he didn't want to hear what she had to tell him.

"They just brought Kayla and her fiancé into the emergency room."

"Oh God, please."

"She has some broken ribs and lots of scrapes, but she's going to be okay. The young man is in surgery. His legs are crushed, but he is stable."

Jim tried to speak, but no words would come out. He handed the phone to Paula.

Kayla was strong. She would survive. In Maple Springs or New York City or someplace else, it didn't matter where. She would survive. They all would.

CHAPTER 36

6:40 PM

WAYNE

A tangle of branches and bushes had been deposited on the trail when the tornado ripped down the river. For a few euphoric moments after he had escaped the truck, Wayne felt great. But as he started to fight his way through the muck and the brambles and the bushes, he quickly became exhausted. Every couple minutes he had to stop and rest. Every ragged breath felt like a knife was turning in his chest.

His ostrich-skin boots were useless in the muck, and Wayne abandoned them soon after he started his trek. The river was calmer now, and the wind had died completely. The sun broke through the clouds just above the horizon creating long, crazy tree shadows. Had there really been a tornado?

He wanted to shout Dancer's name, but it was too much of an effort with the searing pain in his chest. Even shallow breaths made him nauseous. He staggered sideways into a scrub pine. The branches scratched his face. His eyes stung and he could feel a trickle of blood run down his neck. His vision had blurred and he squinted hard trying to bring the river trail back into focus.

Every step was agonizing and now he was going blind. Even with the sunlight illuminating the way, he could barely see the trail. A tree stump on the bank beckoned him. Just a short rest, to regain his strength. How could that hurt? But that's what he had done when Sonny had needed him. Gave up.

He turned his face away from the stump like it was an evil totem. He continued down the trail. Up ahead the river disappeared around a sharp bend. The sun refracting through the trees and reflecting off the water created a strange glow beyond the tree line.

Wayne whispered, "Dancer. Where are you?"

And then as he rounded the corner, there the man was. Sitting on a big granite boulder in the middle of the river, his legs raw, like they had been scraped with steel wool. But he was smiling. He acted as though he had been waiting for Wayne.

"Are you okay?" Wayne called. The pain in his chest was gone and he could see clearly.

Dancer gave him that glare again. "Do I look okay?"

"You look great for an old man. I hear you saved your dog."

Dancer picked up a rock and tossed it into the river. "Damn dog. More trouble than he's worth. How has your day been? You square things with your lady?"

"She don't love me, Dancer. Says we're not right for each other."

Dancer nodded like he had already come to that conclusion.

"I guess she's right," Wayne said. "She messed up my chance with the C-Pirates. That sort of sucked."

"You need to get out of this town, son. Go to Memphis."

"Memphis?"

"Lots of opportunities for a good musician. Start over there."

"Memphis, huh?"

Dancer closed his eyes and raised his arm like he was some kind of crazy preacher. "If I'm wrong you can sue me."

Wayne shook his head. "How I'm supposed to get you off that rock?"

Dancer grinned like that was another stupid question. "I

don't know. But don't try swimming. I know how that story ends."

"Fuck you, old man." Wayne said, and then doubled over in pain. "Goddamn. That rib is killing me." He clutched his side.

"Phoebe's just around the bend. She'll take care of things."

The river trail was dry and clear of debris. It couldn't be more than a couple hundred yards to the cottage. "I'll come right back, Dancer."

"Hey, Wayne?"

"Yeah."

"Sorry about your truck."

Wayne shrugged. "Yeah." His body felt numb and he was lightheaded. It was as if someone had squeezed all the oxygen out of the air.

"I think Jimmy's running a special on Silverados. Might want to check that out."

"Okay. I better get a move on it. We can talk trucks when I get back."

Dancer lay down on the rock, like he wanted to sleep. "You take care now, son. Remember. Memphis."

Wayne stepped carefully up the trail. As he rounded the bend, he checked one last time to make sure Dancer was okay, but the sun had cast the river into dark shadows.

ABOUT THE AUTHOR

Len Joy had an idyllic childhood, growing up in the gem of the Finger Lakes, Canandaigua, New York. In high school he lettered in four sports and went off to the University of Rochester with dreams of becoming a football hero and world famous novelist. But that didn't happen. Instead he switched his major from English to Finance, quit the football team but started dating one of the cheerleaders. Three years later, Len and Suzanne were married, and four decades later, they still are with three grown kids.

They relocated to Chicago where Suzanne became a corporate lawyer and Len, with his MBA and CPA, became the auditing manager for U.S. Gypsum. Several years later, he bought an engine remanufacturing company in Arizona and for fifteen years comm(nted to Phoenix.

During those many flights, Len read hundreds of novels, renewing his dream of becoming a world famous author. In 2004, he wound down his engine business and started taking writing courses and particpating in triathlons.

Today, Len is a nationally ranked triathlete and competes internationally representing the United States as a part of TEAM USA. He is also the author of three published books, with a fourth (*Everyone Dies Famous*) to be released in July 2020 by BQB Publishing. Len's books and his writing have received shining reviews: "American Past Time" was reviewed by Kirkus as ". . . expertly written and well-crafted." Kirkus also described "Better Days" as "a character-rich skillfully plotted Midwestern drama" and Foreword Reviews found it to be "a bighearted wry, and tender novel that focuses on love and loyalty."